THE BOOK OF REVELATION

THE BOOK OF REVELATION

RUPERT THOMSON

BLOOMSBURY

First published 1999

Copyright © 1999 by Rupert Thomson

The moral right of the author has been asserted

Bloomsbury Publishing Plc, 38 Soho Square, London W1V 5DF

A CIP catalogue record for this book
is available from the British Library

ISBN 0 7475 4439 5

Typeset by Hewer Text Ltd, Edinburgh
Printed in England by Clays Ltd, St Ives plc

Will there ever be anything other than the exterior and speculation in store for us? The skin, the surface – it is man's deepest secret.

– Stefan Hertmans

ONE

I can see it all so clearly, even now. The studio canteen was empty, and I was sitting in the corner, by the window. Sunlight angled across the table, dividing the smooth, blond wood into two equal halves, one bright, one dark; I remember thinking that it looked heraldic, like a shield. An ashtray stood in front of me, the sun's rays shattering against its chunky glass. Beside it, someone's coffee cup, still half full but long since cold. It was an ordinary moment in an ordinary day – a break between rehearsals . . .

I had just opened my notebook and was about to put pen to paper when I heard footsteps to my right, a dancer's footsteps, light but purposeful. I looked up to see Brigitte, my girlfriend, walking towards me in her dark-green leotard and her laddered tights, her hair tied back with a piece of mauve velvet. She was frowning. She had run out of cigarettes, she told me, and there were none in the machine. Would I go out and buy her some more?

I stared at her. 'I thought I bought you a packet yesterday.'

'I finished them,' she said.

'You've smoked twenty cigarettes since yesterday?'

Brigitte just looked at me.

'You'll get cancer,' I told her.

'I don't care,' she said.

This was an argument we had had before, of course, and I soon relented. In the end, I was pleased to be doing something for her. It's a quality I often see in myself when I look back, that eagerness to please. I had wanted to make her happy from the first moment I saw her. I would always remember the morning when she walked into the studio, fresh from the Jeune Ballet de France, and how she stood by the piano, pinning up her crunchy, chestnut-coloured hair, and I would always remember making love to her a few days later, and the expression on her face as she knelt above me, a curious mixture of arrogance and ecstasy, her eyes so dark that I could not tell the difference between the pupils and the irises . . .

Brigitte had moved to the window. She stood there, staring out, one hand propped on her hip. Smiling, I reached for my sweater and pulled it over the old torn shirt I always wore for dance class.

'I won't be long,' I said.

~

Outside, the weather was beautiful. Though May was still two weeks away, the sun felt warm against my back as I walked off down the street. I saw a man cycle over a bridge, singing loudly to himself, as people often do in Amsterdam, the tails of his pale linen jacket flapping. There was a look of anticipation on his face – anticipation of summer, and the heat that was to come . . .

I had been living with Brigitte for seven years. We rented the top two floors of a house on Egelantiersgracht, one of the prettier, less well-known canals. We had skylights, exotic plants, a tank of fish; we had a south-facing terrace where we would eat breakfast in the summer. Since we were both members of the same company, we saw each other twenty-four hours a day; in fact, in all the time that we had lived together, I don't suppose we had spent more than three or four nights apart. As dancers, we had had a good deal of success. We had performed all over the world – in Osaka, in São Paulo, in Tel Aviv. The public loved us. So did the critics. I was also beginning to be acclaimed for my choreography (I had created three short ballets for the company, the most recent of which had won an international prize). At the age of twenty-nine, I had every reason to feel blessed. There was nothing about my life I would have changed, not if you had offered me riches beyond my wildest imaginings – though, as I walked to the shop that afternoon, I do remember wishing that Brigitte would give up smoking . . .

I followed my usual route. After crossing the bridge, I turned left along the street that bordered the canal. I walked a short distance, then I took a right turn, into the shadows of a narrow alley. The air down there smelled of damp plaster, stagnant water, and the brick walls of the houses were grouted with an ancient, lime-green moss. I passed the watchmaker's where a cat lay sleeping in the window, its front paws flexing luxuriously, its fur as grey as smoke or lead. I passed a shop that sold oriental vases and lamps with shades of coloured glass and bronze statues of half-naked girls. Like the man on the bicycle, I had music in my head: it was a composition by Juan Martin, which I was hoping to use in my next ballet . . .

∼

Halfway down the alley, at the point where it curved slightly to the left, I stopped and looked up. Just there, the buildings were five storeys high, and seemed to lean towards each other, all but shutting out the light.

The sky had shrunk to a thin ribbon of blue.

As I brought my eyes back down, I saw them, three figures dressed in hoods and cloaks, like part of a dream that had

5

become detached, somehow, and floated free, into the day. The sight did not surprise me. In fact, I might even have laughed. I suppose I thought they were on their way to a fancy-dress party – or else they were street-theatre people, perhaps . . .

Whatever the truth was, they didn't seem particularly out of place in the alley. No, what surprised me, if anything, was the fact that they recognised me. They knew my name. They told me they had seen me dance. Yes, many times. I was wonderful, they said. One of the women clapped her hands together in delight at the coincidence. Another took me by the arm, the better to convey her enthusiasm.

While they were clustered round me, asking questions, I felt a sharp pain in the back of my right hand. Looking down, I caught a glimpse of a needle leaving one of my veins, a needle against the darkness of a cloak. I heard myself ask the women what they were doing – *What are you doing?* – only to drift away, fall backwards, while the black steeples of their hoods remained above me, and my words too, written on the sky, that narrow strip of blue, like a message trailed behind a plane . . .

∼

It is only five minutes' walk from the studio to the shop that sells newspapers and cigarettes. I ought to have been there and back in a quarter of an hour. But half an hour passed, then forty-five minutes, and still there was no sign of me.

I had last seen Brigitte standing at the canteen window, one hand propped on her hip. How long, I wonder, did she stay like that? And what went through her mind as she stood there, staring down into the street? Did she think our little argument had upset me? Did she think I was punishing her?

I imagine she must have turned away eventually, reaching up with both hands to re-tie the scrap of velvet that held her hair back from her face. Probably she would have muttered something to herself in French. *Fait chier. Merde.* She would still have been longing for that cigarette, of course. All her nerve-ends jangling.

Maybe, in the end, she asked Fernanda for a Marlboro Light and smoked it by the pay-phone in the corridor outside the studio.

I doubt she danced too well that afternoon.

∼

That night, when I did not come home, Brigitte rang several of my friends. She rang my parents too, in England. No one knew anything. No one could help. Two days later, a leading Dutch newspaper published an article containing a brief history of my career and a small portrait photograph. It wasn't front-page news. After all, there was no real story as yet. I was a dancer and a choreographer, and I had gone missing. That was it. Various people at the company came up with various different theories – a nervous breakdown of some kind, personal problems – but none of them involved foul play. My parents offered a reward for any information that might throw light on my whereabouts. Nobody came forward.

All this I found out later.

There was a point at which Brigitte began to resent me for putting her in such a difficult position. She found it humiliating, not knowing where I was; I was making her look ridiculous. It must have been then that it occurred to her that I might have left her – for another woman, presumably. How cowardly of me to say nothing. How cowardly, to just go. Brigitte was half French, half Portuguese, and her pride had always resembled a kind of anger. There was nothing constant or steady about it. No, it flared like a struck match. When she was interviewed by the police she told them that I had abandoned her, betrayed her. She couldn't produce any evidence to support her theory, nor could she point to any precedent (in our many years together I had never once been unfaithful to her), yet the police took her seriously. A woman's intuition, after all. What's more, she lived with me. She was supposed to know me best. So if that was what she thought . . . The police did not send out any search parties for me. They did not scour the countryside with tracker dogs or drag the city's waterways. They did not even put up Missing Person posters. Why would they? I was just a man having an affair.

This, too, I found out later.

One other thing. The last person to see me before I disappeared was not Brigitte, but Stefan Elmers. Stefan was a freelance stills photographer who worked for the company. He took pictures of us dancing, black-and-white pictures that were used in programmes and publicity. Both Brigitte and I counted Stefan as a friend.

As I was walking along the canal that afternoon – and this could only have been moments before I turned into the alley – Stefan happened to drive past me in his car. Usually he would have stopped and talked to me, or else he would have shouted out of the window, something cheeky, knowing Stefan, but there was another car behind him, right behind him, so he just kept going.

Apparently, I looked happy.

For the next eighteen days no one had the slightest idea where I was.

TWO

When he came to, there was a taste in his mouth, a kind of residue, that was sweet yet chemical, like saccharine. His eyes didn't work properly. Things spun round, tilted, misted over.

He lay still, with his head on one side.

Floorboards. A white wall.

In the distance he could hear violins. Or it could have been cellos. He listened to the music, as if it might afford him an insight into what had happened. It just went on and on, though, indefinite, unchanging. It fed on itself without ever seeming to consume itself.

Time passed.

The music was still there, but he couldn't be sure where it was coming from – or even, in the end, if it was real.

At last he felt able to lift his head. He was lying on his back, his wrists and ankles held by stainless-steel rings. Each ring was attached to its own individual rail by a second, smaller ring. Each rail was firmly bolted to the floor. All four of the smaller rings had been locked into position on their rails, using metal eyes that were built into the floor at certain strategic points. The structure puzzled him. It was so intricate, so carefully designed. But why, what for?

His mind was slow and cloudy. Answers would not come.

He looked around. It was a large room, rectangular in shape. A single door stood in the far wall, just above the toe of his right shoe. There were three lights in the ceiling, each fitted with a wide metal shade; the light they gave off would be merciless, unflinching, like the light in an abattoir, he felt, or a laboratory. Everything had been painted white, even the pipes that ran from floor to ceiling on his right, even the wall to his left, which was built out of naked brick. There were no windows in the room, only one small skylight that looked as if it had been nailed shut. Floorboards stretched away in all directions – bare, unvarnished, slightly dusty.

He lay back, aware of the black rubber mat beneath his body. It reminded him of being in a gymnasium. It had the same smell. Hot-water bottles. Sweat. He stared up at the skylight. A white window-frame, a simple square of blue. It seemed only distantly related to the narrow strip of sky he had seen while walking down the alley.

The cigarettes, he thought. *I never bought the cigarettes.*

He saw the women as he had seen them then, their faces concealed under conical black hoods, their black cloaks swirling round their bodies. The fabric flapped and rippled, making him think of rays, the way they move across the ocean floor, and he could hear their voices overlapping – *We saw you dance last week, we were in the second row, it was wonderful* – so much so that it was hard to tell exactly who was speaking. He was used to receiving praise from strangers, of course. He had learned to be patient, gracious . . . Though he had the feeling that one of them had not talked at all. Instead, she had simply inclined her head, as if she was paying close attention. Or was she shy, perhaps? Even at the time, something about the encounter had struck him as being wrong – and yet he didn't think it was the enthusiasm; the enthusiasm had seemed genuine, unfeigned. He had been about to excuse himself and turn away when he felt that sharp, cold pain in his right hand. He shivered as he remembered how the needle had left the vein, how smoothly it withdrew, how stealthily, like a snake that has just released its venom . . .

A hypodermic, presumably.

A syringe.

He could still remember the sunlight falling across a steep roof at the far end of the alley, the tiles gleaming as if coated in gold leaf, but he could remember nothing after that – nothing until this white room with no windows, this imprisonment . . .

Once again he raised his head to look around. This time he noticed that the walls were studded with unusual fixtures – all kinds of brackets, hooks and bolts; they did not set his mind at rest since he could think of no innocent explanation for their presence. To his right, and slightly behind him, was a shallow alcove. Inside it stood a washing-machine and a tumble-drier, both German-made. The sight ought to have reassured him – such appliances were familiar, domestic, part of everyday life – and yet, in the context of the rubber mat and the stainless-steel rings, in the context of the fixtures on the walls, they took on a threatening air, they became accomplices.

Fear surfaced on his skin like a sharp, hot scent.

He felt the sudden urge to urinate.

∼

He had no memory of hearing the door open, and yet it must have done, for there they were, the women, moving towards him, the hems of their black cloaks snagging on splinters in the floorboards. They stood above him, peering down, as though he lay far below them, as though he was lying at the bottom of a well.

'You're ours now.'

He could not tell which one of them had spoken. His gaze

13

lifted beyond them, to the skylight. That square of blue, empty and indifferent.

The same woman spoke again. She was the tallest of the three. She had a slight accent, as if she had learned her English in America.

'You belong to us,' she said. 'You're ours.'

His first instinct was to ask her what she meant, but he fought against it. He didn't want to give her the satisfaction of hearing his voice. Not yet, anyway. He wanted to deny her something. Perhaps it was the only thing he had that he could still withhold.

Though she seemed content simply to stare at him – to run her eyes down the length of his body, and then up again . . .

A plane appeared behind her shoulder, a single speck of silver in the blue. It was strange to think of all the people up there, reading magazines, listening to music, drinking drinks. It was strange to think they didn't know that he was lying in a room below them, held by chains . . . He watched the plane cross the top right-hand corner of the skylight, its progress steady, smooth, impervious –

Then it was gone.

The women were murmuring to each other now, their voices lowered, intimate, distorted by their hoods. He couldn't distinguish one voice from another, nor could he make out what any of them were saying, even though they were still standing over him.

At last, and without warning, they withdrew. He lay still. The air had a muffled quality to it, a deadness. He wondered whether the room was sound-proofed. It seemed likely. If so, the music he had heard when he came round must have been playing in his head, his blood making one thin sound as it ran through his veins, like fifty bows drawn slowly over fifty sets of strings . . .

And now, in the same way, the woman's words floated in the air above him, haunting, constant, the meaning just out of reach:

You're ours now. You belong to us.

~

It was hard for him to work out exactly how much time had passed. The blue in the skylight had darkened, though it was not yet night. He was just beginning to feel the first stirrings of hunger when the door swung open and a woman walked into the room, a tray balanced between her hands. She moved towards him cautiously, so as not to spill anything, setting the tray down on the rubber mat. There was cold meat, salad, cheese, fresh fruit and bottled water. In the context of the room, which was so bare and colourless, the food looked exotic, almost absurd.

Kneeling beside him, the woman reached for the water. For a few moments she struggled to undo the plastic top. Either she had no strength in her hands, he thought, or else she was nervous, perhaps. The air gushed out of her as the seal broke and the top finally came free. She filled a glass and held it to his mouth. He gulped the water down. She had to do everything for him, dabbing his chin with a napkin when he drank too fast and almost choked.

By now, his head had cleared. He felt he should start to take things in, to gather information. He watched as the woman peeled an apple, green skin curling away from moist white flesh and dangling in the air below her thumb. Her hands were raw, he noticed – red, slightly swollen knuckles, bitten fingernails. Her head remained lowered, which made it difficult to see her eyes, though he sometimes caught a glimpse of them, a momentary glitter, as she helped him to a piece of lettuce or a slice of meat. Once, the faint, ticklish smell of mothballs lifted off the sleeve of her cloak as she reached towards him, making him think that it had only recently been taken out of storage. Where had the cloaks come from? Did the women own them?

Was this the first time they had attempted something like this?

All of a sudden he saw the theatre floodlit for the evening's performance, with people crowding into the foyer, taxis drawing up outside –

'What's the time?' he asked.

The woman shook her head, her way of signalling that he shouldn't talk. But he wanted to. He had to.

'Look,' he said, 'I've got a performance tonight.'

She gave no sign that she had even heard him.

'I'm due on stage at seven-thirty.' Then, though he felt stupid saying it, he added, 'I'm a *dancer*.'

She might as well have been deaf.

'So I can't ask you anything?' he said.

When the woman saw that he had eaten and drunk enough, she rose to her feet, picked up the tray and moved towards the door. He watched her go, his head lifting off the rubber mat, his neck muscles at full stretch. She had not spoken to him, he realised. Not even once.

Lying back, he wondered if he was being held to ransom. The thought of his father receiving a ransom note – his father who had always been so careful with money! – was almost enough to make him laugh out loud.

～

Later on that first day, when night had fallen and the overhead lights had been switched on, all three women returned. This

16

time they stood by the door at the far end of the room. They seemed to be conferring.

At last they turned and swept towards him. They gathered round him, as before. Disturbed by their approach, tiny complex galaxies of dust floated away from him, across the floor . . .

He had decided to hide anything he might be feeling, in much the same way that the women were concealing their identities. He would reveal as little of himself as possible. At the same time, there were things he needed to know. He had to try and find out who the women were, where they had taken him, and what they had in mind.

'What do you want?' he said.

The women glanced at each other.

'Do you want money? Is that it?'

'Money?' one of the women said. 'No, we don't want money.'

This was not the woman who had spoken to him earlier. This woman's voice was lower, huskier, as if she smoked. She had almost no accent.

'So what *do* you want?' he said.

The woman reached up with one hand to ease the hood away from her neck. Though the material did not look particularly coarse, it appeared to be chafing her. Her skin must be sensitive, he thought. She had white hands, with short, tapering fingers, and her nail-varnish was a dark purple-black, the colour of dried blood or cheap wine. He was noticing hands; hands were all that he was being shown.

'We already have what we want,' the woman said. Then, turning to her two accomplices, she said, 'Don't you agree?'

They nodded.

Yes, this was a different woman. She seemed to have more

17

authority. Maybe she was even the leader. In any group of three, there would have to be a leader.

'We have some rules . . .'

The woman turned away and walked towards the alcove that housed the washing-machine and the tumble-drier. She moved slowly, and with a certain gravity, a sense of self-importance, like a judge. She told him that he should not, under any circumstances, try to escape. There was no point, actually. They had taken all the necessary precautions. They had thought of everything. She also warned him against any attempts at violence. She was sure, in any case, that it was not in his nature. If he behaved well, she said, he would be treated well. She paused, waiting for him to speak, perhaps, but when he chose to say nothing, she continued. There was a device close to his right hand. If he was hungry or thirsty, or if he needed to go to the bathroom, then all he had to do was press –

'Actually,' he said, 'I need it now.'

'The bathroom?'

He nodded.

From where she was standing, the woman signalled to her two accomplices – a simple lowering of her head, a granting of permission. They turned and left the room. While they were gone, he examined the 'device'. A square piece of metal – aluminium, by the look of it – had been screwed into the floor next to the mat. In the middle of this metal plate was a round white button. It looked like a light-switch or a door-bell. He pressed it once, but heard nothing.

'Only when you need something,' the woman warned him.

Her two accomplices returned, carrying handcuffs and leg-irons. One sat by his feet, the other by his head. For the first time, he noticed how each individual rail doubled back on itself, resembling the handle of a traditional umbrella. When he looked at two of the rails together, the two that held his feet, for instance, he saw they had been laid out in such a way that they formed a kind of fractured S:

The woman sitting by his feet released the two smaller stainless-steel rings so they could run freely along their rails, then she brought his ankles close together and secured them with the irons. Only then did she unlock the larger stainless-steel rings. Once his legs were securely shackled, the second woman performed an almost identical manoeuvre on his hands, using the cuffs to fasten them behind his back. The two women worked in unison, in silence. At no point was any part of his body free. The routine was so efficient that it had to have been worked out in advance.

They helped him slowly to his feet. Though he had only been lying down for a few hours, he felt an impatience in his muscles. Something fidgety. His body had been denied its afternoon's exercise. He stood between the two women, moving his arms and legs, moving his head on his neck, as if he was going to give his performance after all . . .

The chains that bound him chinked and rattled.

Taking one arm each, the women led him towards the door. With his hands cuffed tightly behind his back and his ankles shackled, it was hard to do more than shuffle.

He had been wondering what lay beyond the room. This proved a disappointment to him. All he could see was a passageway, its walls and ceiling painted white, its carpet a hard-wearing, industrial shade of grey. There were two white doors, one to his left, the other at the far end of the passageway. There were no windows. The only sound he could hear was the steady, drowsy murmur of the fluorescent lighting overhead. The building felt as if it might have been refurbished recently, but he couldn't imagine what it would look like from the outside, let alone where in Amsterdam it might be — if indeed it was in Amsterdam.

The door to the bathroom was the door on the left. One of the women remained in the passageway, like a guard, while the other guided him inside. The room was no more than eight feet long and four feet wide. In front of him was a toilet with a black seat and a white cistern. A small hand-basin jutted from the wall to his right. The brand-name on both the toilet and the hand-basin was *Sphinx*, one of the most common makes in Holland. He smiled grimly when he saw the name and said, 'That's perfect,' but the woman standing behind him did not react. Like the passageway, the bathroom had no windows. There was no mirror either.

Without a hint of shyness or hesitation, the woman pulled down his track-suit trousers and took his penis out of the jockstrap he was wearing underneath. He sat down to urinate, something he had never done before. He had the idea it might make things easier, somehow, even though it meant he had to face the woman who had escorted him into the room. She seemed the more bizarre for being shut in such a confined space with him . . . In the silence before his urine came, he heard her breathing. It must be hot, he thought, wearing a hood and cloak — and, almost immediately, he imagined he could smell her sweat, bitter as the sap in a spring flower. He knew which woman she was. The raw knuckles, the chewed nails . . . She had served him his first meal. She was also the only one whose voice he had not heard as yet. All of a sudden a feeling of power ran through him. It seemed so out of place, so utterly unfounded, that it made him catch his breath. But it was fleeting, too. No sooner had it registered itself in him than it was gone, leaving not even a flicker of itself behind.

When he had finished, the woman pulled up his jockstrap and his track-suit trousers, then, reaching past him, flushed the toilet. Once again, there was no hint of awkwardness or prurience on her part, only a kind of methodical efficiency; a task needed doing, and she was doing it. Still, it felt odd to be handled in that way. It had brought back a period of his life that he had thought was lost for ever. With just a few simple actions, she had closed a gap of thirty years, returning him to his first few moments in the world.

~

The two women who had taken him to the toilet wasted no time in chaining him to the floor again, then they hung the handcuffs and leg-irons from conveniently placed hooks on the wall behind him and retreated to the left side of the room.

The woman with the white hands and the darkly painted nails stepped forwards. She stood so close to him that he could see a small, right-angled tear in her cloak, about hip-high, as if it had caught on a nail, and there were spots of something that looked like dried mud along the hem.

'Better?'

He nodded.

She stood over him, peering down. Her shoes showed below her cloak. They were black, with rubber soles. 'Are you cold?'

He shook his head.

'No,' she said, 'it is quite warm in here.'

She kneeled beside him, looked right at him. Perhaps because her eyes were framed by the fabric of her hood, they seemed to glitter with an almost supernatural light.

'You see, we don't want you to suffer,' she said. 'On the contrary . . .'

As if responding to a signal, the other women approached and kneeled. One sat at his feet while the other took hold of his sweater and eased it gently over his head. Underneath, he wore nothing except his old torn shirt. Starting at the collar, the woman began to undo the buttons. Her fingers were elegant but strong. This undressing was quite unlike the undressing he had just experienced in the bathroom, and not simply because a different woman had taken over. There was stealth in this. There was anticipation.

Wanting to make things difficult for her, he tried to move sideways, but with his wrists and ankles secured by the stainless-steel rings, there was very little he could do. He could only watch, in fact, as, one by one, the almost transparent pearl-white buttons sprang out of their holes.

'Ah yes,' one of the women said – or, rather, breathed.

Their interest was in the air; it was palpable, like a vibration or a pressure.

He closed his eyes, darkness as a form of denial, darkness as escape, but found he could see more vividly than ever, the women's hands, what they were doing. Their fingers on the drawstring of his track-suit trousers, slowly teasing the knot undone, slowly loosening the waistband . . .

'You're very beautiful,' he heard one of them say.

'Such smooth skin,' said another.

A third woman spoke, a murmur of corroboration.

He felt them begin to touch him. Sometimes their hands were tender, sometimes they were only curious, but there was no part of him, no curve or hollow, that they did not, in the end, explore.

He couldn't have said how long this adoration of his body lasted.

Once, the colour of the inside of his eyelids altered, and he opened his eyes to see that one of the women had switched the main lights off and that another was bringing tall candles into the room. The atmosphere became intimate, but also oddly medieval. That flickering, unstable light, and his clothes laid open, peeled back, like the skin of an animal that was being dissected. His nakedness – three figures, hooded, crouching over it . . .

He shut his eyes again.

There was a moment, too, when he felt the beginning of an erection, that gradual tightening at the base of his penis, that slow, almost luxurious rush of blood. It was as if his body was taking sides against him. Betraying him. Though his eyes were still closed, he could hear the women's voices:

'Look.'

'He's ready.'

'Who's going first?'

～

The ceiling was no longer there, the walls slid away, and he had views at last, wide open spaces, the bright sky arching over him, the dark vault of the earth. And the landscape kept changing before his eyes. He saw glittering salt flats that stretched for miles, and fields of tall grasses shifting under heavy dark-grey clouds. He saw a yellow prairie bounded by a range of mountains; they stood in shadow, tilting slabs of black and indigo. A fresh wind moved over his face, into his hair. It wasn't raining, but the air smelled of rain; rain had fallen recently, perhaps, or else it was on its way.

The air smelled of distance.

Land all around him, vast and dramatic, land as he had

rarely seen it in his life, and he was alone in it. Alone, but not lonely. There was that sense of being at the centre, of being somehow fundamental, the hub of a wheel that includes the universe in all its aspects and dimensions. He had felt this before, though not for many years. Perhaps it was simply the feeling of being young.

Sometimes he was standing still, sometimes running, but he was always alone, untroubled and curiously absorbed – a kind of rapture . . .

Though there was a part of him that knew a door could open and lights could flicker on, brilliant and merciless, and then something could take place that would fix him exactly where he was, in that white room, his wrists and ankles shackled.

Even in his dreams there was a part of him that knew.

~

Waking in darkness, not knowing where he was. Then noticing a faint light falling from the window high above. Landing on his body, soft as snow.

Night now.

He lay still and listened. There were no sounds coming from outside. No police siren in the distance, no drunk man singing – nothing.

Knowing nothing, and then remembering. The smell of rubber. Thin. Almost comforting. The cold grip of the stainless steel. The delicate, metallic chinking of the chain's links shifting as he turned over . . .

After the women were done with him, after they had finished, they adjusted the rings so as to give him more freedom of movement. By sliding the rings along their rails, he found that he could alter the position in which he slept. He could lie on his stomach, if he wanted. Or turn on to his side. He could bring his hands close to his face or draw his knees up towards his chest. He was freer, but not free.

What had that woman said?

You're ours now. You belong to us.

He felt nothing but shame and humiliation. No, wait. That wasn't entirely true. There had been another feeling there, a feeling that lurked behind the others, shadowy and sly – insidious: a feeling of excitement . . .

Once he had an erection, it had taken him almost no time at all to come, the sperm seeming to leap out of him, to catapult across his stomach. The women had taken it in turns to lick him clean, bending over him with warm, wet tongues. They had even argued over who should have the cloudy pearl of liquid that had formed at the tip of his penis, the last remaining evidence of orgasm. There had been a moment when he tried to say something, but one of the women put a hand over his mouth, a hand on which he could faintly smell himself.

'No, don't talk. You'll spoil it.'

Afterwards, he needed to urinate. This time they chose not to take him to the toilet. Perhaps they were afraid that it might break the spell. Instead, they allowed him to use a metal bedpan, which they had brought into the room with them.

Later, they removed his clothes completely and washed him, every part of him. He felt as if he was in a painting, the darkness all around him, a tin bowl full to the brim with water, his naked body, and everything lit by candles. Shadows jostled on the walls, like people who had been drawn to the event. Like crowds.

When the women had dried him, they dressed him in clean clothes, then slipped a pillow underneath his head. They left the room in silence, blowing out the candles as they closed the door.

'Sleep now,' he heard one of them say.

~

He woke again at first light. He was lying on his side, one hand under his cheek. Two or three drops of candle-wax had landed on the floorboards close to him; they could have been old coins, coins that had been handled for so many years that they had been worn quite smooth. He looked down at his body. He was wearing a white T-shirt and white underpants. They were not his clothes. The events of the night came back to him, and he felt a sudden queasy hollowness in the pit of his stomach. He had allowed the women to do exactly as they wished. He had submitted without an argument, without a struggle. What sort of man is it, he thought, who just submits?

He turned on to his back and watched a cloud drift through the skylight. There was another dimension to what had happened too, a dimension that was even harder to acknowl- edge: the excitement he had felt, despite himself. Had the women identified some kind of need in him? Had he tacitly encouraged them? Was he, in some fundamental sense, responsible for all this?

This was a version of himself that he didn't recognise.

Perhaps, in the end, he had simply been taking the path of least resistance.

He still had not decided what he thought when the door opened and a woman appeared. She was carrying the bowl they had used for washing him the previous night, and, judging by the angle of her head and the cautious way she moved across the room, the bowl was full of water. She set it down on the mat, no more than a foot away from him, then

26

left the room again, returning moments later with a towel, a flannel and a washing-bag. Settling beside him, she unzipped the bag and took out a disposable razor and a can of unscented shaving-foam. She shook the can a few times, sprayed foam on to the palm of one hand, then used her other hand to smooth it on to his face and neck. She had bitten her nails so far down, he noticed, that they were almost circular, which made her fingers look blunt, like roots.

She shaved him quite differently to the way he would have shaved himself. She started with the groove that ran from the base of his nose to the middle of his upper lip, small vertical strokes of the razor, then she moved along the right side of his upper lip and out across his cheekbone towards his ear, still using the same small strokes. After finishing the right side of his face, she returned to his upper lip, the left side now, and repeated the same manoeuvre – or, rather, its mirror-image – before dropping downwards to his chin, and then still lower, to his neck. He noticed that she held her breath each time she laid the blade against his skin, then let the air rush out of her as she leaned back and rinsed the razor in the bowl, and he thought of children, how they do exactly the same thing when they're drawing. He couldn't remember if he had ever been shaved by anyone before. He didn't think he had. She was surprisingly good at it. He never once had the sense that she might cut him.

As she was about to complete the job, a sharp pain twisted through his lower abdomen, just above his groin. He told her that he needed to use the bathroom. She withdrew immediately, returning a few moments later with one of her accomplices. He watched the two women as they went through the ritual of locking and unlocking, and, once again, he was struck by how smooth the operation was, as if they had rehearsed it many times. As before, one of the women, the tall one, waited outside the bathroom door while the other one, the one with no fingernails, escorted him inside. She stayed in the room with him throughout, even though he was doing more than urinating this time. It was like water, what fell out of him; it had the pungent, almost rotten smell of game. For once, the woman's hood seemed fitting – a display of delicacy on her part, as if she were averting her gaze.

When he had finished, she wiped him clean, pulled up his underpants and flushed the chain. She behaved exactly as she had behaved the night before: she was methodical, efficient – matter-of-fact. Afterwards, she stepped back to the hand-basin. There was a flaw in the white porcelain, at the base of the hot tap. He saw her touch it with one finger. She seemed to think it was something that could be dislodged – a hair, perhaps. When it didn't move, though, when she realised it was just a crack, a murmur came out of her, as if she felt she had been the victim of a practical joke.

While the woman held her hands under the hot water – how odd, he thought, to have someone wash their hands on your behalf – he stood back and looked around, trying to find out more about the room. A naked light-bulb hung from the ceiling. Philips. Sixty watts. The floor was lino – white dots on a dark-grey ground, a kind of stippling effect, like a TV screen when all the stations have closed down. To the left of the toilet there were two larger splashes of white that didn't appear to be part of the original design. Looking closer, he discovered they were paint. They must have dropped from some decorator's brush. He nodded quickly to himself. Other people's carelessness was something he needed reminding of. He had to believe that people could slip up. Make mistakes.

~

Back in the white room he waited until the women had gone, then he turned on to his side and faced the wall. The room still smelled of candle-smoke from the night before, a smell that reminded him, curiously enough, of Brigitte. Whenever Brigitte found herself inside a church, she always lit candles for members of her family, not just for those who were dead, but for the living too, even her cousin, Esperanza, whom she had never met, one candle after another, and her face as mystical, as solemn, as a three year old's. *What would the candle-makers do without you?* he had said to her once, outside the basilica in Assisi, a comment that drew an uncomprehending look from her, and then a smile and a remark about English humour and how she would never understand it, not if she lived to be a hundred.

Now that he was absent, would she light a candle for him as well?

He saw her as he had seen her last, no more than eighteen hours ago . . . She was standing by the canteen window, staring down into the street. He remembered how she had walked towards him, frowning slightly, as if something was troubling her. She had asked him to buy her some cigarettes. He had told her she'd get cancer. She had shrugged and said she didn't care. It had been a stupid argument. Pointless. Petty. He ran through the scene again from the beginning, seeing it the way it should have been. This time, when she crossed the room, she didn't have to ask him anything because her cigarettes were lying on the table where she had left them, forming a kind of still life with the ashtray and the coffee cup. She reached down, took a cigarette out of the packet and lit it, then she stood beside him, with her left hip almost touching his right shoulder. He saw how her left hand supported her right elbow, and how she held the cigarette close to her lips, even when she wasn't actually inhaling, and how the smoke

29

altered from grey to blue as it tumbled upwards through a shaft of sunlight . . . When she had finished the cigarette, crushing it out in the ashtray, they returned to the studio to rehearse the ballet that was opening in two weeks' time. The rehearsal ended at seven, after which they showered and changed. Then they drove home, as usual.

A different version of events.

A fantasy . . .

He wondered what Brigitte would be doing now. Would she be looking for him? How exactly do you go about looking for someone when they disappear without warning, without trace?

He thought of the time he took her to Crete. They had stayed in a village on the south coast, at the foot of the mountains. Every day they climbed on to their rented Vespa and drove to a deserted beach a few kilometres away.

One morning, while Brigitte was swimming, he lay down on a flat rock to read a book. When he looked up he saw her in the distance, halfway along the beach. She was washing herself in a fresh-water spring they had found by chance the previous day. She was naked, her olive skin already darkened by the sun, her bikini a small splash of scarlet on the rocks beside her. Smiling, he turned back to his book.

The next time he looked up, the beach was empty.

He was calm at first, thinking she must have gone swimming again. He scanned the bay. The mid-morning light had a brilliance that hurt his eyes; the water was a mass of ripped silver foil. She wasn't there. His calmness began to change shape inside him. He felt a kind of panic take its place.

Sitting on his rock, he scoured the beach for minutes on end, but Brigitte did not appear. She simply wasn't there.

He stood up, put on his swimming-trunks. He felt as if he was moving too slowly, and yet he couldn't see what good hurrying would do. He felt stupid. Perhaps he should just sit down again. Read his book.

He began to walk.

His walk turned into a kind of run as he realised how long it had taken him to think that something might be wrong. He had already wasted so much time. All of a sudden every second counted.

He reached the place where he thought he had seen her last. Yes, look. There was the shape of her foot in the wet sand. He was aware of the weight of the sun on his head, on his shoulders. The beach, grey and ochre, curved away towards a rocky promontory. Its emptiness seemed natural. It even had a quality of indifference about it, as if any feelings he might have were of no interest, no relevance.

What if somebody had raped her, then hit her with a rock? What if somebody had killed her? What if she just vanished?

Brigitte, who he couldn't live without. Brigitte, who he adored.

He had an image of her with nothing on, drinking water from the spring. At a distance of a hundred yards, it was not her face you recognised her by, it was the way she bent forwards from the waist, as only a dancer can, the way her spine and the backs of her thighs formed a right-angle, a perfect right-angle . . .

This is how it happens, he thought, when someone disappears. An empty beach. A stillness. Brigitte had been his responsibility. Her disappearance, if that was what it was, would be his fault. Her death, his fault.

He swallowed.

Turning away from the spring, he began to walk towards the promontory, but he had no hope now. She had been missing for an hour at least. He couldn't imagine circumstances that would account for that. He couldn't come up with a single explanation.

Then he heard a voice call his name. He stopped, looked up. Brigitte was standing on a rock above him, her body pale-grey, every part of her pale-grey, in fact, even her face, and, for a moment, he thought that his nightmare had come true, that she had been killed and was now returning as a ghost . . . The truth was far less dramatic, of course: while exploring the promontory, she had discovered some special mud, mud that was good for the skin . . .

That evening, as they sat outside the village bar, drinking glasses of chilled retsina, he watched her turn her head to blow her cigarette smoke into the street. He was still astonished that she hadn't come to any harm. He couldn't quite believe she wasn't dead and gone, as he had feared.

'What is it?' she said.

He shook his head. Being Brigitte, it had never occurred to her that he might have missed her, that he might have been worried, and he knew her well enough to realise that, if he told her, she would not have understood. She might even have thought less of him for it. She would herself have been astonished.

'Nothing,' he said. 'It's nothing.'

In retrospect, you could resent people who lived so entirely in their own skin that they had no idea of what it was like to be in yours. Not just no idea either, but no interest in trying to find out. The thought simply wouldn't have entered their heads.

This was why he was finding it so difficult to envisage how Brigitte would react to his disappearance. She was so used to being the centre of attention – how would it be when that situation was reversed? Every time he tried to imagine what she might be doing, all he saw were the ordinary things, some element or other of her everyday routine. She was sprinkling food into the fish tank. She was lying in a hot bath, listening to Bob Dylan tapes (which she loved, and he always teased her about). She was sitting on the floor in the corner of the studio, stretching her legs out sideways, or touching her forehead to her knees. She was behaving normally, in other words. She was behaving *as if he was still there*. Was there a grain of truth in these images (not that his absence wouldn't affect her, but that she would carry on regardless)? Or did they simply indicate the poverty of his own imagination?

Another memory came to him. It had happened years ago, when they first knew each other. After rehearsal one afternoon he had gone to fetch his car, which he had parked a few streets away. He waited for her outside the studio, the engine running. At last the door opened and she climbed in, her skin smelling of the Chanel soap she always used back then, her hair still wet.

'You're staring at me,' she said.

He could not deny it. He was captivated by her beauty, and there was nowhere he would rather look.

Even then, or especially then, perhaps, she had felt his love as a weight, a pressure, and at times it had exhausted her. This is not to say that she didn't love him, only that his love had preceded hers. His love had been instant, irrepressible and overwhelming, while hers had grown slowly, as a complement to his, as a response.

But if that was still true, if she sometimes felt his love weighed on her too heavily, and if that weight was then removed, in its entirety, would she, at some deep level, admit to a feeling of relief?

Or would she feel unanchored suddenly, unstable?

∼

Towards sunset on that second day the women appeared, each one dressed identically in black, as usual. They were like

33

doors, he thought, doors into the dark. None of which you would ever choose to pass through.

'We have a request.'

This was the tallest of the women, the one with the slight American accent. Her voice had an abruptness to it, a strident quality, as if she was used to giving orders. He said nothing, waiting for her to continue.

'We want you to masturbate for us.'

He turned his face away. During the day, while on his own, he had been thinking about the dangers of co-operation, one of them being that the women would never be satisfied, that they would keep asking more of him. This 'request', as they called it, seemed to prove the point.

But they were talking to him now, their voices seductive, insistent, overlapping one another, just as they had in that narrow alleyway.

'We want to see the expression on your face – '

'The way it changes – '

'Like you're lost inside yourself. Like when you dance – '

He shook his head and turned on to his side. The early evening sunshine struck through the skylight, making a rectangular shape on the bare boards. The rectangle was slightly wider at one end than the other. It looked as if a bright-orange coffin had been delivered to the room.

The women were still trying to persuade him. Though he didn't want to listen, he couldn't shut the voices out.

'All you have to do is masturbate – '

'Is it really so much to ask?'

One of them stepped closer, until she almost filled his field of vision with the folds of her black cloak. For a moment, he felt he might be losing consciousness.

'Do you remember what happened last night?'

This was a voice he recognised. It belonged to the woman

34

with the darkly painted nails, the woman he thought of as the leader. It occurred to him that he was already beginning to be able to distinguish between the women. It might be useful if he could give them separate identities, somehow. Name them even.

The woman repeated her question. 'Do you remember what happened?'

'Of course I remember,' he replied.

'Well,' she said, 'we filmed it all. On video.'

He looked up at her in disbelief.

She turned away, walked a few paces. 'Of course, it's mainly for our own pleasure. Our own,' and she paused, 'delectation.' She leaned against the white pipes that ran from floor to ceiling. 'However,' she went on, 'we could always make a copy. We could send it to your girlfriend, for example. You have a girlfriend, don't you. Or we could send it to the people who employ you . . .'

'Why are you doing this?' he murmured.

The woman who was standing to his left kneeled awkwardly beside him. 'Because you're beautiful,' she said in a curious, low monotone. 'Because,' and she hesitated, and then looked down at the floor, 'because we love you.'

The woman standing behind her laughed.

'Well?' said the woman who he thought of as the leader. 'What have you decided?'

He felt instinctively that she was not bluffing. Though he hadn't noticed any filming equipment, it seemed obvious that in a room of this type there would be a hidden camera somewhere. It went with the handcuffs and the rubber mat; it belonged to the same family of objects. If he refused to submit to their demands, they would put the video in the post, and he didn't want even to begin to imagine Brigitte's face if she were to receive something like that.

'OK,' he said quietly.

'You will do it?'

'Yes.'

The leader walked back towards him, her hands clasped almost ceremonially in front of her. Under that black hood of hers, he knew she would be smiling. He looked beyond her. The piece of bright-orange sunlight had changed shape and moved in the direction of the door. It no longer bore the slightest resemblance to a coffin. He wasn't sure if this was a good omen or a bad one.

'If there is anything we can do,' the woman said, 'to make it easier . . .'

He stared at her, not understanding what she meant.

'Men often need something,' she said. 'Pornography, for instance.' She paused. 'You know,' and she was still smiling, he was sure of it, 'a lot of men would pay to be in your position –'

'If I was paying,' he said, 'it would be my choice. This is not my choice.'

'But you will do it,' she said, 'won't you.'

∼

That night he woke up to find he couldn't move. Something was resting heavily against him, pinning him to the floor – something warm, alive . . . It took him a moment to realise that it was one of the women.

She was lying next to him, her head turned sideways on his chest. He could just make out her hair, which was thick and wiry, and the curve of her left shoulder, edged in silver, thin light falling from the window high above.

She appeared to be naked.

He wondered whether he should say something. What, though? Suddenly the situation seemed ridiculous.

Only a few hours earlier the women had put on a show for him. Two of them sat on moulded plastic chairs while a third stood in front of him and slowly, teasingly, undid her cloak. Underneath she had nothing on except expensive-looking, flame-red underwear. What struck him first was the difference between her body and that of a dancer. Her body was softer than the bodies he was used to, and less defined. To his trained eye, she looked curiously indistinct, almost blurred, and, just for a moment, he seemed to see another, leaner figure, the dancer within her, bending, stretching, preparing for a morning class . . . She reached behind her and unhooked her bra. It came away. Though her limbs were slender, her breasts were heavy – out of proportion to the rest of her, somehow. She drew her knickers downwards, past her knees. She had a faint bikini-line, as if she had been in the sun that winter, and high up on the outside of her left thigh there was a small round scar, the size of a guilder. He began to masturbate, as he was required to, but found that he couldn't even achieve an erection.

One of the women thought he wasn't trying.

'I am trying,' he protested. 'Anyway, you can't *try*. It doesn't work like that.'

The woman who had just undressed for him stooped quickly, clumsily, and gathered up her clothes. Then, wrapping herself in her black cloak, as if for warmth, she turned towards the door. He almost felt he should apologise to her.

The other women rose out of their chairs.

'Please don't send the video,' he said.

They left without another word, without a backward glance, which made him wish he hadn't pleaded.

But now one of them had returned . . .

As his eyes adjusted to the darkness, he discovered that he

37

could make out a pale mound, which was her hip, presumably, and, to the left of that, the two much smaller curves of her heels, one resting on the other.

He could feel her breath against his skin, as light as feathers landing.

'Don't worry,' he heard her say. 'It's only a dream.'

'But I'm awake,' he said. 'I'm not asleep.'

'A dream . . .' she murmured, 'only a dream . . .'

~

In the end, he did what they wanted him to do. In the end, he managed it, though only by drawing on erotic memories of Brigitte. There had been a moment when he opened his eyes and saw that one of the women was touching herself, her movements perversely echoing his own. It had been like looking into a distorting mirror. At the same time, the connection between himself and the woman had seemed so intimate that he felt as though he was indulging in an obscure form of infidelity.

Afterwards, they left him alone for the rest of the day, but he knew this was only a temporary reprieve, a sort of natural interval. He had detected a greed in them. There would be more requests, and they would not get any easier, of that he felt quite certain, and yet he had no idea what they might involve; he could not see into the women's heads, could not predict the direction their fantasies would take.

His only consolation, if you could call it that, was that he now felt able to distinguish between the women. Even in a physical sense they were beginning to lose their mystery. Once, for instance, when the woman he thought of as the leader turned to one of her accomplices, he noticed how the tip of her nose pushed against the fabric of her hood. A prominent nose: it wasn't much, but it was something. He could add it to the sensitive skin, the darkly painted nails, the smoker's husky voice. It was as if their hoods and cloaks were gradually becoming transparent. As if their disguises were subject to some kind of unavoidable decay.

There was much that still puzzled him, of course. What was it that the women had in common? What were the circumstances that had brought them together? This curiosity about the nature of their connection threw up dozens of still more basic questions. What did the women do when they weren't in the room? How did they earn money? Who were their friends? How long had they lived together? Had they grown up together? If so, where? Were they related in any way?

Slow down, he told himself. Slow down.

From his point of view the women formed a unit, a sort of edifice, but he had to remember that they were individuals as well. Two of them had determined and uncompromising characters, and they would be difficult to get the better of, but there was a third who was softer, who rarely spoke. She was the one who had crept into the room at night and laid her head against his chest, content, it seemed, simply to be close to him. Possibly, he thought, just possibly, he had found a weakness in the structure – though, as yet, he wasn't sure how, or even if, it could be exploited. In the meantime, he had to concentrate on building up as clear a picture as he could of each of the three women. He had to look beyond their hoods and cloaks. He had to turn them into human beings.

~

You don't choose anger. No, anger chooses you. Ever since he had surfaced from the anaesthetic they had given him he had been calm. In fact, given the circumstances, his calmness had been unusual, if not unnatural. Perhaps it was shock. Or disbelief. Or perhaps, at some deep level, he was taking stock of the situation, developing a strategy. He didn't know. All he knew was, something was beginning to change in him. To shift. Something was beginning to accumulate.

One evening a woman walked into the room holding a lighted candle and a glass of water. He knew from the uncertainty in her footsteps that it was the woman with the bitten fingernails. She placed the candle on the floor, close to his head, then settled beside him, grunting slightly as she eased down on to the mat.

'How long are you going to keep me here?'

It was the first time he had asked the question, and he heard a tremor in his voice, a kind of nervous violence, which surprised him.

The woman did not answer. Instead, she held the glass to his mouth. Her shadow ducked and shuddered on the wall behind her.

He lifted his head and drank. When he had swallowed he looked up at her.

'I said, how long are you going to keep me here?'

Again she did not answer.

The next time she held the glass to his mouth, he turned his head violently to one side. She was affecting humility, the way a servant might, and yet she was the one who wielded the power. There was something self-righteous about her, something almost pious, that he could no longer stomach. He began to shout at her.

'I asked you a question. I asked you how long you're going to keep me here. What's wrong with you? Are you deaf?'

Perhaps someone had sensed anger coming because he had been locked face-down on the floor, his body fixed in an X shape. Each time he shouted he had to lift his head up off the mat, which put a strain on his throat, and if he wanted to look at the woman he had to peer over his shoulder. She was sitting there, staring mindlessly into the candle-flame. She was still holding the water glass, even though it was empty. She had started humming to herself. There was no tune to this humming – at least, none that he could recognise. It was just a sound, unvarying, unending. It only added to his fury. He swore at her, using the worst language he could think of.

At last she picked up the candle and rose to her feet. He thought she might have glanced at him. Just once. Furtively. Then she turned away, withdrew into the shadows at the far end of the room. He heard her blow the candle out. She closed the door behind her. She was gone.

Though he was alone now, and in the dark, he went on shouting. He shouted until his throat felt raw. Until he thought he could taste blood.

Nobody came.

That woman he had sworn at, she was the one who had visited him the night before, the one who lay there quietly, just holding him. *Don't worry. It's only a dream.*

For who, though?

Not for him.

~

There was a limit to the time that he had left. A male dancer's career doesn't last long – all that lifting: the body can only take so much of it – and his career would be shorter than most. His own personal history of injuries had started at the age of twenty-four. He had been born with a very straight back. It didn't flex, which meant that it took a huge amount of impact when he jumped. It often stiffened after a performance. He even had trouble doing up his shoes sometimes.

Every so often, when he was on stage, he would sense the injury returning. It was like watching clouds gather. Like watching weather moving in. There was nothing he could do to stop it, not a thing. He just had to use his experience to get through the performance. Afterwards Brigitte would come up to him. *Was your back bad tonight?* The physiotherapist would try and persuade him to take a few weeks off, but he never listened. Rest was like a form of torture to him. He was a dancer, and dancers want to be on stage. There's just no substitute for that.

In three months, he would be thirty, and he had to face the fact that he was rapidly approaching the end of his career. Yes, he had the choreography to fall back on – he was lucky to have that talent – but dancing had always been his first love, his one true passion. Yet here he was, locked in a room somewhere, unable to move . . .

His last moments were being stolen from him.

∾

It had been dark for several hours when the door opened and someone switched on all the lights. In the abrupt, fierce glare he blinked, trying to adjust his eyes. He decided not to look round. He was tired of looking round. Instead, he stared at the back of his right hand, the place where the needle had gone in. There was a slight discolouration around the vein, an area of yellow and faded purple. It still ached a little.

Footsteps crossed the bare boards behind him. He felt so defenceless lying on his stomach. It was almost impossible to resist the urge to glance over his shoulder; he felt as if he was fighting some kind of instinct.

At last a woman appeared, taking slow, measured steps, circling the very edges of his field of vision. She was wearing skin-tight leather shorts, a lace-and-satin bra and a pair of thigh-length boots, all of which were black. Instead of the usual hood, she had pulled on a rubber mask. It enclosed her entire head, but left holes for her mouth and eyes. The rubber was a dusty matt-black, which made her lips look unnaturally red. The smell of alcohol and perfume rose off her skin. Cigarette smoke too.

'Have a nice evening?' His sarcasm was muted by the fact that he was forced to whisper. His throat still hurt from all the shouting.

'You've been making noise,' the woman said.

She was the one who had taunted him. *We want you to masturbate. Is it really so much to ask?* She was also the one who had taken off her clothes for him. Her body was the kind of body you see in tabloid newspapers or pornographic magazines: young, firm – top-heavy. He didn't really know how to look at her.

'You've been shouting,' she said, a hard edge to her voice.

He turned his head sideways so that his right cheek lay flat against the pillow and his eyes were on a level with the floor. He had noticed something in her left hand. It had straps attached to it. Buckles too. He swallowed suddenly.

'You upset my friend,' she said.

She took a diagonal path across the room until she stood directly in his eye-line. He could see the toe of her left boot – patent-leather, mirror-bright. He could see the sharp stiletto heel.

Her voice tightened. 'You upset my friend.'

'I was asking a question,' he said. 'She wouldn't answer.'

'So you started shouting – '

All of a sudden his patience abandoned him. Since the

43

beginning he had had the feeling that, if he met this woman in real life, on equal terms, he would dislike her. That abrasive manner. That superior, hectoring tone.

'So I started shouting,' he said. 'So what?'

She stepped back to the wall and leaned against it, her hands behind her. She appeared to be studying him.

Her slender arms, her heavy breasts – what else had she revealed to him? She had a faint bikini-line, he remembered, and a coin-shaped scar on her left hip. Otherwise her body was flawless, the kind of body most men dream about. He thought she might be a year or two younger than he was. Twenty-seven, twenty-eight.

As he watched her, she left the wall and strolled past him, towards the door. Was she leaving? He heard several dainty, metallic sounds that he could make no sense of. Before he could glance over his shoulder, she appeared on his right. He had wondered what it was that she was holding in her hand. Well, now he knew. Strapped to the front of her leather shorts was a dildo, with every detail luridly recreated – the glans, the veins, the urethra . . .

'You know, I've always wondered what it would be like,' she said slowly.

She moved away from him, then turned, moved back again, more than the hint of a swagger in her walk.

'Feels good,' she said.

She smiled, but only with her mouth. Her eyes were cold.

He rested his head against the pillow. A bitter fluid had risen on to his tongue. He wished he could go to sleep.

'We can only take so much,' she went on, 'before – well, how should I say it? – before we feel the need to punish . . .'

'I won't shout any more,' he muttered grudgingly. 'I promise.'

'Ah, you change your tune. But it's too late, you see? Too easy now. Like the dog when it sees the stick.'

A tiny ball of fear formed in his solar plexus. It did not move at all; it just sat there, as if held in place by some slight hollow or depression.

'I told you, I won't do it again.' He tried to think of more words. 'I'm sorry about your friend. I didn't realise she was so sensitive.'

The woman squatted on the floor in front of him. She brought a small bottle out of her pocket. It was olive-oil, produced in Italy. The label said *Extra Virgin*.

'A nice touch,' she said, 'don't you think?'

He looked at her, not following.

'It will make things a bit more comfortable for you,' she said. 'Of course, I'm assuming it's your first time . . .'

The ball of fear rolled slowly out of its hollow and down into his belly. He pulled hard at the rings, but only succeeded in grazing the inside of both wrists.

'It's not so bad,' she said. 'You might even get some pleasure from it.'

She took the pillow from under his head and folded it in half, then wedged it beneath his stomach so that his buttocks were lifted into the air. He was facing the right wall, which was made of brick. All of a sudden his focus altered, and he saw himself reflected in the stainless-steel ring that held his right hand. He could only see an eye, the right one. It didn't look like his.

The woman had positioned herself behind him, with her knees between his thighs.

'I always wanted to do this,' she whispered in a silky voice.

He cried out as he felt the dildo penetrate.

'You can struggle if you like,' she whispered.

She held him by the hips and pushed in deeper. The

stranger's eye stared out at him forlornly from the narrow, curving strip of stainless steel.

'You know what you are, don't you,' she was saying. 'You're a cunt.'

After a few moments she kneeled upright, unfastened her bra and dropped it on the rubber mat beside her. Then she leaned over him again, her breath hot against his neck. Cigarettes and perfume. Alcohol.

Her nipples brushed his shoulder-blades as she moved in and out.

'Cunt,' she whispered in his ear.

And then, in time with the rhythmic motion of her body, 'Cunt . . . cunt . . . cunt . . . cunt . . .'

Afterwards, when she had loosened the rings and he was lying on his side, she spoke to him again. 'That question you were asking before. Well, the answer's no. We're not finished with you yet, not by a long chalk.'

She paused.

'Is that the correct phrase? It sounds kind of strange.'

∿

Later that night, when the door opened again, he tensed. He knew it off by heart by now, that sequence of sounds – a squeak as the handle turned, a click as the lock slid sideways in its chamber, a creak as the door moved on its hinges . . . It meant that something was about to happen, something that could neither be predicted nor controlled. He lay motionless, his bowels stinging, oddly wet, and watched through half-closed eyes as one of the women dimmed the centre-lights. A sigh came out of him. For hours now, the glare of those three lights had burned through the thin skin of his eyelids, seeming to illuminate the whole of the interior of his head. There had

46

been nowhere he could go for privacy, not even inside himself.

He saw two women move towards him, bringing a tin bowl brimming with hot water and a pile of soft white towels. They kneeled on either side of him. Steam rose from the bowl, a ghostly flickering. One of the women dipped a flannel in the bowl, then wrung it out. The glassy trickle of the water . . .

He flinched when they first touched him, and one of them murmured in Dutch, words that were probably intended to reassure or comfort him. He found unexpected tenderness confusing. Once again, he had the impression that the women were not all of one mind, that the actions of one could invoke the disapproval of the others, that there were differences, in other words, but he still did not feel capable of exploiting these differences to his advantage.

In fact, if anything, he felt less capable now. After his humiliation of that evening, he had plunged into a kind of apathy. The feeling had stayed with him, not so much the feeling of being violated, but the orgasm that had occurred as a result, an orgasm in which he had played no part, an orgasm that had been involuntary, autonomous. It had been like a lesson in which he had been taught the true meaning of the word 'powerlessness'.

You might even get some pleasure from it.

How cynical that woman was. How vicious. He would never have called it pleasure – though he had been aware of a definite physical response, like a series of pulses passing along the length of his penis, pulses which he visualised, oddly enough, as rings. It was the opposite of a normal orgasm since it had been triggered from the inside, and, at one particular point, he had experienced a curious and unpleasant sensation of delay: he felt as if he was coming when, in actual fact, the sperm was still deep inside him, still on its way. Just then the

47

woman had murmured something in his ear, though he couldn't remember what exactly. Another piece of mockery, no doubt.

He stared at the women kneeling on either side of him, one with shiny, slightly swollen knuckles, the other wearing nail-varnish that looked black. Though they were washing him with their usual patience and thoroughness, he thought he detected a brittle quality in the air, a wariness, even a resentment. He had broken the rules. He had been violent. Realising he could not afford to provoke them any further, he lay there quietly, with his eyes closed, as if asleep. He tried to rid his body of all longing, all tension. He tried to think of nothing . . .

At last, the women left him. He waited until they had switched off the lights and closed the door behind them, then he opened his eyes again. He suddenly saw the room for what it was: an artificial space, a setting – a kind of stage. This was something he was familiar with, of course. The difference was, he had no say. He felt as if he was being asked to sustain a performance with no knowledge of how long it was supposed to last. If he was to survive he would have to look on it as a test of his discipline, his stamina.

It would almost certainly be the hardest test that he had ever faced.

~

In the middle of the night, with rain falling carelessly across the skylight, he woke up in possession of the names. He didn't know where they had come from. He didn't even seem to have played a part in their selection. They were just there, ready to be put to use.

Astrid, first of all. This was the name he would give to the tallest of the women, the one with the faint American accent and the photo model's body. From the very beginning, he had detected a grudge in her. Trouble, he had thought instinctively, would come from that direction. Well, he'd been right about that. What's more, when she took off her clothes for him and he failed to respond, he had almost certainly insulted her, which had only fuelled her hostility, a hostility she had unleashed on the night of her assault on him. She had claimed to be punishing him, but she had administered the punishment with a ferocity and a relish that bore little or no relation to the offence. Astrid suited her. It was beautiful, as she was, but it also cast a cold, astringent shadow. Rearranged, it almost spelled 'disaster'.

The next name that had come to him was Gertrude. A name like Gertrude had connotations of strength and leadership, which made it ideal for the woman with the white hands and the darkly painted nails. She had laid down the rules on the first day. She did most of the talking. She wore the type of shoes that the police wear. He had the feeling she had been the brains behind the plan to abduct him; she seemed to display all the right qualities – clarity, authority, audacity. He thought she might be older than the others, though this was a hunch based on nothing more than the sound of her voice and the way she moved around the room. True or not, he would still have been prepared to bet that she was the principal decision-maker.

That left Maude. At best, there was something cosy and dependable about the name. At worst, it was heavy, lumpen, just plain slow. It would act as a net for the many unlikely characteristics of the woman with the bitten nails. After all, she carried out most of the chores. She fed him, washed him, shaved him, took him to the toilet. She was reliable and willing. She did not complain. There was also a naïve side to her that didn't seem at odds with a name like Maude. She seldom spoke, but, when she did, the others usually found her entertaining. *Because we love you. Because you're beautiful.* And, once, he had woken to discover her – it could only have been her – lying against him in the dark, her body pressed to his. Perhaps that was all she asked of him, that physical proximity, that solace . . .

The rain was still falling, flecking the skylight's glass with silver.

Gertrude, Astrid, Maude . . .

The names seemed peculiarly appropriate, suggesting a hierarchy, a secret court, in which each woman played a distinct role. And yet, at the same time, they had that 'd' in common. Almost as if they shared the same root. This link between the names acted as a kind of understudy to the far more complex link between the women themselves, a link which he had not, as yet, been able to divine. But, lying there, an idea occurred to him: Astrid's open hostility towards him, Maude's downtrodden, almost masochistic nature . . . and Gertrude? – well, he didn't know, but might it not be true that the three women were all, in their different ways, damaged somehow, and that it was the damage they had suffered that had brought them together?

His heart was beating loudly now. He moved his face towards the ring that held his right wrist, located his right eye in the narrow bar of stainless steel and gave himself a wink.

It was a long time before sleep took him.

~

They came to him early in the morning, dark clouds above his head, the skylight trembling as thunder rumbled over it. They came and stood in front of him, all three of them, in their

50

usual hoods and cloaks. He grinned despite himself. He had named them, and they did not know. He had discovered for himself a kind of power – a modest power, admittedly, no match for theirs, but valuable all the same. In their new ignorance, the women seemed less daunting.

'You feel good today?' Astrid said.

His smile lasted, but he did not reply.

Gertrude stepped forwards. They had a proposal, she said. If he went along with it he would be rewarded. He looked up at her, imagining her pointed nose, her skin that flushed too easily. And what would his reward be? he wondered. Freedom? It seemed unlikely. Still, he was in no position to bargain.

'What's the proposal?' he said.

On the following night, she said, there was to be a banquet, and they had decided that he would play a special part in it. In fact, the event was to revolve around him – quite literally: instead of arranging the food on a table, they would arrange it on his naked body. They would sit around him, on cushions. It was a wonderful idea, wasn't it? An inspiration.

Before he could react, she informed him he would have to wear a hood throughout the dinner. Clearly, he could not be allowed to set eyes on the guests. That was one reason. But also, if he wore a hood, his identity would be protected. The guests would see him as a beautiful man – beautiful, and anonymous.

Maude murmured something, but Gertrude ignored her.

His feet would be chained together, she went on, but his hands would be left free. However, he should not move at all, or make a sound, not unless it was absolutely necessary. He should not speak – obviously. That would break the spell.

'If you do,' Astrid said, 'there will be repercussions.'

He didn't need to ask her to elaborate.

51

'And the reward?' he said.

'That will be negotiated afterwards.' Gertrude paused. 'Can we trust you?'

He nodded slowly.

'Really?' she said. 'We're expecting some important people.'

'Do I have a choice?' he said.

~

That night he dreamed that Milo, a dancer in the company, had died. In the dream he was travelling on a bus through a country that he didn't recognise. He supposed he must be on tour, between performances. Vivian and Carmela were sitting behind him, talking about how sad it was. Turning in his seat, he interrupted them, saying that he didn't know, he hadn't heard. Was it really true?

Oh yes, Vivian said, her eyelashes dark and wet. *His heart just stopped.*

But I only saw him on Friday –

I know, Vivian said. *It happened really suddenly.* She put her arm round Carmela, who had started to cry.

He sat back and stared out of the window. The bus shifted into a lower gear. They were passing through mountains now, lush green mountains draped in mist . . . He could see Milo so clearly – his pale, almost sickly complexion, and his compact, muscular physique. He thought of the histrionic stomach pains that Milo had in class most mornings – his nickname in the company was Milodrama – and yet, despite these afflictions, whether real or imaginary, despite his size too, Milo could jump higher than anybody else, Milo could make space crackle . . . He remembered how Milo had drunk three glasses of champagne in a restaurant in Buenos Aires once, and how he had then danced an extraordinary, impromptu tango with

52

Fernanda. When it was over, the people eating there had given them a standing ovation . . .

Little Milo, dead.

When he woke up he lay there quietly. Though he was sure it wasn't true, the dream had nonetheless disturbed him. It had the stillness of a premonition, the eerie tangibility of the future tense. Yet, at the same time, paradoxically, it felt like reality, or even memory, and because of that, perhaps, it reminded him of what he had lost. Most people have no knowledge of the dancer's world – how small it is, how intimate, and how complete; it's a world within the world, and everything you need is there – work, friendship, passion, laughter, love. It was the world he had lived in since he was fourteen years old, and now he had been torn away from it, and it was going on without him. He had no news of it, and he felt alone, so terribly alone. The dream had made that clear to him, more vividly than anything the three women had said or done. He kept going over it and over it, trying to bring back something else, another moment from the journey, another fragment of conversation, until at last the door-handle at the far end of the room turned slowly clockwise and the woman he called Maude walked in.

~

She kneeled on the mat beside him. 'You're unhappy?'

'I had a bad dream,' he said.

'You can tell me, if you like . . .'

He shook his head. 'No.'

'Well,' she said, 'I'm sorry for your dream.'

Perhaps it was her imperfect English, or perhaps it was just that she had tried to show him sympathy, but, in that moment, he felt as if he knew exactly what she looked like. Her face was round, with features that seemed to crowd into the middle – all cheeks, in other words, but no chin to speak of, and not much forehead. When she found something amusing, her eyes would half close like a cat's, and small tucks would appear at the corners of her mouth. She would age well, he thought. In fact, she probably would not age at all.

He allowed her to wash him, to clean his teeth, to take him to the toilet. The sight of the word *Sphinx* raised its usual, wry smile. Back in the room, she brought him his breakfast. They had started giving him the sort of food that he was used to: breakfast was cereal and fruit, for instance, and two or three cups of herb tea.

Almost as soon as he had finished eating, the preparations for the banquet began. While the work was going on, he was kept blindfolded. He lay there and listened to the women talking quickly among themselves in Dutch. Every now and then they called out to him, as if they wanted him to share in the excitement, but he still felt weighed down by the melancholy that he had woken with that morning.

On the removal of the blindfold an hour or two later he found that he was lying inside a structure that resembled a tent, only it was a tent built out of the most sumptuous fabrics, crimson and violet and gold, and furnished with tropical plants, carpets of hand-woven silk, and leather cushions that had been embroidered with velvet, mirror-glass and suede. He could have been transported to a Berber dwelling high in the Atlas Mountains.

'Well?' Gertrude said. 'What do you think of it?'

He hadn't been expecting anything quite so elaborate, and he told her so, which seemed to please her.

The day passed slowly. He had the strangest feeling that he was involved in the venture with them – that they were, all four of them, collaborating . . . Towards nightfall he was taken to the bathroom. While he was there, they told him that this would be his last visit to the toilet until after the banquet. They could not afford to have any interruptions, they said. They wanted the evening to be seamless.

On his return to the room, they spread a length of gold material over the rubber mat, then asked him to lie down on his back with his arms by his sides and his legs together, like a soldier standing to attention. This created a long, narrow trough which they then began to fill with all kinds of *antipasti*. They placed artichoke hearts between his ankles, then piled a selection of olives, gherkins and pickled onions on to his calves, along with carrots, sticks of celery, cherry tomatoes and green beans. On either side of his knees they put a risotto of asparagus and prawns. Along his thighs lay salads of rocket and watercress, arugula and radicchio, already dressed with a light vinaigrette. Nestling close to his testicles were wedges of fried aubergine and seared red pepper, with crescents of white onion and thick half-moons of wild garlic. On the soft bed of his pubic hair they arranged the shellfish – mussels, clams, oysters and scallops – all bought fresh that morning, so they claimed. On his belly lay a whole baked salmon, garnished with lemon and parsley. On his solar plexus the sauces and relishes were to be found: mustard, horseradish, aioli, hollandaise. His chest was decorated with medals of cold meat – salami, prosciutto, bresaola. Roast quails nested in his armpits and his collarbones, and, on his shoulders, like armour, lay overlapping slices of turkey, duck and veal. It took more than an hour to arrange the meal, and, by the end, there was scarcely a square inch of his body that was not a receptacle for one delicacy or another. Though naked, he felt strangely clothed.

Maude left the room, returning with two candelabra, which

she positioned carefully, one at his head, the other at his feet. His food-encrusted body glistened in the warm, gold light.

'A feast,' Gertrude said. 'A real feast.'

'A work of art,' Astrid said.

'Remember,' Gertrude said, and she was addressing him directly now, 'not a word from you. Not a sound. Not unless it's absolutely necessary. If you have to move, move slowly. Nothing sudden or violent. Is that clear?'

He nodded.

At that moment, from somewhere deep in the house, came the clumsy jangle of a bell. Maude leaned down and gently drew a hood over his head, a cloth hood with a drawstring round the neck. One of his hands rose involuntarily towards his face.

'You will be able to breathe quite easily,' Gertrude said.

'Yes,' Maude said. 'I have tried it myself.'

∼

It was a long evening – seemingly endless, in fact. So far as he could tell, ten people attended the banquet, seven women and three men. Two of the men were American, and both spoke Dutch fluently. Somebody – a woman, presumably – was wearing bangles, which were tortoiseshell, he imagined, or amber; they clicked loudly as they slid up and down her forearm. Somebody else smoked throughout the meal. He could hear the brisk rasp of a lighter in his left ear.

At first he could feel people touching him in different places as they helped themselves to the food that was laid out in front of them. After that, it only happened sporadically, and often took him by surprise, making him jump. Oddly enough, about halfway through the banquet, he fell asleep. Maybe he was lulled by the darkness inside his hood, or maybe it was the effect of listening to three conversations at the same time, none of which he fully understood.

A smell woke him. The heavy, sickly scent of marijuana. One of the American men was talking – in English, this time.

'So tell me,' the American said. 'What's for dessert?'

Somebody chuckled. Glasses chinked.

Astrid spoke next. 'It's a surprise. Can you guess?'

'Well, as far as I can see,' the American said, 'there's only one thing left on the table . . .'

This was obviously very witty because everybody burst out laughing. But, as soon as the laughter had died down, a silence descended, the silence of anticipation, soft and dense as velvet.

Inside the hood he could hear his blood humming.

A warm and slightly oily hand reached between his thighs. Was it the same person, or another, who then grasped his penis, which was already, for some reason, half erect, and put it in their mouth?

He gasped.

Just then he felt a hand on his upper arm. It was one of the women, he was sure. Though her touch was subtle – perhaps it even went unnoticed by the others – he knew it was a reminder, a warning. At the same time she was telling him that he should relax. Let things take their course.

Remember, not a word from you. Not a sound.

His chest expanded as he took air deep into his lungs. A pool of fluid slid out of a hollow where it had been resting and trickled sideways across his ribs.

Meanwhile the guests were taking turns with him, it seemed. Some were rough, almost greedy. The prickle of a beard, an unshaven chin. The grazing of a tooth. Others were reverential. Delicate. A touching that was on the edge of touching. He found himself thinking of a butterfly alighting on a leaf. That almost negligible weight.

And then, when it took off again, he followed it, past huge garish blurs of colour that were flowers, up into the air, where it was buffeted by the smallest gust of wind, its wings fluttering gamely . . .

~

When the women finally removed his hood, the lighting in the tent was dim and intimate, just candles, most of which had burned down low. Even so, after the hours he had spent in total darkness, he found it difficult to see at first. Through half-closed eyes he stared down at himself. Blackened strands of salad clung to his legs, almost translucent, like seaweed, and empty clam shells tangled in his pubic hair. His whole body was stained with sauces, juices, traces of saliva. He looked like a piece of wreckage that had washed up on an unknown shore. Curiously, he ached too, as if he had been thrown about by waves.

Gertrude was leaning against the wall to his right, her arms folded beneath her breasts. Her head was covered with a conical black hood, and a bracelet of beaten silver gripped her upper arm. Otherwise she was naked. The candle-flames sent lascivious tongues of shadow flickering across her skin. It was the first time he had been allowed a glimpse of her. She was solid, but slim. Her shoulders were the same width as her hips. She had no waist. Though her breasts were oddly elongated, they did not interfere with the impression her body gave of spareness and economy. She reminded him of the Ancient Greek statues that hold up the roofs of temples – the caryatids – and this was something he could not have predicted. From the way she moved when she was wearing clothes, he had

58

expected her to be much heavier, more fleshy. On his left was Astrid. She was lying on her side on a heap of lavish cushions, her head supported by one hand. She was also naked, her face concealed by a matt-black rubber mask that he recognised from the night of her assault on him. She was smoking a cigarette. On the middle finger of her left hand she was wearing a ring that had several inch-long spikes protruding from it. He wondered where Maude was. Downstairs, probably. Washing the dishes.

'A successful evening,' Astrid said, inhaling deeply.

'It was a triumph,' Gertrude said. 'A real triumph.'

'The dessert was especially good . . .'

Both women laughed.

He looked from one to the other. Though they were probably quite close in age – or, at least, much closer than he had originally imagined – Gertrude's skin was anaemic, almost ghostly, while Astrid's had a glow to it, like treasure. Astrid had a neat round head, with even features and hair that she kept cut short. Her tight-fitting rubber mask revealed as much. Was Gertrude secretly jealous of the way Astrid looked? Was that why Maude was there, to act as a foil, a distraction, something for them both to ridicule? He wished he knew how the women behaved when they were alone together. But the door that led out of the room was like a science fiction gateway. As soon as the women passed through it they seemed to dematerialise, to become invisible; they crossed into a different dimension.

'You behaved well,' Astrid said, studying the end of her cigarette.

'You behaved impeccably,' Gertrude agreed. 'We'd like to reward you.'

She walked towards him, her breasts lolling complacently, the insides of her upper thighs rubbing lightly together. To

59

his surprise, he felt his penis harden. She didn't seem to notice, though – or, if she did, she took pleasure in pretending that she hadn't. Up close, her eyes looked bloodshot. He thought she was probably drunk.

'What would you like?' she asked him.

'Within reason, of course,' came Astrid's voice from behind her.

As he looked up at Gertrude, the air seemed to warp suddenly, to shudder. At first he didn't realise what it was. Then he saw it. A single hair had fallen from beneath her hood. A single hair had come loose and floated downwards through the air between them. It had fallen past his face, too close for him to focus on, and landed on the gold fabric of the tablecloth, just inches from his right elbow. He could see it lying there, about the length of a finger, with a slight curve to it. It was red.

Gertrude seemed quite oblivious to what had happened. 'Tell me what you'd like,' she was saying, breathing wine fumes over him, 'what you'd like for a reward . . .'

'You could let me go,' he said.

She turned away. 'No. That's not an option.'

'Within reason,' Astrid reminded him, crushing out her cigarette.

He looked down at the red hair again – a give-away, a clue, a piece of evidence. How long had he spent imprisoned in this room? Five days? Six? He was beginning to lose count. He had been taken on a Monday afternoon. Could it be Saturday already? His eyes shifted to his body, which he no longer felt as if he owned. He could almost see the weakness spreading through him. His body was his only clock, he realised, and he had no way of measuring time except in terms of wastage, atrophy, decay. Disgust collected like a kind of bile in his throat.

60

'There must be something you would like,' Gertrude was saying.

His lungs had filled with dust. He could hardly breathe.

'I need to move,' he said. 'I need some air.'

～

He thought he sensed tension as the women walked into the room the next morning, the tension that follows an argument that has yet to be resolved. He had the feeling that there might have been some disagreement over the granting of his request. There was a certain stiffness in their body language. He saw hips and elbows. Thumbs. Watching them arrange themselves in front of him, he realised that this was a sequence he could have choreographed. What music would he have chosen for a piece like this? Would it have been full of jarring dissonance, in keeping with the mood, or would it have flowed sweetly, providing an ironic counterpoint?

Once both his hands and feet were shackled, the women helped him to stand up. Maude slipped a hood over his head. It was the same hood that he had worn the night before; he could smell meat on it, and wine, and smoke. The women led him towards the door. He must have looked like a man being taken to the scaffold.

'So this is my reward,' he said.

He felt unaccountably light and skittish; he could not resist making jokes, but there was no reaction from any of the women.

They passed out of the white room and into the passage-way. The toilet, he knew, would be on the left, and there would be a second door ahead of him, about fifteen feet away, but that was where his knowledge ended. He could see nothing, of course, and anything he might have heard was drowned by the sound his chains made as he moved. His sense of smell was complicated by the hood. He had to try and ignore what was left over from the banquet. He had to filter all that out. Smell beyond it, somehow. Through the second door they went and out into what felt like a larger space. A landing, perhaps. This was new ground now.

They turned to the left, took a dozen steps, then turned to the right and stopped. There are stairs here, one of the women told him. He reached out cautiously with one foot, as if testing the temperature of water. The air that brushed against his bare forearms was cool, reminding him of the air in a cellar. He thought he could smell plaster, a smell he usually associated with new buildings, but the staircase was wide and steep, which led him to believe that he was in an old house. Though there were women on either side of him, he found it easiest to climb down sideways, like somebody on skis. He reached the bottom of one flight, and then embarked upon another, one of the women holding him by the upper arm as a precaution.

At last they reached ground level. The surface beneath his feet was no longer carpeted. Tile, he guessed. Or concrete. Down one step, along, down another step, along again. One of the women turned a key in a lock and pushed at the door, which seemed to resist her for a moment, then they walked out into the air . . .

Even through the hood his first breath was exhilarating. He had forgotten air could be so intricate. He could smell the wind and rain in it, and earth, dark earth, and the bitter milk that leaked from the stems of plants. He could also smell the mildewed panes of a glass-house and the rusting screws on the handle of a watering-can. Then the warm, slightly gritty smell of a red-brick wall. Beyond that, he could smell the city, faintly, but in all its richness and variety: bicycle tyres, canal water, pickled herrings, a tram's electric cables, spilled beer in the entrance to a bar – and, in the distance, at the very limit of his sense of smell, the pungent salty spray that lifted off the North Sea as it hurled itself repeatedly against the land. He stood outside the door and breathed. Just breathed.

'Nice garden,' he said after a while.

He was only guessing, of course, but the stillness of the women told him that he had guessed correctly. Beneath his hood he smiled. He felt so sharp all of a sudden. He felt humorous. Though he was bound and chained, though he had three people to contend with, strangers, it seemed to him that he was master of the situation.

He shook his head. 'You know, I think you might have made a mistake.'

The stillness deepened. It was almost as if the women were no longer there, as if he was talking to himself. At the same time, though, he could sense the glances arrowing between them.

'You should never have let me out of that room.' He took another draught of air, took it to the bottom of his lungs. 'You were too nice,' he said. 'Too kind.' He gave that last word a sardonic twist. 'I mean, it's such a risk . . .'

He shuffled forwards. No one restrained him. No one spoke. He found that he was standing on grass. He loved the spongy quality it had, the way it gave slightly beneath him. He could feel its dampness through the thin soles of his shoes. Just then, from somewhere to his right, there came the wincing of a train's brakes. Two streets away. Maybe three.

'First of all,' he said, 'you didn't gag me. I could start shouting. I could draw attention to myself. And, who knows, somebody might come – '

'So, are you going to shout?'

This was Astrid's voice, dispassionate but menacing. He ignored her.

63

'Or somebody might see me,' and he lifted his head, looked upwards, 'from an upstairs window – and what would they see? Three women in black cloaks and a man wearing a hood. All standing in a garden on a Sunday morning. Now that's not exactly normal, is it, even for Holland – '

'It isn't Sunday,' Gertrude said.

Once again, he ignored the interruption.

'And then,' he went on, 'and this is more serious, perhaps, you're giving me the chance to gather information . . .'

He could no longer hear the train. Instead, in the distance, a church bell started tolling. What did she mean, it wasn't Sunday? Of course it was Sunday.

'Yes,' he said. 'Little details. Sense data.' He nodded to himself. 'It all helps me to put a picture together. Of where I am. Of who I'm dealing with.'

He looked round at the women, even though he didn't know exactly where they were. He felt elated, slightly giddy. It was probably the sudden influx of oxygen into his body after days of stale, recycled air.

'Take me to a donkey,' he said. 'I bet I could pin a tail on it.'

'A donkey?' Astrid said. 'What donkey?'

He laughed at her.

'If I was you I'd never have allowed me out. Fresh air indeed!' He snorted in derision. 'Who needs fresh air? But, of course. I forgot' – he would have slapped his forehead, but his hands weren't free – 'You love me. You'd do anything for me.' He was laughing again. 'You think my work is wonderful.'

A woman took him by the arm. She just held him, though; she didn't try to move him.

'You see, you had a really good set-up,' he explained, 'but now you've gone and undermined it. You've introduced an element that's volatile. Do you understand that word? I don't know what it is in Dutch. Something ugly, I expect.'

64

Chuckling to himself, he shook his head.

'Yes,' he said, 'while I was in that room, everything was under control. Now, though . . .'

He released the thought into their minds like a virus, hoping it would take root and spread, weakening their confidence, their resolution.

'It's time to go back in,' Gertrude said.

Your hair is red, he thought. *I've seen it.*

He felt a hand push him in the small of the back, push him towards the door. He detected a brusqueness in the gesture, a sense of irritation, and he was glad that he had finally got under the women's skin.

'I don't think you've been listening,' he said, 'not properly. I don't think you've really taken in what I've been saying.'

He allowed himself to be led through the door and back along the passageway. As he placed his right foot on the bottom step, about to begin the climb back to the room, he heard a ringing sound somewhere behind him.

'That's the phone, isn't it?' he said.

There was no reaction from the women, no response.

'Don't you think you should answer that?' he said. 'It might be someone important.'

∿

Perhaps he shouldn't have talked so much. Something irrepressible had taken possession of him, though; all of a sudden he had been flooded with adrenalin – and this despite the handcuffs and the hood . . . The women thought they were doing him a favour by letting him out of the room for a few minutes. They thought they were rewarding him. Well, the whole thing was absurd. He had tired of their arrogance, their condescension. He had wanted to make them feel stupid.

Careless. And if his reading of their silence in the garden was correct, then it was possible he had succeeded. Would there be reprisals? He couldn't tell. Probably it would have been wiser to hold his tongue. Probably he should have stood there like some dumb animal and breathed the air.

He stared bleakly at the skylight, a square of blotchy white and grey. It was dismal weather. But still, those moments he had spent outside – the smell of rain-soaked grass, the touch of the raw spring breeze on the back of his hands – had cruelly reminded him of everything he had lost. He thought of Brigitte, and the pain was oddly sharp, abdominal. He thought of how little sex they'd had recently, and that saddened him, though he knew it happened to other couples too, especially when they were working hard and always tired. He remembered how it had been at the beginning, on their first holiday together, in Elba. They had stayed in a small, family-run hotel in the back-streets of Portoferráio. Their room had a high ceiling and a milky, pale-green marble floor. There was an old-fashioned double bed, with a metal headboard and a counterpane made of a satiny pink material. Above the bed was a painting of a gypsy woman with her white blouse pulled down off her shoulders and her chin raised in defiance. Brigitte said the place reminded her of her mad spinster Aunt Cecile's apartment in Marseille. He watched her unfasten the dark-green shutters and lean on the windowsill, looking out over the town, the strong, slender muscles showing in the back of her calves . . . Later, while they were making love, a gap had opened in the middle of the bed. It wasn't a double bed at all, he realised, but two single beds that had been pushed together. The china lamp on the bedside table swayed, then disappeared from view. Amazingly, it didn't break. A woman's voice downstairs kept shouting, *Mario? Ma-rio?* Afterwards, they found themselves between the two beds, on the floor, the counterpane still underneath them. They could have been lying in a hammock. Twenty to eight on a June evening, the clatter of knives and forks in the restaurant below, the waspy rasp of a passing *motorino*, and Brigitte murmuring, *Where am I?*

Of course she knew, really. But the sex had been so abandoned, so all-consuming, that they had, for a short time at least, been lost to themselves. When they returned, they returned to a room they didn't recognise, a town they didn't know, which was a shock because they had worked so hard that year, rehearsing, performing, rehearsing again, there had been time for nothing else, and now, suddenly, they were away somewhere, alone together, and their removal, that fact in itself, was almost impossible to believe, a cause for wonder. She lay beneath him on the counterpane, her hands reaching above her head, as if in surrender, the palms facing upwards, the fingers curled. He could see the shadowy hollows under her arms, which she always shaved, and her pointed, almost nonexistent breasts, with nipples that were so sensitive that he could sometimes make her come just by touching them. Her body, though slight, concealed huge energy, an energy she would summon in performance. There had been a night in São Paulo once when he had watched her from the wings of the theatre, and his heart had lifted inside his chest and then stayed there, as if suspended, because she was doing things that he had never imagined she might do, not the steps so much, though they were faultless, but the feeling that in-formed the steps, and, at the end, bouquets flew out of the darkness in their dozens, the stage was ankle-deep in flowers suddenly, flowers he had never seen before and could not have named . . . When she walked into the wings towards him, the look of amazement and disbelief must still have been on his face because she said, *I know, I don't know what it was — j'avais des ailes.* And then she laughed and said, *I was flying,* and he held her in his arms and felt her body against his, the muscles taut, heat bursting through her skin, and then someone behind him shouted, *There are drinks at the ambassador's, everybody – drinks at the ambassador's . . .*

Where am I? he thought.

A white room, somewhere in the Netherlands.

Lying there, chained to the floor, he could taste a metallic substance in his mouth. His gums were bleeding again. When the women cleaned his teeth, they brushed too hard – or in a way he wasn't used to, perhaps. That morning, for the first time in his life, he had noticed a thick streak of bright-red in his saliva, and it had shaken him, as if he had been forced to confront his own weakness, his mortality . . .

The next few hours were difficult, his mood careering wildly from nostalgia to despair. They're two quite different places, but the journey from one to the other, it's a journey that takes no time at all.

~

Later that day the door opened and a woman entered. She closed the door behind her, then leaned against it. She was on her own. From where he lay, in the middle of the room, he couldn't tell which one of them it was; she was standing in deep shadow, and she was wearing the usual black hood and cloak. He was slightly apprehensive about the way the women might react to his behaviour in the garden. He decided that it might be best to try and ingratiate himself.

'I'm sorry about what happened this morning,' he said. 'I got carried away. Being outside, even for a few minutes – you forget what it's like . . .'

Slowly the woman eased herself away from the door and

68

out into the room. The uncertainty, the awkwardness. He thought he recognised her now, if only by a process of elimination. It was Maude.

'In any case,' he said, 'I just wanted to apologise.'

She kneeled on the mat beside him, as she had done many times, her head averted, her hands laid, palms down, on her thighs. In that moment he found that he could imagine her as a child. She had been unwanted, unloved. Perhaps she had even been beaten. It would explain the way she moved, as if she was trying not to take up any space. It would also explain her voice, which, though monotonous, had a curiously indignant ring to it, almost a kind of reverberation, reminding him of the sound geese make. It was the voice of somebody who had never been allowed to express herself, or had never dared.

She put one hand on his left ankle and ran it along the side of his foot until she reached the toes. 'A dancer's foot...' The tips of her fingers lingered on the places where his skin had hardened, where his bones had changed shape. 'It's good when what a person does, it leaves marks on their body,' she said. 'The hands of a gardener, for instance ...' She touched a white scar on his ankle. 'What happened here?'

'A calcium spur,' he said. 'The calcium builds up and forms a kind of spike on the bone. I had to have an operation to cut it out. It's common for dancers.'

She took a breath. 'I'm not going to do anything bad to you.' Her eyes shifted behind the two holes in her hood.

He wanted to talk to her, to have a normal conversation, but he couldn't think of a good place to begin.

'I would like to lie next to you,' she said, 'if you don't mind.'

'No,' he said, 'I don't mind.' He kept his voice gentle.

'I have to be naked,' she said.

She pushed her cloak back from her legs to reveal a pair of black work-boots. The toes were scuffed, and the tread on the

69

soles had almost worn to nothing. As she untied the laces she began to hum in that tuneless way she had, which he now understood to be a sign of nervousness. Not wanting to embarrass her, he looked away. He felt he could have predicted those boots that she was wearing. They fitted the image he now had of her, of someone who was both stubborn and neglected.

'My body is not exciting to you,' she said.

He turned to her again. Her thighs were heavy and dimpled, and her ample belly folded in on itself. She had the solid, rounded shoulders of a swimmer – though he couldn't really see her swimming – and small, oddly delicate breasts that seemed as if they must belong to someone else. Her body showed you all the colours and textures flesh could be. A painter would have loved it.

'It's all right,' she said. 'I don't want to – I don't want anything.' She paused. 'I'm not like the others.'

He waited for her to elaborate, but nothing came. She was too deeply embedded in her own thoughts. This was the damage that had been done to her. All of a sudden he knew what he could say.

'It was you that night, wasn't it.'

She became so still then that he could see her pulse sending tremors across the surface of her skin.

'I woke up a few nights ago,' he said, still using the same gentle voice. 'Someone was lying next to me. It was you.'

She turned and fitted herself against him, her left leg drawn up over his thighs, her head resting on his shoulder. He looked at her left hand lying on his chest, her short, pale fingers aligning themselves with the gaps between his ribs. He could feel her heart reverberating through his body. It was beating as fast as a small animal's.

'I must warn you,' she said.

'Warn me? What about?'

'They have things planned.'

'What things?'

'Things I could not have thought of.'

'They're angry with me . . .'

'Perhaps. But also you are here. It is because you're here.'

'Can you talk to them?'

'Talk to them?'

'Stop them.'

'I don't think so.'

'Please,' he said.

Lifting her head, she reached out with one hand and touched his lips. This was her way of saying that she couldn't help him. Her fingers smelled of onions and candle-wax.

He lay there quietly, beneath her weight.

'It was you I shouted at,' he said after a while.

'Yes.'

'I'm sorry if I shouted,' he said. 'You don't know what it's like.'

'You frightened me.'

'I'm sorry.'

He heard rain on the skylight and thought of people cycling home with their heads lowered, the metal tramlines shining . . . In his mind he leaned on black railings and stared down at a canal. The water looked studded, punctured – sharp, somehow. Like a bed of nails.

They have things planned.

Sometime later he woke up to find that Maude had gone, though the smell of candle-wax and onions was still there, rising into his nostrils from the places on his body where her hands had rested.

~

His dreams were fuelled by a terrible anxiety that night. There were no landscapes any more, no views at all, only the bare white walls of the white room, only the skylight with its empty square of sky. He would see himself suspended upside-down, hoisted on a complex web of ropes and pulleys. He would be turning slowly in mid-air, like a carcass on a hook, his body trussed, blood flooding into the cramped spaces, the cavities and hollows, behind his eyes. There would be a woman in the room with him, a naked figure in the shadows near the door, and all she would be wearing was a hood of deepest black. It would look as if her head was missing, as if a headless body was standing in the room, and he would hear it whispering, this headless body, *Beautiful, so beautiful* . . . Then he would wake again, and it would be hard to know whether he was alone or not, he couldn't always see into the corners, not at night, and the darkness hissing, buzzing, like a thousand shrunken voices all muttering at once, and he would look down at his body, which was laid out in the manner of an offering, a sacrifice, and he would find that he no longer knew what was a dream and what wasn't, and he would wonder which was worse . . .

In a way, being awake was easier. At least he could make an attempt to control things. Awake, he could try and hypnotise himself into a different place, his only refuge being the obvious one, that of his past life, but it was difficult to sustain, and in the end it was pointless too, perhaps. As soon as the images he summoned from the past began to falter, the room would assert itself, parts of it becoming visible, like skin showing through wet clothes. There it would be, stark and white, but never quite dispassionate, somehow, how could it be with all those rings and straps and bolts, every one of which, he now knew, had been designed with some exquisite torture or perversion in mind. The hooks and rails. The washing-machine. The dull-black rubber mat. A blandness about it all, an everyday brutality – predictable, unchanging, remorseless.

The room was always there.

~

And so it came, the day of his mutilation.

He was lying on the floor, as usual, when the door opened and the women filed in, one by one. All three of them were wearing red hoods over their heads. All three of them were naked. They looked like the cardinals of some arcane or sacrilegious church. The hairs lifted on his arms. There had been a change in the women. He could feel it. It was as if, in stripping themselves of their clothes, they had removed all decency, all inhibition. As if, naked, they might be capable of truly monstrous things.

Just then, the sun came out. The shaft of light that reached from the skylight to the floor was so rich in colour, so thick and golden, that it gave the impression of being solid, like a buttress. The women stood beyond it, plunged into a kind of shadow suddenly. When they moved towards him, passing through the sunlight, it was an eerie moment, almost super-natural, like watching ghosts walk through a wall. He felt as though the fabric of the world had been tampered with, which only added to his suspicion that the women were beyond all natural law.

Maude was carrying an oblong metal box, he noticed, and Astrid had a screwdriver in her hand. For a moment, he was reassured. They were going to adjust the rails that held him to the floor, perhaps. Tighten something that was loose. Later, he would look back on that thought with grim amusement.

Was it another punishment? They didn't say. In the end, he

didn't think it was. It was simply that they had exhausted one line of fantasy, and now they were about to explore another. No hard feelings, nothing personal. What had Maude said?

Because you're here.

They gathered round him, all scarlet hoods and pale flesh. His eyes darted from the turquoise vein that twisted down into Maude's groin to the scar on Astrid's hip, which was like the imprint of a coin, to Gertrude's pubic hair, shot through with hints of darkest red, settling at last on the box that Maude had placed on the floor beside him. He had seen something like it once before. It had belonged to his grandfather, who had acted in amateur theatricals, and it had contained all kinds of make-up – eye-liner, grease-paint, rouge . . . But why had Maude brought it into the room with her?

'This will be painful,' Gertrude said.

He looked up at her, his throat constricting. 'What do you mean? What are you going to do?'

'Perhaps it's better we don't say.'

She took hold of his underpants and pulled them down to his ankles.

'No,' he said suddenly. His voice sounded almost strident in the silence and – odd, this – exactly like his father's.

'There could be advantages,' Astrid said. 'There could be benefits. In time.'

There was no comfort in the woman's ambiguities – he had learned that early on. He stared at the screwdriver she was holding. It had a transparent, bright-yellow handle. The tip was half a centimetre wide.

'You're not – ' He faltered, unable to put his feelings into words.

'The reason why this will be painful,' Gertrude said, 'is because we have no anaesthetic.'

'A screwdriver, though,' he said uselessly.

He turned to the woman he called Maude, wishing that he knew her real name.

'Help me,' he said. 'Please.'

But she only turned her head to one side, as if embarrassed or ashamed.

The other women spoke to her quickly in Dutch, their voices calm, insistent. What were they telling her? That she shouldn't listen to him? That everything was going to be all right? He watched as Maude opened the metal box and took out a packet of cotton swabs and a bottle of what looked like iodine.

Not make-up, then. First-aid.

'And now,' Gertrude said, motioning to Astrid.

The women crouched around him on the floor, Gertrude to the left of him, Astrid on his right, Maude between his legs. Gertrude pinched his nostrils, and when he opened his mouth to breathe, she put a piece of balled-up rag in it, then reached into Maude's metal box and lifted out a roll of silver insulation tape. She tore off a strip of tape and stuck it over the lower half of his face. The rag tasted of diesel oil.

Astrid took hold of his foreskin between her finger and thumb and lifted it away from his penis, stretching it until the light shone through it. She placed the tip of the screwdriver against the skin and then pushed firmly. The screwdriver broke through. He could see the wide, sharp tip poking out the other side. He remembered being surprised by how red the blood was, a red that was so bright and clean that it looked new. He remembered seeing drops of blood lying in his pubic hair, like berries, as if they had grown there.

All this, as if from a great distance . . .

By the time he came round, the women had fixed a ring through the hole. At first he could not understand how they had managed it, then he saw that one section of the ring was thicker, and had a lock built into it. The ring was a dull silver colour, an alloy of some kind, and measured more than an inch in diameter. He supposed they must have bought it specially.

They had not pierced his penis, only the foreskin, and now Maude was bending over him, a cotton swab poised between her fingers. The bright flash of pain as she dabbed iodine on to the punctured skin was almost enough to make him pass out for a second time. With his mouth taped up, though, he could hardly make a sound. His pain stayed inside him. They didn't want to hear it. As he lay there, floating in and out of consciousness, he had a keen sense of the hopelessness of his predicament: they could do anything they wanted – anything at all . . .

~

Later, when the wound had been cleaned, the women brought a length of chain into the room. They attached one end to the ring in his penis and the other to a solid iron staple that had been driven into the wall behind him, then they freed him from the stainless-steel rails and clustered round him. Their hoods had the effect of making them appear utterly without feeling, without conscience, and this contrasted oddly with their voices, which sounded tender, concerned, even encouraging. Though his wrists and ankles would often still be shackled, they told him, he would have more freedom of movement from now on. He would be able to stand up, walk a little. Maybe even dance. It's what we want most of all, one of the women said, to see you dance. He shook his head. What they were saying seemed like mockery. How could they put him through these endless, grotesque ordeals and still claim that they cared for him? And another thing. He had given up the idea of distinguishing between their voices. If he thought he could find an ally, or win some kind of leverage, he was fooling himself. Their voices were neither human nor individual. They were the voices of a single creature: his jailer, his tormentor.

One of them held out two white tablets on the palm of her hand. Codeine, she said. She put the tablets on his tongue, one at a time, holding a glass of water to his mouth so he could wash them down. He lay back on the mat. The sky had clouded over. The golden buttress no longer angled down into the room. In the new half-light the stinging at the centre of his body was like a colour. Not a colour he could name, though. No, it was too brilliant for that. Every now and then it grew in size until it surrounded him completely. At times, he felt as if he was actually inside it.

Through this haze he heard the women's voices:

'You should rest now – '

'We'll check on you in the night – '

'We'll take care of you – '

'The wound, it will heal. Don't worry – '

'Rest now – '

∼

Though he was given pain-killers at regular intervals throughout the night he slept fitfully, the skin that divided sleep from waking membrane-thin, translucent. It must have been a form of delirium. His dreams, when they came, were specific and repetitive, almost circular, and they never strayed too far from reality. Once, he woke, or thought he woke, to see the bright-orange coffin lying on the floor beside him. It did not change shape, though, or move across the room. It stayed exactly where it was, for hours. Another time, he dreamed that he had been chained to a brick wall. His penis had a rusty iron padlock attached to it, such as you might find on the door of an abandoned barn, and the wound was raw, sticky with pus. He let his head fall back against the wall. The bricks had a blackened quality, as if they had once stood too close to a fire, as if they had been scorched. A wind roared and rattled in the air.

In that dream, as in almost all the others, there were two levels of consciousness, two levels that coexisted and sometimes even overlapped. On the one hand he was bewildered, shocked and numb with horror at the situation in which he found himself. On the other he was looking forward to the moment when he could shake off what he knew to be a dream, when he realised that none of it was true.

The cruelty of waking to the soft chink of the chain's links moving . . .

The truth lay in the dream, of course, outside it too, and the misery that he experienced as he shifted on the mat was hard to bear.

Sometimes he would catch a glimpse of himself in one of the steel rings that held his wrists. He could only ever see himself in fragments. A cheekbone, an eyebrow. Part of an ear. He was like a vase that had been broken thousands of years ago. He would never be whole again. He only existed in pieces. In memory.

He turned slowly, gingerly, on to his side and pushed his shackled hands towards his groin, as close as they would go. Somehow, the mere fact of proximity was soothing.

A milky glow spilling from the skylight.

The ticklish, slightly peppery smell of dust between the floorboards.

That low groaning he could hear, a sound that was so constant, so present in the room that it seemed to have a form

– a dog run over by a car, a coat thrown on the ground – that groaning sound, that was him.

$$\sim$$

He no longer knew what day it was, no longer cared. His suffering had made an irrelevance of things like that. There was only pain, and the need to be delivered from it. Sometimes, when the codeine floated him beyond its reach, people would appear in the room. He could not be certain, then, if he was dreaming or hallucinating. Probably it did not matter.

Brigitte was the first to come. She sat on his left, facing the door. Her legs lay flat on the floor, at right-angles to one another. Her hands rested in her lap. She was wearing a loose-fitting, pale-blue T-shirt he had never seen before, but her hair was tied back with the usual scrap of mauve velvet. As he watched, she bent her forehead to her right knee, then straightened up again, her right arm lifting into the air beside her ear. This series of movements had the ease, the fluidity, of a reflex, as though she hadn't really been aware of what she was doing. Her dark eyes stared into the middle distance.

'Our time is almost over,' she said.

He could feel his heart push against the inside of his chest, like something trying to escape. What did she mean?

'You and me,' she said, as if his thoughts were audible. 'Our time together.'

'No,' he said, 'you're wrong.' His throat was dry. He swallowed. 'You just have to wait till I get out of here. Wait till I'm free.'

She reached up with both hands to adjust the piece of mauve velvet, then she turned to face him. In her eyes he could see nothing but indifference. She had the look of somebody who didn't know him. Who had never known him.

'You'll never be free,' she said.

'I will,' he said. Though, suddenly, he wasn't sure.

She shook her head and stared into the distance again. 'No,' she said.

He looked away from her, unable to find the words with which to contradict her. When he turned to her again, she was no longer there.

Sometime later, in the middle of the night, his family appeared – his mother and his father, both still young, in their fifties, and his brother, Edward, who worked for a bank in Tokyo. His father and his brother had dressed for the occasion, in identical grey suits. His mother was wearing a cardigan over a pleated skirt. People often said that he took after his mother, though he couldn't really see it, except in the eyes, perhaps, which were hazel and sloped upwards at the corners, giving them both a faintly Slavic look. She seemed more preoccupied than usual, her head craning on its slender neck, as if she was peering deep into the corners of the room. 'Well,' she said at last, 'this isn't so bad, is it.' His father nodded in absent-minded agreement, one hand lifting to smooth his thinning hair. Edward, meanwhile, had tucked one highly polished heel against the far wall and was measuring dimensions, as if he was thinking of putting in an offer for the property. That was just like Edward. He watched his family, half despairing, half amused. Eventually, his mother came and stood beside him. She did not appear to find the situation out of the ordinary at all. She simply smiled at him, and then repeated herself: 'Really, darling, it's not that bad.'

He wasn't sure how to interpret their behaviour. Did they genuinely not notice that he had been mutilated, that he had been chained to a wall? Or were they *pretending* not to notice, so as to disguise their embarrassment, their shame? Or – more subtle, this – were they trying to offer him a message of hope, trying to give him strength, but using an oblique, almost coded approach in case his captors overheard? Before he could decide, his mother caught sight of the full moon floating in the skylight. A gasp came out of her, a soft sound that signified both shock and wonder, and she began to spin, some part of her knowing that everybody's eyes were fixed on her, the other part not caring. Her skirt flared out all round her, making the shape of a mushroom in the ghostly, silver air . . .

Other people came to visit him as well, all sorts of people from his life. Bert Gischler, the company director. Stefan Elmers, the photographer. Even his mentor Isabel van Zaanen appeared, wearing an ankle-length fur coat and diamond earrings, as if she had arrived straight from a première. Isabel had worked for the company as a guest choreographer for many years, and he owed much of his success to her advice and inspiration. Standing by the wall, she lit one of her Egyptian cigarettes. 'Remember what Balanchine said,' she told him. ' "First comes the sweat, then comes the beauty." ' She smiled to herself – Balanchine had been a friend of hers – then she walked over and bent down so he could touch his lips to her cheek.

None of his visitors acknowledged his predicament – or even seemed to notice it. All the same, he was glad that they had made the journey, and he drew no little comfort from their presence. He needed to be reminded that there were people beyond the room. People who knew him, loved him. People who missed him. Even if they were not actively looking for him, they would be thinking of him. It was a link, a kind of lifeline.

Though sometimes, it was true, they brought messages he didn't want to hear:

You will never be free.

81

Our time is over.
You and me.
Our time together.
Over.

~

The wound healed slowly, almost grudgingly. Perhaps he was
to blame, turning over in his sleep and irritating it, or perhaps
it was the chafing action of the ring. In any case, he was being
given antibiotics to prevent infection and codeine to neu-
tralise the pain. Most of the time he felt glassy, sluggish –
drugged. Every so often, though, the air would seem to clear,
and he would notice that the women were naked as they
carried out their tasks. They still had hoods over their heads,
of course, and they often wore something on their feet –
Astrid and Gertrude chose shoes with spiked heels; Maude
preferred her work-boots – but they had thrown aside their
cloaks. They had become more open, more flagrant, and, at
the same time, more voyeuristic. In the beginning the vision
of a chained man had been enough in itself. Now it was his
injury which they found stimulating – the nature of that
injury, and its location. When they took him to the toilet they
would shackle his wrists and ankles, as usual, but one of them
would lead him by the chain, as though he was an exotic but
domesticated animal. When he was lying on the mat, they
would walk round him, almost as if they were stalking him,
with their hooded faces angled hungrily in his direction. They
would lean down and touch the chain, their breathing quick-
ening as they bent over him, their voices thickening in their
throats like beaten cream. Sometimes they would lift the
chain – gently, though, so as not to disturb his penis, the way
you might try and remove an empty cider bottle from the

82

hand of a sleeping drunk. Other times he would wake out of a medicated daze to find one of the women sitting in front of him, her head tilted back, one hand moving rhythmically between her legs . . .

He had never watched a woman masturbate before – no girl he had gone out with had ever done it in front of him – and he was intrigued to see that each of the women had their own quite different techniques. Maude always began in a kneeling position. Then, at some point, though, she would fall forwards, panting, her right arm reaching back down the middle of her body, her right hand hidden. All the weight would be taken by her other arm, the skin creasing at the wrist, her small round nails reddening as the blood rushed in underneath . . . Astrid masturbated standing up. She would lean against the white pipes that ran from floor to ceiling, or sometimes she would stand close to him, only just beyond the rubber mat. Unlike Maude, she touched herself all over, her hands fluttering this way and that across her body. They seemed oddly fidgety, distracted, almost disconnected from the rest of her. They would circle one of her breasts, flicker across a hip, brush against the inside of a thigh, but they would never settle anywhere for more than a few moments, just long enough, presumably, to bring that part of her to life. When she came, her legs would buckle slightly, as if she had been given a strong muscle relaxant and was having to fight to remain upright . . . Gertrude was more explicit than Astrid, and more visceral. If this surprised him a little, it was only because she had been the last to reveal her body, and he had sometimes wondered whether she might not be the most modest of the women. But there was nothing modest about the way she lay on her back in front of him, with her legs wide apart and her knees raised. Her cunt was palest pink, almost pallid, with labia that were uneven, swollen, slightly ruffled, like the pages of a book that has fallen into water and then dried out. She would sink the middle fingers of one hand so deep into herself that her hand looked disfigured, and red blotches would appear on her neck, or her breastbone, or on the soft skin of her belly . . . There was only one thing the women had in common. They all shuddered at the moment of orgasm. They seemed to be responding to some distant violence, as though they were the topmost branches of a tree that was having its trunk shaken. It reminded him of stories he had heard about tidal waves. When a tidal wave has travelled a thousand miles, it becomes just another wave, one among many on a beach. Watching the women, that was how far away he felt from what was happening. He was seeing just a fraction of the power. He was watching ripples.

~

Before too long they wanted to see him in what Astrid called 'a state of arousal'. The hole in his foreskin had not mended yet, but he was no longer feeling too much discomfort. You might think that he wouldn't get erections after being hurt like that, but you'd be wrong. The erections happened despite the injury – in fact, there were times when they almost seemed to happen *because* of it. When the women noticed this, they couldn't conceal their delight. They appeared to find the sight of his penis struggling to lift the chain particularly exquisite. They got wet just watching. He closed his eyes, but he could still hear the delicate, liquid sound of their fingers in their cunts . . . They did everything they could think of to excite him. They showed him pornographic movies. They fed him a diet of aphrodisiacs. Astrid, especially, was in her element. She wore a series of fetishistic outfits that catered for every male fantasy, from the standard to the highly specialised, the bizarre. Once, she put on a nurse's uniform. Another time, she dressed up as a cowgirl, in a ten-gallon hat and denim cut-offs. She would appear with sections of her body wrapped in clingfilm, or tightly bound with rope, or just exposed. In general, she favoured skirts that were so short that they revealed her knickers (which could be crotchless, straight out of a sex catalogue, or plain white cotton, like a schoolgirl's, tight-fitting and yet demure) – and, every now and then, of course, there were no knickers. He became fascinated by her cunt – as she intended him to, perhaps: it looked so neat, so *stuck-on*, somehow, that he began to feel as if it didn't belong between her legs at all, but had lodged there, accidentally, like some exotic, plum-coloured shell . . . And, all the time, they kept him naked, with the heat in the room turned up and that ten-foot chain running from his pierced foreskin to the iron staple in the wall, like a surreal version of an umbilical cord . . .

~

It was during this period of exhibitionism that he thought he noticed a shift in the relationship between the women. There had always been a difference between the behaviour of Maude and that of the other two, but the difference was becoming more pronounced. Maude began to distance herself from what was happening in the room. She did not make the slightest attempt to arouse him, for instance, and she no longer seemed to want to satisfy herself. Instead, she tended to hang back, in the shadows. Or she would turn away, as if she did not care to watch. She no longer spoke to him either. Astrid and Gertrude did not appear to have noticed this new reticence, or, if they had, they had decided not to acknowledge it.

Then, one morning, his theory was proved correct – though not in a way he would have chosen. He was still half asleep when the door opened. It was Maude, and she was alone. He leaned up on his elbows, yawning. She stood in front of him with her feet turned slightly inwards, the insides of her knees touching. Her shoulders sloped downwards, as if drawn earthwards by the weight of the rest of her. For the first time, he saw that she had a mole just to the right of her navel.

'You've been very quiet recently,' he said.

She sat beside him, the breath crushing out of her. She was so close to him that he could see the fine cross-hatching on her knuckles. She was holding an old-fashioned quill pen, he noticed, and a bottle of blue ink.

'Lie down, please,' she said.

Her voice had a hard, neutral sound to it, as if she had made up her mind about something and was determined not to be influenced or distracted in any way.

He lay back slowly. The weather in the skylight was overcast, the light bleak and watery. In the distance he thought he could hear a church bell ringing. Surely it couldn't be Sunday again already?

'It's not right,' she said, 'what is happening.'

He wondered what she meant. He didn't ask her, though, thinking it might be better just to let her talk.

'They think they can do what they want.' Putting the quill down, she picked up the bottle of ink and started to unscrew the top. 'They should not be doing all these things.'

'You're upset,' he said.

'Yes.'

When she had opened the ink she placed it on the mat in front of her. Once again, he noticed how blunt her fingers were, and how the nails were almost circular, and it suddenly occurred to him that she might be retarded. Images of her flashed before his eyes like evidence. He saw her as he had seen her first, standing in the alley with her head at a peculiar angle. Not listening, as he had thought. Not shy. But cut loose, floating – adrift in a world of her own. He remembered the time that he had called her names, and how she had failed to react, how she just sat there, staring down . . . Then, one night, he had woken to find her lying next to him with nothing on, her heartbeat twice as fast as his. In retrospect, the cruelty of the other women seemed in keeping with the room, whereas Maude's tongue-tied adoration felt eccentric, if not simple-minded. Perhaps it even explained the speed with which Astrid had sprung to her defence and punished him. *My friend.* It all fitted in. Made sense.

He watched as she dipped her pen gingerly into the ink and then touched the nib against the bottle to drain off the excess.

'If you struggle,' she said, 'it could be painful.'

'What are you going to do?'

She hesitated, pen in hand. 'Now they will know the truth,' she said. 'Now they will know.' Then she added something in Dutch.

Her belly pushed forwards, flattening against her thighs, as she leaned over him. Pressing down with the gold nib, she broke the surface of his skin about halfway between his left hip and his navel. He flinched, and took in air.

'The pain's not so bad, I think,' she said, as she worked the dark-blue ink beneath his skin.

'You startled me . . .'

'Please do not struggle.'

'No. All right.' He peered at her across his chest. 'What are you doing?'

He knew what she was doing. She was tattooing him, using the only materials that were available to her.

It took her something like an hour to complete. She would

87

hold her breath as she leaned over him, just as she did when she was giving him a shave, then, sitting back, she would release it all at once, the air gushing out of her, as if some sort of valve had opened. Then she would dip the gold nib into the ink, touch it gently to the bottle's thick glass lip and lean down once again. She worked slowly, painstakingly, with a degree of care which, in the circumstances, seemed exaggerated, if not comic. He couldn't see her face, of course, but he suspected that the tip of her tongue would be showing in the corner of her mouth. If she wasn't actually retarded, there was clearly a side to her that was naïve or immature.

Though he had flinched in the beginning, and though it still hurt when she bent down with the pen, drawing what felt like hundreds of short lines on him, it was almost a relief to have pain occurring in a different place. It took his attention away from the nightmare of the ring, it was something new to think about . . . After a while, he found that he could hardly feel the scratching of the nib at all, and he would lift his head to see what, if anything, was happening. He would watch in a kind of stupor as the beads of blood welled up on to the surface of his skin, mingled with the ink, and then spilled sideways in quick, dark lines, reminding him of the way a girl's mascara runs when she is crying. He could only stare as the woman etched a single word on to his body, a four-letter word, the most possessive pronoun that exists:

MIJN

～

Gertrude noticed the tattoo almost as soon as she stepped into the room that evening. It would have been hard not to. By that time, the skin around and underneath the letters was thoroughly inflamed; the whole area had lifted into a raw, red weal. For a moment she stood still. Then her head turned and she looked into his face. Her eyes glittered fiercely inside her hood.

'Who did this?'

Somehow, he didn't feel like making things easy for her.

'I don't know,' he said.

'You don't know?'

'You all look the same. How am I supposed to know which one of you it was?' He paused. 'It could have been you for all I know.'

She bent down, both hands braced on her knees, her elbows jutting sideways into the air. She inspected the tattoo at close range, her face just inches from it, then she straightened quickly and walked out of the room.

When she returned a few minutes later she had the others with her. For the first time in days all three women were wearing their black cloaks, which he took to be an indication of how serious things were. He watched Gertrude take Maude by the upper arm and point at the tattoo. She wanted an explanation, but Maude leaned away from her, resisting her, the way a child might. Gertrude persisted with her questioning. When Maude finally spoke, he heard the word *ziekenhuis*, which he knew was Dutch for *hospital*. But no sooner had Maude used the word than she broke off in mid-sentence and lowered her head, as if chastened. Both the other women glanced sharply in his direction. Though this puzzled him, he didn't ponder it for long. The injury to him didn't seem sufficiently severe to warrant talk of hospitals – and anyway, he was more interested in the fact that there had been anger in Maude's voice, something he couldn't remember hearing before. She was standing up for herself for once.

At some deeper level, she was also standing up for him, of

course. She had disapproved of what the others were doing to him, and the tattoo she had inflicted on him was testament to the strength of that disapproval. In tattooing him, she was attempting to reclaim him; she was saying that he belonged to her, only to her, because only she truly cared for him. He had always assumed that the women's behaviour was governed by a code – at the very least, there had to be some kind of understanding – but this was his first real glimpse of it. Obviously, in this case, Maude had acted alone, without permission, and against the spirit of the group. As he lay there, listening to her being scolded, he realised that a crack had opened right in front of him. Why not try and drive a wedge into it?

Lifting his head, he said, 'It's all right. There's no need to argue.'

He felt Gertrude turn and look at him.

'The tattoo,' he said, 'it's really not a problem. You don't have to be angry with her.'

'This isn't your business,' Gertrude said.

'I was the one who was tattooed,' he said. 'Whose business is it, if it isn't mine?'

Gertrude turned to Astrid and spoke to her rapidly in Dutch, then all three women left the room, with Gertrude still gripping Maude by the upper arm. When the door had closed, he lay back with a faint smile on his face.

~

It had always been Maude who had taken care of the menial tasks. The next morning, though, Gertrude and Astrid appeared in her place. He could only imagine that Maude was in disgrace, and that all access to him had been denied. Perhaps, like him, she had been confined to a room somewhere in the

90

building, and was now lying on a single bed, her big round face turned sullenly towards the wall. When he asked Astrid where 'her friend' was – he used the words deliberately, provocatively – Astrid refused to answer. He sensed that the two women had had just about enough of his impertinence. If he wasn't careful, another punishment would come his way.

Towards the middle of the day Astrid stepped into the room. She was alone this time. She had replaced her black cloak with a brown suede jacket, jeans and a pair of brown leather boots with low heels. Though he was always apprehensive when she appeared on her own – understandably so, since it often preceded some new form of violation she had dreamed up – he discovered that he was smiling. So many Dutch girls dressed that way. It almost amounted to a uniform. He wondered if her face was also typical. Just for a moment he could see her on a bicycle, with short blonde hair, a wide mouth, and steady grey-blue eyes that looked bold or unimpressed.

Astrid seemed to consider his smile, then decide not to comment on it. Instead, she told him that he had a première in two days' time. He would be required to dance in front of an invited audience.

He stared at her, nonplussed.

'I can't dance,' he told her. 'I'm out of condition. I haven't trained for – ' He did not even know how long it was since he had last trained.

'You will dance to the best of your ability,' she said.

'And what about this?' He held up the chain. 'What am I supposed to do with this?'

'That's part of it. A test of your,' and she paused, 'of your ingenuity.' She turned and walked a few paces, her hands in the pockets of her jeans. Then she stopped and looked at him across one shoulder. 'You're a choreographer, aren't you?'

He lay back, said nothing. Wind gusted across the roof, a full, low sound, like someone blowing across the top of an empty bottle.

'It will be worth your while,' he heard her say.

His laughter was bitter, sardonic. 'Where have I heard that before?' He lifted his head again, watched her move smugly towards the door. 'That hood with those clothes,' he said. 'It looks ridiculous.'

She paused with one hand on the door-handle. 'And you,' she said, 'what do you look like?'

~

He leaned against the wall in the half-dark, the cold iron of the staple just to one side of his head. The number of times that he had tried to pull that staple out of the wall . . . He had tugged and heaved and strained, but it hadn't moved at all, not even minutely. He had examined the chain as well, to see if he could find a weak link. There were none. He had even thought about taking the chain in both hands and ripping the ring free of his foreskin –

But no, he couldn't do it.

He couldn't face that bright flash of agony as the flesh tore, and then the pain that would follow it, spreading outwards like a brilliant, unearthly colour until it enveloped him completely. And there was always a chance that he might seriously injure himself.

Perhaps he was just a coward . . .

In any case, he had reached a point where he had begun to feel as if his fate was no more or less than he deserved. There was nothing random or accidental about what had happened to him. There was nothing *unlucky* about it. All those years of performing on stage – exhibiting himself . . . What was dance if it was not exposure of the body? It was as though he had advertised himself. He pressed his forehead against the wall, but its coolness did not soothe him. He felt impotent and useless. He felt dull-witted too. Whether he deserved his fate or not, he still had no idea what that fate might be. His only vision of the future was a present that endured and did not alter. He stayed sitting by the wall in a kind of trance or dream-state. His whole mind seemed to be floating, as if there was no gravity inside his head.

He remembered Astrid's proposal. Almost despite himself, he found that it appealed to him. Even if the performance was a travesty, at least he would be dancing. And it would occupy him, give him a sense of purpose. He returned to the rubber mat. Lying down on his side, with one hand under his cheek and his knees drawn up towards his chest, he tried to think of a ballet that might be appropriate. He quickly rejected his own works as being unequal to the occasion. After all, this was his chance to comment on what had happened to him, and for that he would need a classic, he felt, something that everybody knew and loved, something that was virtually a cliché. He wanted irony, a sense of paradox.

Sometime during the night he woke up knowing that his choice would be *Swan Lake*. He hadn't danced classical ballet for at least ten years, but he had seen countless performances of *Swan Lake* while studying in London, and he knew it well enough. He was thinking particularly of Act Three, often referred to as 'the black act'. During Act Two the Prince has met Odette, who has been turned into a white swan. She can only be freed by a man who loves nobody but her, and the Prince has sworn that he will be this man. In Act Three, however, he meets Odile. Odile bears a striking resemblance to Odette, the only difference being that she dresses in black. Assuming that they are one and the same person, the Prince falls for Odile and announces that he intends to marry her. In doing so, he betrays Odette, the woman he actually loves. What has been done cannot be undone, and the ballet ends tragically for both of them, with Odette condemned to remain a swan and the Prince drowning in the lake.

He glanced down at the chain, ten feet of dimly glinting metal coiled on the floor beside him. His smile was thin-lipped, mirthless. He would have to improvise, of course. Many of the steps would be impossible, given the restrictions he would be working under. In fact, during the next twenty-four hours, he would have to choreograph the sequence all over again. But that would be a challenge, wouldn't it?

What an unusual *Swan Lake* it was going to be – a version that had never been seen before, and would never be seen again.

A special performance, one night only.

Swan Lake In Chains.

~

The following morning, as he rehearsed, ideas came quickly to him. The strange thing was, Astrid was proved right. She had said the chain would be a test of his ingenuity, and that was exactly what it turned out to be. Obviously, there were certain jumps, such as the *double tour en l'air*, that he would be unable to attempt, but that, in itself, was a kind of provocation. It allowed him to alter one of the most famous set-pieces in classical ballet. Even Nureyev, who had re-choreographed *Swan Lake* for his performance with Fonteyn in 1966, even Nureyev would not have tampered with the four pirouettes that end the Prince's solo in Act Three. Ironically, then, the chain gave him freedom. It not only prompted him to change the actual steps, it was also a metaphor around which he could construct his own personal vision of the ballet. It became a way of reinterpreting the story. The solo that the Prince dances after meeting Odile, the black swan, is supposed to communicate his euphoria at having found the love of his life, but if the Prince dances the solo as a man in chains, then his euphoria is undermined, and he begins to look deluded, almost laughable. The real beauty of this new *Swan Lake*, then, was its sub-text: he would be using the ballet both to expose and to ridicule the whole idea of the women's love for him, which was not a tribute or a celebration, whatever they might say, but an entirely destructive force.

It was Gertrude who brought him lunch that day. 'So,' she said as she set the tray down beside him, 'you have decided to dance for us.'

He nodded. 'I'm going to perform *Swan Lake*. Well, part of it, anyway.'

'A wonderful choice. I think our audience will enjoy that very much.'

'Of course, I've had to alter it a bit.' Smiling brightly, he held the chain up in the air between them.

'Yes,' she said in a slightly puzzled voice. 'Of course.'

It was a conversation she was having trouble with, and she seemed relieved when, turning to more practical matters, he told her that if they wanted him to dance *Swan Lake* for them he would need to be able to listen to the music.

During the afternoon Astrid appeared with a sound system and a CD of *Swan Lake* that had been recorded in the sixties, with von Karajan conducting the Vienna Philharmonic. Once she had connected the CD player and the speakers she stood back with her arms folded and stared at him. As usual, he seemed to arouse a mass of different feelings in her – hostility, wariness, triumph – and these mingled uneasily, making it difficult for him to bring her into any kind of focus. The way she would fall still in front of him sometimes reminded him of a humming-bird's wings: it wasn't stillness at all, in fact, but the illusion of stillness, created by rapid movement, agitation.

In her opinion, she said, he should not have been provided with the equipment, and if he used it for anything other than listening to music, the consequences would be severe. He nodded, to signal that he had understood. Then, with hardly an alteration in her tone of voice, she told him how much they were looking forward to his performance the following evening, and how they were sure it was going to be a great success. He nodded again, wishing she would leave the room. She stared at him for a moment longer, then she turned away.

As soon as she had closed the door behind her, he put on the CD. Turning the volume up almost as high as it would go, he sat down by the wall and waited.

The music began.

For days, if not for weeks, he had been held in virtual silence, with only the creaks of the building to listen to, or the rattle of the skylight, or the whisper of the women's cloaks across the floor. Music had been denied to him; he had almost forgotten such a thing existed. The power of it, though. The power and the sweetness. Even though it was *Swan Lake*, a piece that had never had any great significance for him. He listened to the whole ballet, from beginning to end. He could not move. Usually, if music was playing, it had an immediate physical effect on him – he would walk around, he might even dance – but on that afternoon he remained in the same position for an hour and a half, with his legs stretched out in front of him and his back against the wall, and, once or twice, to his surprise, to his bewilderment, he reached up, touched his face and found that it was wet.

∼

Standing in the brilliant white spotlight he couldn't see them clearly. There seemed to be both men and women present, all of them in formal evening dress. He caught glimpses of their masks, one with eye-holes ringed in sparkling stones, another made entirely of green feathers, and he could also just make out the starched shirt-fronts of the men, white triangles that gleamed softly in the darkness. What struck him most, though, was the smell – a smell that consisted of new spring leaves, exhaust fumes, alcohol and rain, a smell that seemed both exciting and forbidden. They had brought the night air into the room with them; it clung to their clothes, their skin, their hair . . . Who were they, he wondered, these thirty men and women? Were they part of some secret society, people united by their love of the perverse, which took them, on certain nights, to anonymous houses on the outskirts of the city? And did the women who had organised the entertainment belong to that same underworld, the damage that had once been done to them now finding expression in clandestine rituals, barbarity, a pursuit of the bizarre? He listened to the low buzz of a dozen whispered conversations. Where had they all come from? Who *were* they? There was only one thing he could say for sure. It was the strangest audience that he had ever had.

He had already warmed up before they were ushered into the room, and he was eager to begin, but it took several minutes for the murmuring to die down. A few last coughs, a throat being cleared, one long and oddly pleasurable sigh – and then a crackle in the speakers behind him as the third act of *Swan Lake* began . . . He had decided to approach the performance as he would approach any performance, with absolute dedication and commitment. If he was going to get through it he would have to lose himself completely in the dancing (perhaps, after all, he knew no other way). His

97

nakedness, which the women had insisted on, would become a fundamental part of what he was doing. Like the chain, it had to be incorporated. He had to treat them both as elements without which the piece simply would not work.

And he thought he succeeded pretty well. From the first moment of his entrance, the music starting quietly, poignantly, the notes ascending in a minor key, he used the chain as a stand-in for Odile. Whenever he was required to dance with her he danced with the chain instead, holding it, lifting it, parading it about. This had worked the day before, in rehearsal, and it worked even better now, especially in the slow waltz that formed part of the *pas de deux*. He liked the jingling of the chain across the floor. It sounded like somebody fingering loose change, like impatience, in other words, or nervousness, and it seemed to comment directly on the music, almost in the way percussion does, adding to the atmosphere of unease. Not until the Prince's solo, which is long and technically demanding, did things become tricky. He had trimmed many of the jumps, but, even so, he had to take care that he did not trip and hurt himself. He had covered himself by injecting humour into the choreography. Once, for instance, when he should have been launching himself into a *grand temps levé*, a difficult jump at the best of times, the chain appeared to intervene, preventing him from even attempting it. If the solo forfeited some of its athleticism, it gained in both astringency, he felt, and pathos. The chain became a symbol of the Prince's wayward sexuality: it was clear for everyone to see that, in pursuing Odile, he was being led by his most basic desires. At the same time, in hampering the Prince's movements, the chain was trying to warn him, to enlighten him. *Open your eyes. This isn't love.* When he had finished the solo he stood still, his chest heaving. He could feel his lack of fitness now, and he wondered whether anyone had noticed. The music was continuing, though. He looked on as a phantom Odile danced her own solo – a raunchy, triumphant series of steps that celebrated the fact that she had succeeded in seducing him. *It worked. I've got him. He's mine.* He turned his head this way and that, as if he was actually following her progress across the stage, as if he was admiring her, then he threw himself into the coda, which was like an array of circus tricks, pausing once again to watch Odile execute one of the most famous sequences in ballet – the thirty-two *fouettés* in a row. He danced right up to the moment when the Prince realises that he has been deceived, and that everything is over. Instead of running off stage, though, as Nureyev had done, he slowly pirouetted towards the back wall, allowing the chain to wind itself around him, so that, by the time the music built to its crescendo, he was standing by the iron staple at the back of the room, his entire body imprisoned, paralysed. He immersed himself so deeply in his performance that, when the act finally came to an end and he looked up, he expected to see the gilt balconies and red plush seating of a theatre, he expected to hear applause rush towards him out of the darkness like a wave, but there was only a bare room, with thirty people clapping, so he slowly freed himself and stood there, with the chain in his right hand, then he bowed once, ironically, and, turning his back on them, walked out of the spotlight, into the shadows . . .

❧

It was late. The sound system and the spotlights had been dismantled; the chairs had been stacked, and then removed. The room looked as it had always looked, brutal and unadorned, though he felt he could still smell the night air, that distillation of spring leaves and recent rain. For the last hour,

Gertrude had been giving him a massage – some kind of reward for his efforts, he supposed – and, to his surprise, she was at least as good as Hendrik, the masseur who worked for the dance company. Her fingers were more powerful than they appeared to be, reaching down into his muscles, easing tension and spreading a feeling of luxurious well-being. He had almost drifted off to sleep when he heard her murmur something:

'You will not be here tomorrow.'

He did not know what to make of Gertrude's announcement, coming as it did from somewhere far away, beyond the soothing mists and perfumes that enveloped him. Were they going to kill him? That could happen, couldn't it, in situations such as these? His mind grappled sluggishly with the idea . . . No, surely he must have misheard her. Or perhaps she was having trouble with her English, and what she was trying to say had come out wrong.

'I'm sorry,' he said. 'What was that?'

'You will not be here tomorrow. You will be free.'

He looked round, wide awake now, his heart beating in his throat. 'This is a joke . . .'

'No,' she said in that humourless way she sometimes had, 'this is not a joke.' She picked up a towel, began to wipe her hands.

'Why?' he said. 'Why now?'

She paused for a moment, seeming to stare into space. 'It was a difficult decision, but it was necessary.'

'I don't understand.'

She gathered up the massage oil and the towel, rose to her feet and started for the door. He called out after her, but she ignored him, pausing only to switch off the lights. It was the most peculiar feeling of frustration suddenly. He felt it was impossible, no, *inconceivable*, that he should simply be released,

100

with no questions asked and none answered. He felt that the whole thing should be explained to him. But they weren't going to do that. They weren't going to say another word.

It was necessary.

He lay back in the darkness, thinking. What if the women had decided that it would be dangerous to hold him for any longer? What if they felt they would be risking exposure? After all, they had already given a banquet, with several guests, and then there had been his performance in front of an invited audience . . . How many people had seen him so far? Thirty? Forty? Surely it was only a matter of time before the secret got out. In the end, only two courses of action lay open to the women: either they had to dispose of him, or they had to let him go. They appeared to have chosen the less drastic option, which was a relief, of course, but still —

You will be free.

It was unthinkable, after all this time. It was absurd.

It was almost frightening.

~

All that night he stayed awake, pacing at the end of his chain, unable to come to terms with what he had been told. Perhaps he could not afford to. The risk of disappointment was too great. But it had created a kind of havoc in his head, a chaos of possibilities . . . Most likely it was some exquisite new torture the women had devised for him, a shift from the physical to the psychological. Yes, he could imagine that. And yet she had announced it with such evident regret . . . He paced. He sat with his back against the wall. He paced again. At last he saw dawn appear in the skylight, a subtle easing of the darkness, a breath of pink across the glass . . .

Only moments later, it seemed, a woman brought him

coffee and a plate of fruit. One glimpse of her hands, strong yet elegant, with nails that were filed square across the top, told him that it was Astrid. Identity no longer interested him, though. He was looking for a variation in the routine, a change of mood, some hint or sign that he was about to be released. He noticed nothing.

Not long after breakfast the door was thrown open, and a cloaked and hooded woman burst into the room. The floorboards bounced as she ran clumsily towards him. She came to a standstill some distance away, as if she had forgotten something and was thinking of turning back. Though he could not see her legs he could imagine them – the feet pointing inwards, the knees touching: Maude.

'I saw the performance,' she said in a quiet, breathless voice.

'Did you enjoy it?'

'Oh yes. Yes. Very much – '

'Are you all right?' He tried to look into her eyes. 'Did they punish you?'

Her head turned in the direction of the door. 'I must go.'

Alone again, he lay there on the mat. Maude didn't seem to know that he was being freed, but that didn't prove anything. They probably wouldn't have told her. Uncertainty had lodged in him like an ache. His eyes stung from lack of sleep.

Then, sometime in the middle of the day, while he was dozing, the door opened again and all three women appeared. He sat up, rubbed his eyes. The sky had darkened since breakfast, and the light in the room was murky.

Gertrude came towards him, holding the clothes he had been wearing on the day of his abduction. Everything had been washed and folded. Everything was clean. Working with Astrid, Gertrude chained his hands behind his back, then helped him to his feet. Maude stood off to the left, he noticed, with her head turned to one side. From beneath her cloak Gertrude produced a silver key, which she used to unlock the ring that they had fitted through his penis. When she had removed the ring she handed it to Astrid, who placed it in a small black box she had brought into the room with her. He looked down at the jagged hole in his foreskin, wondering if it would ever heal.

Gertrude reached for his clothes, pulling on his jockstrap, his track-suit trousers and his socks. She slipped his shoes on to his feet and tied the laces. The wistful quality that she had seemed to have the night before had gone. She was brisk, unsentimental, and he did not attempt to resist her; he allowed her to dress him, as if he were a child. It was beginning to sink in now, the knowledge that they were about to let him go, and yet a feeling of suspense hung in the room, like mist, making it difficult to see too far ahead; he didn't want to say anything in case he broke the spell.

While Gertrude was buttoning his shirt, he suddenly realised that his hands were free. He could have reached out and taken her by the throat. He could have strangled her. She seemed to guess what he was thinking because she looked up quickly. She was standing so close to him that he could see a burst vein in the white part of her left eye. He looked away from her. The moment passed.

Once she had finished dressing him she offered him a choice. If he was prepared to co-operate, they could simply slip a hood over his head. Otherwise, they would have to inject him with anaesthetic, as before. He told her he would rather wear the hood.

Astrid stepped forwards.

'It's all right,' he said. 'You don't have to warn me.'

As Astrid reached up with the hood, he had his last glimpse of the women, an image that seemed to print itself on to his mind, as motionless, as fixed in time, as any photograph. Gertrude had positioned herself at Astrid's shoulder, with one hand folded over the other and held just below her breasts. Slightly to the left of Gertrude, and standing deeper in the room, was Maude, her head still angled away from him, as if she could not bear to look. Then just the bare floorboards, with their dust-balls and their splinters, stretching off into the thick grey light . . .

~

They led him down the two steep flights of stairs. Instead of turning right at the bottom and doubling back towards the garden, they moved straight ahead, taking a right turn, then a left turn, until at last they walked, not into the open air, as he had been expecting, but into a large indoor space. The temperature dropped, and he could smell damp earth and paraffin. He might be in a garage, he thought – or some kind of warehouse, maybe. Though there was movement all around him, the rustle of the women's clothes, nobody spoke. A key scraped in a lock. Then, just as he was being bundled into the van – he could tell it was a van because of the double-doors at the back and the corrugated metal floor inside – he heard the strangest sound, a sound that was somewhere between keening and wailing. Only later did he identify the source of it, and by that time they were driving. It was Maude, of course. It could only have been Maude. Perhaps she had learned that he was being freed. Or else they had told her that she couldn't come with them. Once again, she had been mistreated, overlooked.

It was hard to sit with his wrists shackled behind his back. When the van pulled away, he almost toppled sideways, and one of the women had to reach out and steady him. He wondered if she had a loaded syringe with her, just in case. For the first ten minutes there were constant twists and turns. There were potholes too, which made him think that the road was being repaired. Either that, or it simply had no surface yet. Then only smoothness for a long time, smoothness and the roar of traffic. A motorway, presumably. Once or twice the woman sitting next to him shouted to the woman who was driving. She spoke so fast, though, and the engine was making so much noise, that he didn't understand a word.

They reached what he thought must be a built-up area. The van stopped and started every thirty seconds, which told him there were traffic-lights or traffic-jams. Was it rush-hour already? He wished he could work out what make of van it was by listening to the engine. Some people could do that. But he had never known the first thing about cars . . .

At last, after driving for about an hour, they stopped. He heard the abrupt creak of the hand-brake, but noticed that they kept the engine running. A woman walked round to the back of the van and opened the double-doors. She unlocked the leg-irons first, then the handcuffs. Though he was still wearing the hood, he could smell fumes rising from the van's exhaust. Taking him by the arm, the woman helped him to climb out into the open air. He felt grass beneath his feet.

'Lie down on your stomach,' she said.

He did as he was told. The thought that he had had the night before came to him again, only it was stronger now, more urgent. *They're going to kill me. I'm going to be killed.*

'Start counting,' the woman said, 'and don't move before you reach one hundred.'

He began to count under his breath. A door slammed shut. The van revved twice and drove away.

He lay on the grass and counted. He did not move.

Even when he had reached one hundred he did not move.

~

He lay there with the hood over his head long after he had finished counting and all he could feel was the earth beneath him, which he pressed himself against, which he clung to, as if it was a piece of wreckage that would carry him to safety. There was even a rushing sound, as if of waves.

At last, he sat up. Sat motionless, with the hood still on, and listened. Traffic. In the distance, though. Somewhere behind him. He slowly loosened the drawstring and pulled off the hood. Daylight burst against the surface of his eyes.

He was sitting on mown grass, next to a pavement. There were trees above his head. In front of him stood a small boy, four or five years old. The boy was wearing a pale-blue cardigan and red trousers, and he was clasping one hand in the other, as priests do when they deliver sermons. Behind the boy there was a row of houses. The glass in the apartment windows looked black.

'Don't be frightened,' he told the boy, in English.

The boy's eyes had opened wide, and his bottom lip stuck out.

'It's all right,' he said gently, switching to Dutch. 'There's nothing to be frightened of.'

The boy turned and ran off down the street, his legs jerky, oddly stiff, like a puppet or a cripple. The boy was screaming as he ran.

He watched the boy disappear round a corner, then he stood up. His eyes were still adjusting to the glare. The sky was grey, but strangely dazzling, and a light breeze pushed against his face. He began to walk.

The street felt private, secretive, almost as if a curfew had been declared. Perhaps it was simply an effect created by the overhanging foliage. Or perhaps it was just him. A strip of city parkland lay directly to his left. The trees were part of it. A footpath curved past an empty wooden bench and on through areas of grass that looked too green. Beyond the path, beyond the trees, he could just make out the tarnished silver of an artificial lake. To his right, on the other side of the street, stood a row of semi-detached houses. They were made of pale-red brick, and all the window-frames had been painted white. Newspapers stuck out of many of the letter-boxes, which seemed unusual, given the time of day. He saw a man sitting at a table in a ground-floor window, doing a crossword. Everything would make sense, he thought, if he was calm, methodical. Everything would fit together.

He walked on until he reached a main road. The name seemed vaguely familiar. He thought he must be in the outskirts of Amsterdam, though he couldn't have said where exactly. If he looked in one direction he could see a flyover. He could hear the steady, hypnotic roar of cars travelling at high speed. He turned round, faced the other way. A girl of about eight was running up the pavement towards him with one hand raised above her head. She was holding a broken cassette. Half the tape had wrapped itself around her, en-circling her blue denim dress and her bare legs. The rest trailed in the air behind her, yards and yards of it. She was laughing. Beyond her, in the distance, he could see a row of shops. Perhaps he could ask there.

He had to choose between a bicycle shop, a supermarket, and a bar with small gold and silver trophies in the window. He chose the bar. It was dark in there. The woman behind the bar was smoking. He saw the end of her cigarette glow red as he walked in. He sat down on a stool and ordered a beer. He hadn't realised how thirsty he was, and the beer tasted delicious, more delicious, possibly, than any beer he had ever drunk before.

'This is very good,' he told the woman behind the bar.

She smiled at him, but did not say anything.

'How far is it from here to the centre?' he asked.

'Three kilometres,' she said. 'Maybe four.'

'How long would it take me to walk?'

'Half an hour,' she said, tilting one hand in the air to indicate that this was only a rough estimate.

She had bronze hair – it had been dyed, presumably – and there was a smooth, pale bump in the middle of her left cheek. It had been a long time since he had seen somebody's face, and he found it impossible not to stare. He was noticing her clothes too – the crocheted turquoise cardigan, the rust-brown skirt. But she caught him staring, and she stared back. He thought he had better say something.

'How much do I owe you for the beer?'

'Two seventy-five.'

His hand dropped to his track-suit trouser pocket. Suddenly he wasn't sure whether he had any money. He reached into one pocket, and then another, and finally into his zipped back pocket. His hand closed round a note. Ten guilders. This was the money he had taken out with him so he could buy Brigitte her cigarettes. He stared down at the note as if it held the key to what had happened. In that moment he felt that he should buy the cigarettes, and that, if he did so, he would be closing a circle, he would be bringing the story to its natural, its intended, conclusion. He looked up again. The woman was still watching him suspiciously.

He handed the ten-guilder note to her.

'Do you have a cigarette machine?' he asked.

'It's behind you.'

He swung round on his stool. The machine stood by the door that led to the toilet. On top of it, oddly, was a plaster bust of Marilyn Monroe.

'Could you give me some change for it, please?'

He fed the coins into the slot and watched the packet drop

108

into the stainless-steel lip at the bottom of the machine.

Outside, on the street, he slid the cigarettes into his back pocket. As he turned away from the bar he had the feeling he was being watched. He looked up. Yes, there. Somebody was standing in the window, watching him. It was several seconds before he realised that he was staring at his own reflection. He moved closer to the window, closer still, until he was standing less than eighteen inches from the glass. Though he did not think that he had changed at all, he hardly recognised himself. He remembered how he had looked into the stainless steel of the handcuffs and seen nothing except his left eye or a fragment of his neck or hair. He had wondered if he would ever be whole again. Was this part of the same thing? How long had it been since he last saw himself in the mirror? How long had he been gone?

He turned and walked back into the bar, then hesitated just inside the door, uncertain how to phrase the question. The woman in the turquoise cardigan watched him warily, one hand rising to touch the pale bump on her left cheek.

'Do you know what the date is?' he asked.

'The date?' The woman's eyes narrowed, as if she suspected him of laying a trap for her.

He nodded, smiled. 'Today's date.'

'It's May the fourth.'

May the fourth. And he had been abducted on the sixteenth of April. Which meant that he had been missing for eighteen days.

Eighteen days.

He thanked the woman, then he walked out of the bar again, and this time he did not look back.

∾

He had been abandoned in a suburb of Amsterdam, about three and a half kilometres west of his apartment. After buying the beer and the cigarettes, he didn't have enough money left for public transport, so he began to walk. He walked fast, ignoring his surroundings. He wanted to cover the ground as quickly as possible; he wanted to be home. *Brigitte*, he thought. Just that. No other thoughts would form.

As he moved through the city he had a feeling of intense exhilaration, a feeling that was close to euphoria. And yet, at the same time, he felt as if he was on the verge of tears.

It took him twenty minutes to reach streets that he recognised and, with that recognition, the sense of urgency grew. Through Hugo de Grootplein, across the wide sweep of Nassaukade. A motorbike hurtled past him at such speed that it sounded like a person sneezing. Over Lijnbaansgracht. The sun was shining now. A bar released the slightly medicinal perfume of *jenever* into the air . . .

Then he was walking down Egelantiersgracht. Pots of red geraniums glowed on the decks of houseboats. The trees looked greener than he remembered, their reflections un-dulating hypnotically on the canal's dark surface. There was a drowsiness about it all, the drowsiness of three-thirty on a warm spring afternoon. As he approached the house he saw that the windows on the fourth floor were open. His heart turned over. He felt the sudden irrational urge to flee.

He took out his keys and looked at them for a moment, then he opened the door and walked into the cool interior. The letter-box was empty. He climbed the stairs. The fawn-coloured carpet, the chalk-white walls. That faint, sweet smell of grain, as if the building had once been used for milling flour.

He was breathing hard by the time he reached the door of the apartment. He felt under his shirt, found that his chest was slick with sweat. Sliding the key into the lock, he turned it once. The door opened with its usual steeply ascending whine. Air from the apartment pushed past him, into the stairwell. He stepped over the threshold, closing the door gently behind him. And there she was, standing at the far end of the living-room, watering the plants . . .

She must have heard the door open, she must have realised who it was, and yet she didn't put down the glass jug she was holding and she didn't move towards him. She didn't say anything either. She just glanced over her shoulder, with her weight on her left foot, her face alert and yet composed, almost expressionless. It would have been the perfect place to end a ballet, he thought, because the action had been interrupted halfway through, because her position was so beautifully incomplete, hold it, he would have said, just hold it, and the lights go out right there.

THREE

I stood just inside the door with my hands by my sides. All my lightness and purpose had gone, and there was only a feeling of paralysis. I felt like a bad likeness of myself, a souvenir carved crudely out of wood. Then – almost a reflex, this – I reached into my pocket, took out the cigarettes I had bought and held them out to her. She was still standing by the row of windows that over-looked the canal. The glass jug she was holding, half full of water, glinted with an unearthly silver light, like a holy object, but Brigitte herself was hard to see, virtually a silhouette.

'What are those?' she said.

I tried to smile. 'Your cigarettes.'

'Is that supposed to be a joke?'

When she said those words, something collapsed inside me. I thought back to that sunlit afternoon in the studio canteen, my notebook open on the table, the empty ashtray, the coffee cup. . .I thought of how Brigitte had walked towards me in her dark-green leotard and her laddered tights, a piece of velvet showing in her hair. I could still hear her footsteps, light and yet resourceful. I could still see the frown balanced between her eyebrows, two tiny furrows – a j and a j reversed. . .If she did not understand why I had bought the cigarettes, if she did not *remember*, then what chance did I have of explaining things to her, how could I even begin?

~

'You left me,' she said.

She was watching me across the kitchen table. Close up, she looked as if she hadn't slept, the skin beneath her eyes dark-brown, like the flesh of olives.

'I didn't leave you,' I said. 'How could I leave you?'

'There was someone else . . .'

Her eyes drifted away from me, and the fingers of one hand lifted and curled against the corner of her mouth. She looked so sad just then, so genuinely forsaken, that I wanted to reach out and touch her, but I had the feeling she would only pull away. I stared down at the table, shook my head. Outside, a clock was striking six. Though I had been back for less than three hours, it already felt like an eternity.

'There was someone else,' she said, 'another woman.'

'No, Brigitte. There was no one else.' I hesitated. 'Well – '

'There. You see?' A kind of triumph rose on to her face, a triumph that was wounded and perverse.

She had wrongfooted me the moment I walked into the apartment. She had her own theory about where I had been for the past eighteen days. I had been unfaithful to her, she said. I had embarrassed her. Betrayed her. The conclusion she had jumped to in my absence had become the truth.

You left me.

Her certainty took me by surprise. I was certain of nothing. Also – and crucially, perhaps – I didn't have the strength to challenge her. I felt tugged in too many different directions at once; I couldn't seem to anchor myself in one clear feeling.

At some point I went into the bathroom and ran myself a bath. It was all I could think of doing. I soaked in the water until my skin turned pink and the sweat stood out on my forehead . . . Afterwards, I gathered up all the clothes that I had been wearing earlier, carried them out to the kitchen and pushed them into the rubbish bin, deep down, where nobody

116

would find them. I could hear Brigitte on the phone upstairs, but I couldn't make out what she was saying. As I stood there, up to my elbows in wilting lettuce leaves and ugly scabs of orange peel, I realised that I had eaten nothing since breakfast.

When Brigitte appeared a few minutes later, I was sitting at the kitchen table with a sandwich and a glass of milk. The fact that I was eating seemed to upset her. That I should be hungry at a time like this . . . Brigitte had always expected absolute loyalty. If you were with her, you had to be there for her. That was the way she needed to be loved, and I had never had a problem with it. I *wanted* to be there for her. One hundred per cent, no matter what. When I disappeared, though, I think she saw it as abandonment – and from abandonment to infidelity, well, it's not such a big leap to make. Brigitte was the kind of person who would rather believe in something definite, even if it hurt her, than go on living in a state of ignorance or doubt.

There was someone else.

Each time I tried to prove her wrong, my mind would fill with images from the room – the black steeples of the women's hoods, their cloaks swirling around me like unconsciousness itself . . . I couldn't bring myself to tell her what had happened. I couldn't admit to what I'd been through, I suppose, not even to myself. I didn't want it to be true. Each time I tried to speak, my tongue just froze.

Finally, at seven o'clock, Brigitte stood up. 'I have to leave,' she said.

My right elbow jerked sideways, knocking a knife to the floor. 'Where are you going?'

'I have a performance tonight. I'm due on stage in an hour.'

I rose to my feet, then stood there uselessly and watched her take her coat down from the coat-rack in the corridor. 'Don't forget to do your exercises . . .'

She gave me a suspicious, almost hunted look, as if I had succeeded in acquiring information that should not have been available to me. And yet I always used to remind her to warm up properly before a performance. It had been my way of wishing her good luck.

When she had finished buttoning her coat she looked at me again, this time across one shoulder. 'Will you be here when I get back?'

I stared at her. 'Yes. Of course. Where else would I – '

She nodded to herself, then turned and let herself out of the apartment.

~

Exhaustion hit me with the force of something coming from outside. I could have fallen asleep on my feet, standing exactly where I was. I fought it, though. I had to. If I had given in to it, I would have felt as if I was taking things for granted.

I stayed awake by walking through the apartment. As I moved from one room to another I had the sense that I was somewhere I did not belong – that I had broken into the place, in fact, and was about to steal something. I felt edgy and remote, both at the same time. I stared at the fish swimming in their tank, the exotic plants under the window, the contents of the fridge. I opened the wardrobe and looked through all my clothes. I studied photographs, read letters . . . Everything that came under my scrutiny appeared to regard me with supreme indifference. I meant nothing to any of it. Even a book on iconography that Brigitte had given me (*avec mon amour, toujours* – *B*), even framed pictures of us dancing together . . . The sense of being an intruder would not lift. Instead, it began to seem appropriate, and, as the minutes

118

ticked slowly by, it deepened into a feeling that was not unlike loneliness.

I climbed the stairs and, opening the french windows, stepped on to the terrace. I sat on the wrought-iron chair that we kept out there. The night was cold and damp, and a fine mist had settled over the city; the church bells ringing in the distance had a fragile, glassy sound. Four floors below, a single street-lamp gave off a soft-edged orange glow. The air moved towards me warily, the way a wild creature might. I went on sitting there, and, after a while, it came up close and pressed itself against me. I was shivering by then, but it didn't matter. I felt as if I had been acknowledged at long last. I could tell where I began and ended, how much space I occupied. I knew the limits of myself, and it was something, to know that.

Back inside, I prepared for bed. I left two lights on, one downstairs, the other in the corridor outside the bathroom; I didn't want Brigitte to walk into a dark apartment and think that I had gone. Leaving the bedroom door ajar, I undressed quickly and slid between the sheets. All I could see then was a thin column of yellow light at the far end of the room. It reminded me of childhood, the way all the brightness was in the distance, and how it faded as it reached towards me, how my own warm darkness swallowed it. As my eyes began to close, the little boy appeared in front of me. I remembered his pale-blue cardigan and his red trousers, and I remembered how his face had altered when I spoke, as though it was not the sight of a man in a hood that frightened him, but communication, language – speech itself. I kept seeing his mouth open into a round black shape. I kept seeing him turn and run off down the street, like a jerky clockwork toy . . .

~

Though I woke when I heard Brigitte come in, I pretended to be asleep. I felt one side of the bed dip. There was a stillness then, and I was sure that she was looking down at me. I tried to keep my breathing regular. At last, the mattress tilted again as, turning in the bed, she drew the covers over her and settled for the night.

Sometime later I woke again, the sheets all wet and twisted. The windows to my right – a set of pale rectangles – seemed to be in the wrong place; they didn't correspond to any windows that I knew. If you had asked me where I was, I could not have told you. I turned my pillow over, then lay still, waiting for my heart to slow down. I must have been dreaming that I was back in the white room, with only one small square of glass above my head – or at my parents' house, perhaps, in Hampshire . . .

In the morning I heard the bed creak and, opening my eyes, I saw Brigitte reach out and switch off the alarm clock. Once again, I was tempted to touch her, to place one hand against her naked back as she leaned away from me – the skin covering her ribs the way snow covers fallen branches, her shoulder-blades like little buried shields . . . Instead, I waited until she looked in my direction, then I smiled at her. I wanted to reassure her, wanted to let her know that things were going to be all right. She acted as if she hadn't noticed. Since she saw me in a guilty light, I suppose she thought I was just trying to ingratiate myself.

I watched her leave the bed. She pulled on a T-shirt with details of our recent tour of South America on the back – São Paulo, Caracas, Buenos Aires – and I had a sudden image of her painting her toenails on a hotel balcony at dusk, the sky stretching behind her, immense and soft, the wind so warm that it could dry your hair in sixty seconds . . . The memory was proof of something, it was evidence, and I wanted to recall it for her – *Remember the time we* . . . but it was too late, she had already walked out of the room. I listened to her opening and shutting cupboards in the kitchen, lighting the gas, making a cup of Chinese tea. Later, I heard the bath running. Her usual routine. I lay back against the pillows, my eyes already closing. I was aware of my body only as a weight. My fatigue seemed inexhaustible.

The next time I woke up, Brigitte had already left for the studio.

~

On the third evening after I returned, she did not have to give a performance. When she came home at half-past seven she found me sitting by the window in the dark. The house opposite our house had all its lights on, and the bright golden rooms were reflected in the surface of the canal. The water lay so flat and still that the reflections didn't waver. A quiet night in Amsterdam, as if the city existed in a vacuum . . .

She folded her arms across her breasts and leaned against the doorway, watching me. 'Perhaps you should come to class tomorrow.'

I thought about it, then slowly shook my head. 'I'm not ready.'

A silence fell between us.

'I think it will take time,' I said. 'To readjust.'

I looked up. Her body appeared to warp and then swim sideways. And yet she hadn't moved. I pushed my thumb and forefinger into my eyes. To my surprise I heard myself begin to tell her what had happened to me.

'There were three of them – I don't know who they were . . . They took me to a room . . . a white room . . .'

121

My sentences were tentative and unconvincing, but I forced myself to carry on.

'They did things to me – things I can't describe . . .

'Three of them . . . three women . . .'

Once, while I was talking, I glanced at Brigitte. She had the strangest look of pity on her face – not just pity either, but sadness too, and even a kind of admiration; she was almost in awe of the lengths to which I was going in my attempt to exonerate myself. At the same time, it was clear that she didn't believe a word of it. And who could blame her, really? The story she had concocted seemed so much more probable than mine. In desperation, I unfastened my trousers and showed her the tattoo, the scars. She reeled away from me, the back of her left hand pressed against her mouth. Her eyes had filled with anguish, but also with disgust. *What about me?* I wanted to cry out. *How do you think I feel?* Somehow I couldn't, though.

How difficult it is, sometimes, to find the right words. Or any words at all.

The marks on my body became proof not of my story but of her theory: I'd had some kind of affair, some perverted liaison, which, naturally enough, I felt I had to lie about. It also confirmed something she had always suspected about the English, namely that our politeness, our diffidence, if you like, is just a cover for some deep unpleasantness that flourishes precisely because it is concealed.

Throughout that evening I clung to the feeling that everything could be explained if only I could find the correct approach. But when I told her how much I had missed her during those eighteen days, when I told her that I loved her, more than she could ever imagine, she turned away, exasperated, and once she even put her hands over her ears and shouted, 'No!'

She returned to the same point again and again, as if it had magnetic qualities. She kept asking who the woman was, and I kept shrugging and telling her I didn't know.

'You don't know?' She stood in front of me, with both hands on her hips. 'How can you not know?'

I gazed at the floor.

'You didn't even know her name?'

'It wasn't like that,' I said.

'So what *was* it like?'

'That's what I've been trying to tell you. That's what I've been trying to explain – '

'*Merde.*' She paced the length of the living-room. '*Je ne peux pas croire que tu aies fait ça.*'

'*Mais je n'ai rien fait,*' I murmured. 'I didn't do anything.' I put my head in my hands. Veins pulsed against the inside of my fingers.

When I finally looked up again, I saw that she had come to a decision. She couldn't live with me, she said, not like this. She didn't recognise me any more. I frightened her. She would have to leave . . . Though, even as she spoke, her dark eyes swept round the apartment, one wild, despairing look, as if she could not imagine how her life could take place anywhere else.

'I love you, Brigitte,' I said.

It made no difference.

Sometimes, when I look back, I think that what we talked about that night was all irrelevant. The reasons for my absence did not matter. What mattered was the absence itself. I had left her once. I could leave her again. She could no longer count on me. Promises, once broken, can never be mended.

It also seems to me that I colluded in her interpretation of events. I let her believe what she wanted to believe. It saved me from having to tell the story. It meant I could pretend that none of it had ever happened.

Or maybe it had happened . . .

To someone else, though. Not to me.

~

That night Brigitte stayed with her friend, Fernanda, while I lay in our double bed, alone. I was still awake at three-thirty in the morning, my eyes wide open, cool air moving through the room. I heard ducks cackle on the canal outside. I heard the clatter of a loose mudguard as a bicycle went past.

Stefan, the photographer, had called me earlier. Something weird, he said. He had seen me from his car on the afternoon I disappeared. Later, he had talked to Brigitte about it. He had told her how happy I looked, which seemed to confirm some suspicion she had, that I was on my way to meet someone – another woman. And now he had heard that we were splitting up . . .

'News travels fast,' I murmured.

He said he felt responsible. He felt guilty.

I told him, as gently as I could, that he was probably overestimating his own importance, and that he should forget about it, and, by the end of the phone-call, I could hear the relief in his voice. I had given him what he was looking for – a form of absolution.

Of course I'd looked happy, I thought as I lay there. The spring sunlight, the man in the linen jacket singing – and no notion that anything might change. Because, at that point in my life, I wouldn't have changed a thing, not if you had offered me wealth beyond my wildest imaginings. I *looked* happy because I *was* happy.

I turned over slowly in the bed. There were places on my body that still hurt. A clock somewhere struck four. I needed to listen to someone talking, I needed a voice other than my own – I needed not to think . . .

I thought and thought all night, and none of it came to anything.

At half-past five I heard the mutter of a boat as it passed beneath my window. Then it began to rain. The steady grey rain of dawn.

Not long after that I fell asleep.

~

Later that morning I called Isabel van Zaanen. I had known Isabel for years. It was Isabel who had persuaded the company to audition me when I was seventeen. It was Isabel who, being a famous choreographer herself, had encouraged me to try my hand at creating ballets. Despite the difference in our ages, we had become good friends. In her retirement, she had moved to Bloemendaal, which was on the coast, about half an hour's drive from Amsterdam. She lived in an old mansion that had been divided into four or five rambling apartments. I had slept in her spare bedroom once, with Brigitte, and I had never forgotten the window that looked out over the pine forest behind the house, and the smell of the air at night – a mingling of the garden and the sea . . . It was a magical place – timeless, somehow, and at peace with itself.

When I talked to Isabel on the phone I didn't say anything about my disappearance. I didn't even mention the fact that Brigitte and I were separating. I simply asked if I could come and stay with her for a while. Her response was immediate and typical: I could stay as long as I liked – in fact, I'd be doing her a favour, she said, because she had to teach in Oslo that summer, and she'd been thinking she should find someone to move into the place while she was away. This was also typical of Isabel, that she should underplay her generosity, disguise it as self-interest.

That evening I dialled Fernanda's number and spoke to Brigitte. I told her she could live in our apartment. She had her dancing to think of, her career – her life. It would make more sense, I said, if I was the one to leave.

'What about *your* career?' she said. There was a curious flatness in her voice, a sort of reluctance, as if she was only asking out of politeness.

I said something noncommittal. When she asked me where I would go, I told her not to worry. I would find somewhere.

'What about money?'

I didn't follow.

'The rent,' she said. 'I can't pay the rent by myself.'

'Oh, I see.' I paused. 'You'll have to find someone to share with you.'

She took a quick breath, as if I had startled her, and I realised that she was smoking. She often smoked when she was on the phone. She would be holding the cigarette packet and the lighted cigarette in one hand, and the receiver in the other. This whole thing had started with the absence of a cigarette, and now, as we came out the other side, Brigitte was smoking. There was a neatness about it, a symmetry, that was almost comical. But she was saying something.

'Someone to share with me?' She sounded nervous, apprehensive.

'It shouldn't be too difficult,' I told her. 'It's a nice place.'

~

I have heard people talk about the comfort a woman can provide, but it's not something I'm particularly familiar with. Perhaps there's a lack in me, some kind of failing or deformity.

I don't know. Or perhaps it's just that I never looked for comfort, never needed it – at least, not until that still grey afternoon in May when I walked back into our apartment after an absence of eighteen days . . .

Then I needed it more than I have ever needed anything.

Since it wasn't offered, though, since it didn't become available to me, I couldn't begin to unburden myself; I couldn't begin to shift my anger or my sense of shame. I was unable to forge a link between the life I'd had before and the life I would have from that point on. Instead, the two lives became separable, at odds with each other, like stray cats fighting for the same piece of territory, and it would not be long, I felt, before one of them was driven off for good.

I sometimes wonder what would have happened if Brigitte had put down the glass jug she was holding and said, *Come here.* If she had taken my head in her two hands and drawn it gently to her breast . . .

It's a fantasy, of course.

Brigitte was a dancer – an artist. The only thing she was capable of nurturing was her own talent. I don't mean to sound bitter or resentful. I don't even mean to criticise her. It's simply a fact.

The truth is, in the context of our relationship, there was only one person who was capable of providing comfort and support, and that was me.

～

I took almost nothing from the apartment – my notebooks, a few photographs, some clothes. Midday was striking as I walked to my car. I loaded the boxes into the boot, then I unlocked the door on the driver's side and climbed in. Through the windscreen I could see a man of about my own age reading on the roof of a houseboat. He had tangled black hair and wore a pair of oil-stained dark-green Bermudas. He was too deep in his book to notice me. I watched a cat pad past him, its tail curling round one of his thin tanned legs. The sun lay flat on the canal, making the water look opaque. In the distance I could hear a motor launch, a drowsy sound, like a wasp trapped against a window-pane in September. I slid the key into the ignition, but didn't turn it. I wanted to stay exactly where I was, for ever. The man reading the book, the cat, the sunlight on the water . . . One minute passed, and then another. The spell lasted. Then I started the car, shifted into gear and, pulling out into the street, drove in the direction of Haarlemmerweg, which, as its name suggests, would take me to Haarlem, and then on, towards the coast . . .

I felt no sadness as I drove, no sense of bitterness or remorse. No, none of that. Instead, there was a feeling of suspension. As if, after days of weighing too much, I now weighed almost nothing. I noticed how the trees shivered at the edge of the road, and how the sunlight silvered all their leaves. I noticed the rush of cool air through the half-open window, air that seemed delicately laced with salt. I was using only the bright parts of my mind, the shiny surfaces: if I tried to imagine the inside of my head I saw something smooth and concave, something lustrous, and nothing could find purchase there, everything slid effortlessly away.

I think there's a sense in which all dancers are introspective. There's also a sense in which they're vain. It's part of being self-critical, and self-criticism, if you're a dancer, is central to your art: you have to know how to exploit it to your advantage. If you had visited the apartment where I lived with Brigitte you would have seen photos of us everywhere. It wasn't exhibitionism exactly – or, if it was, then it was only because our art revolved around exhibiting ourselves. Dancers spend more time in front of the mirror than any other profession I can think of. They study every aspect of themselves – every muscle, every tendon, every line of every limb. They learn their bodies off by heart. They are exploring their own potential, but they are also looking for limitations, flaws. So they can work on them. In that respect, their vanity is a form of meditation, even of perfectionism. Of course, some dancers take it to extremes. Vivian, for instance. There was always something wrong with Vivian – or not *wrong*, necessarily, but not quite right. Her sensitivity to her own physical condition was so highly developed, so finely tuned, that she would feel injuries coming, injuries that often never actually arrived. If you walked up to Vivian and said, *How are you?*, she would take the question literally. On a good day she would say something laconic like, *Oh, you know, I'll survive.* Otherwise you would have to listen to a whole litany of ailments. And then there was Milo, of course – Milodrama, as we called him . . . This degree of self-absorption was not unusual in the world of dance, but I was outside it now. I had left it behind. I had been freed from something I had lived with for many years – lived *by*, you might almost say. I had been freed from something I had loved. It was a freedom, finally, that had no qualities, neither good nor bad. It was only unequivocal. It was a freedom such as death might give you.

～

The house stood at the top of a small incline, which Isabel liked to refer to as the highest point in Holland. As I drove up the long, curving road I was surprised to see her step out of her garden gate – surprised because I had not told her when I was coming. Even at a distance, she was recognisable; with her straight back and her chin slightly raised, she often looked as if she was reviewing troops. She was wearing a plain white dress that afternoon, and she had coiled her hair into a chignon. Sunglasses hung against her breastbone on a silver chain. I parked the car and walked towards her with a bunch of Montenegro lilies I had bought in a flower shop on the way down.

'I heard the door-bell,' she said, 'but there was no one there,' and she frowned quickly and then shook her head, as if she thought she might be going mad.

'You were a few minutes early,' I said, 'that's all.'

I kissed her three times, as is the Dutch custom, then handed her the lilies. She looked down at them, but only for a moment.

'Exquisite,' she said.

I couldn't help smiling. I had seen Isabel with bouquets so many times – on stage, in dressing-rooms, at parties – and though she often appeared offhand, if not downright unappreciative, I knew this had less to do with arrogance than with its opposite, a kind of modesty, a feeling of general unworthiness, an inevitable dissatisfaction with whatever it was that she had achieved.

We turned and walked into the house. In the hallway we came across a stocky middle-aged man. He had black hair and dark eyes, and he was slitting a letter open with a paper-knife. I remember thinking that the suit he was wearing was exactly the same colour as milk chocolate.

'Isabel,' he said, 'I thought you were in Oslo.'

Isabel said she wasn't leaving until Friday, as he knew perfectly well; she had told him so at least half a dozen times. The man listened to her with an expression that was both sombre and amused. His eyes dropped momentarily to the lilies she was holding, then lifted again – not to her face, though, but to mine. His gaze was oddly appraising, as if he remembered hearing something about me and was now measuring me against it. Isabel introduced us. The man's name was Paul Bouhtala, and he was a neighbour of hers. When she told him I would be spending the summer in her apartment, he suggested we might have dinner together one night – but only if I had time, of course. I smiled and thanked him for the invitation.

'Paul used to be a diamond merchant, among other things,' Isabel told me as she opened the door to her apartment. 'I think he retired, though.' She let out a sigh, which had more to do with how she viewed her own retirement, I felt, than that of Paul Bouhtala.

We sat on her terrace at the back of the house and drank home-made lemonade. I felt sure she noticed the grazes on my wrists, but she didn't ask me what had happened – not on that afternoon, not on any afternoon. She didn't even allude to it. And yet I had the feeling that if I had wanted to talk to her she would have listened. She had worked with dancers for more than half her life She understood when to stand back and give them space, and when to intervene.

These are the people I have learned to value most, the people who know how to do that. That tact, that lightness of touch, that grace – I see it as a form of wisdom. They're not born with it, these people. Nobody is. It's a quality you have to identify in yourself and then develop.

~

That night Isabel cooked a light supper – fettuccine with wild mushrooms, and a salad of tomatoes and fresh basil. We drank a bottle of chilled white wine, following it with small glasses of a pear liqueur that she had distilled herself. With coffee, she smoked several Egyptian cigarettes, which smelled of wood, and also, somehow, of cream. She had started smoking in her sixties, and held her cigarettes horizontally, between finger and thumb, which gave her – or so I always thought – the air of somebody who gambled. Light-headed from the alcohol, I asked her about her early life, the years just before the war. I had heard whispers of a lesbian affair. While still married to a Dutch industrialist, she was supposed to have fallen for a prima ballerina from the Ukraine. The details were shadowy and scandalous.

'You're not really interested, are you?' she said, watching me through smoke that twisted in front of her like pale undergrowth.

I assured her that I was.

'You're humouring me,' she said.

I smiled. 'I wouldn't dare.'

'It's the most terrible thing about being old,' she said. 'Nobody wants to listen to your stories – and you have so many!' She chuckled, then coughed, and, reaching over, tapped a length of ash into the silver dish at her elbow.

That is my most enduring memory of that first night in Bloemendaal – the creamy sawdust smell of the Egyptian cigarettes she was smoking, that and something she told me about the ballerina.

'The most extraordinary thing . . .' Isabel's voice was low, and it had filled with a kind of wonder, as if what was stored in her memory still surprised her. 'This girl had a birthmark on her back, at the bottom of her spine. It was a pale-pink colour, about so big.' She measured two inches in the air with her finger and thumb. 'And you know what? It looked like a sea-horse . . .' She paused, thinking back. 'Exactly like a sea-horse,' she said, and then she shook her head and leaned back in her chair, her eyes lifting past my shoulder, drifting into the shadows behind me.

~

The spare room lay at the far end of the apartment, above the study. I had to climb a wrought-iron spiral staircase, past shelves crammed unevenly with books, then grope my way down an unlit corridor that was so narrow that my shoulders brushed against the walls. Eventually, I came to a door. Easing it open, I reached round to the right and found the light-switch. The room was not quite as I had remembered it. With its metal frame and its white counterpane, the single bed looked spartan, almost monastic – where was the divan Brigitte and I had slept in? – but the walls had been painted a powdery egg-shell blue, and the chest at the foot of the bed looked as if it might once have held a pirate captain's treasure. On the bedside table stood a vase of irises. On the floor lay a simple rug whose rich pale colours made me think of the Sahara, though I had never actually been there. There was only one window, and it was set into the slanting wall that faced the bed, and opened outwards in two halves, the way shutters do. It was so quiet in the room that the air seemed to be making a sound of its own.

On that first night I leaned on the windowsill, a little drunk, and watched the blackness of the forest pulse and swirl. I thought of the pink sea-horse at the bottom of the ballerina's spine, then I thought of the coin-shaped scar on the hip-bone of a woman I had called Astrid. After that my mind went blank.

A wind moved through the trees. There was a delicious smell of pine-needles mixed with sea-salt and damp earth.

I slept heavily and did not dream.

At ten o'clock the next morning I woke to see a thin bar of sunlight lying on the floor like a misplaced stair-rod. Still half asleep, I felt it was telling me I should tread carefully. There were folds and wrinkles in the world. There were pieces missing. If I wasn't careful I could trip and fall.

~

Four days after I arrived, Isabel left for Oslo. She would be away until the beginning of September. From that moment on, I had the apartment to myself. What did I do during those first few weeks? Things I had done as a child, I suppose. In the mornings I would sunbathe on the terrace with Isabel's transistor radio playing close to my ear, or else I would lie on her sofa, reading books. Later, I would go for long walks through the forest or across the dunes; I had never explored the Dutch coast before – I'd never had the time – and I quickly grew to love its wide, bleak beaches, its lack of markings. In the afternoons I slept in the pale-blue room with the window open. Sounds filtered through to me – a car climbing the hill in low gear, the murmur of voices in the garden, a distant plane . . . At least once a day I drove down to the sea and swam – before breakfast, usually, or late in the evening, when there was almost no one else about. This is what I had discovered, that I wanted nothing to do with people. I didn't want to be seen, by anyone.

Odd then that I should take Paul Bouhtala up on his offer of dinner. With his thick waist and his glossy black moustache, Bouhtala looked more Mexican than Dutch. Though his eyes were deep-set, they were large and heavy-lidded, and he would study me with an air of boredom and world-weariness that I found daunting. Still, I ate with him on a number of occasions that summer. He lived in a ground-floor apartment which could only be reached with difficulty: either you had to follow an intricate series of staircases and passageways – this was the indoor route – or you had to work your way round the outside of the house, negotiating a vegetable patch, several beds of nettles, and an orchard of apple trees that had been left untended for years. In his dark rooms, which were hung with lithographs and tapestries, he told me about his travels, his business schemes, his double-dealings (his willingness to make confessions contrasted strangely with his surroundings, which would lead you to expect the opposite – mystery and obfuscation). I would sit on his brown velvet sofa by the window, and I would listen quite happily for hours, losing all awareness of my own existence, losing myself in his. The whites of his eyes were almost too white, I remember, reminding me of porcelain, and he had a disconcerting way of smoothing his moustache. First, he would press two fingers to his upper lip, then, slowly, sensuously, the two fingers would separate into a V. This gesture was so deliberate that I often wondered whether it was not some kind of signal that I ought to recognise, a sign to which I might be expected to respond – but perhaps I was reading too much into the situation. Like Isabel, he asked nothing of me except my presence, and it occurred to me, after a while, that she might actually have asked him to keep me company. At times I felt as if everyone had been told to be kind to me, even people I didn't know, and I realised that, sooner or later, I would tire of this, I would rebel . . .

∿

It was a hot summer, the hottest for many years. I watched my body slowly darken in the sunlight. I watched it heal. In the evenings I sat outside with the french windows open, candles

135

burning on the oak table in the living-room behind me. I would listen to records on Isabel's old-fashioned stereo – Mahler, Puccini, Bach – the candles restless in the dark air, the wild garden below the terrace alive with rustling and shadows. Sometimes the phone rang – a naïve sound, over-eager, somehow, almost desperate. If I answered it, it was always someone asking for Isabel. I didn't feel neglected. I wasn't unhappy either. Words like happiness just didn't seem to apply.

My thirtieth birthday came and went, uncelebrated. In the evening I called my parents, in England. I had last spoken to them on the day after I was released, and my mother's voice had sounded shaky, fearful. I told her it had been a big fuss about nothing. I had wanted to get away, that was all; I had needed time to think (I thought she would believe this because, as a thirteen or fourteen year old, I used to ride out to the New Forest at midnight on my bicycle, only to find her waiting for me in the kitchen, worried sick, when I returned). It had been difficult to lie to her, though, not least because I had the memory of her appearing in the white room and spinning beneath the full moon in her pleated skirt. Even now, it was hard to convince myself that she knew nothing about what had happened.

'Happy birthday, darling,' my mother said. 'How are you?'

'I'm all right. I'm fine.'

'Are you doing something special tonight?'

'Not really, no.'

I could see my mother clearly. When she talked on the phone she would always hold the receiver against her ear so tightly and with such determination that she reminded me of someone gluing a handle back on to a jug.

She told me that she had tried to call me earlier, but that nobody had answered. I wasn't staying at the apartment any

136

more, I said. I had moved out for a while. I gave her the number at Isabel's.

'Are you sure you're all right?' my mother asked again.

'Yes, I'm fine.'

Thirty, I thought. My mind was empty. I felt nothing.

We talked for another five or ten minutes, firstly about my father, who was working too hard, apparently (my father ran a business that supplied industrial vacuum cleaners to big manufacturers), then about my brother, who had said that he would be coming home for Christmas. She asked me when I was coming home, and I told her it would be soon, though I didn't think that that was true.

Later, when the phone-call was over, I drove down to the beach. I walked along the hard flat sand for about a mile, then I turned inland, through the dunes. I couldn't go to England – not yet, anyway. I would never be able to carry it off. I loved my parents, I always had, but this was something they couldn't help me with.

There were times during that summer when the darkness was coming down and the green floorboards in Isabel's apartment looked almost black. The flames of the candles staggered as the cool night air circled the room. I would turn towards the phone, which crouched on a round wooden table in the corner, and I would think of calling Brigitte, but it was funny, even before I rejected it as an idea, I would find that I had forgotten the number, a number that had been my own for the past seven years.

～

Every so often, when I was least expecting it, I would catch a glimpse of a white wall studded with an array of brackets, clamps and rings, or a woman wearing nothing except a scarlet hood. It felt like a story I had heard third-hand, it had happened to someone else, a person I would never meet, a stranger, and yet, when those images flashed before my eyes, my entire body heated up and suddenly my heart was beating too solidly inside my chest, making the same sound that a sledge-hammer would make if you raised it above your head and brought it down repeatedly on someone's lawn.

One night, in Paul Bouhtala's apartment, I was studying the pictures on his living-room walls when I noticed a framed black-and-white photograph of a Japanese man lying on a couch. He was naked except for a loincloth, and his body was covered with tattoos.

'Do you like it?'

I turned sharply. Bouhtala was watching me from the shadows on the far side of the room, where he was mixing himself a cocktail.

'Interesting,' I said.

'I took the picture in Yokohama, more than thirty years ago . . .'

He embarked on the kind of story that was typical of him – one which involved, if I remember rightly, a Korean trans-sexual, a knife-fight and a boat-load of narcotics.

'You don't have a tattoo, I suppose,' he said, already sounding disappointed.

I shook my head. 'No.'

And then, with a start, I realised that I had lied.

'What is it?' Bouhtala asked, still watching me with interest, this time from his brown leather armchair by the fireplace. A maraschino cherry glowed like a gem-stone in the bottom of his glass.

'It's nothing,' I said. 'I was thinking of someone else. A friend.'

Later that night, in Isabel's apartment, I undressed and

stood in front of the bathroom mirror. The marks around my wrists and ankles had long since faded, but Maude's tattoo still showed, her claim on me scratched crudely into my skin.

~

The following morning I drove to the railway station in Bloemendaal and bought a ticket to Amsterdam. I changed trains in Haarlem, then sat by the window, watching the flat green land rush past. I had been away for two months. It seemed even longer. My stomach tightened, and, reaching into my pocket, I took out the notebook I had brought with me. Over breakfast I had copied down the names and addresses of all the tattoo parlours in the Amsterdam phone directory. I opened my notebook and ran through the list, trying to work out which would be the best. I had no way of knowing, of course. In the end, I chose one more or less at random, simply on the basis that I knew the street. Looking out of the window again, I saw apartment buildings sliding by, their façades decorated with dreary squares of yellow, red and blue. The suburbs of the city.

I walked out of Central Station, past the men loitering suspiciously near public telephones, past the tangled mass of bicycles in racks, and crossed that bleak, wide-open area beyond the trams, making for Zeedijk. I had always liked the red-light district during the day, especially when the sun was shining – some bleary, slept-in quality the streets had, the neon diluted, pale, and, every now and then, a girl on her way to work in full make-up and impossible high-heels – but it struck me, as I walked along, that I had been attracted to that world only because of its distance from my own. It had been a kind of romanticism, the naïve romanticism of the inexper- ienced, the uninformed. Now, though, the sight of a woman dressed in latex or plastic felt like something I knew about, felt much too familiar, in fact, and I hurried onwards, with my hands pushed deep into my pockets and my head lowered.

When I arrived at the tattoo parlour, the door stood half open, and loud music pounded through the gap. The window was smoked-glass, revealing nothing of the interior. I hesitated for a moment, wondering what kind of place I had chosen, then I walked inside. A man in a black leather vest sat at a counter with a newspaper in front of him. He was hunched right over, his bare forearms spread on either side of the front page, as if they were guarding it; I could only see the top of his head, his pale hair swirling as it closed in on his crown, like the pattern on a snail's shell. I doubt he could have heard me move towards him, not with that music crashing out of the speakers, but he must have sensed my presence in the room because he looked up as I approached and then reached out and turned the volume down. I explained that I had a tattoo I wanted to get rid of. He asked me where it was. I pointed at it through my clothes. Pushing his paper to one side, he leaned back in his chair. For years, you couldn't get rid of a tattoo, he told me, not unless you used a scalpel, that is. You literally had to lift the top three or four layers of skin away. Yes, he said when he saw the look on my face, that was the only way. He reached for his cigarettes, lit one, then offered me the packet. I shook my head. To remove a tattoo in those days, he went on, it was like surgery. Then, in the seventies, people started using acid. But acid was not so precise, and it could also be painful.

'Now, with lasers – well, it's much easier . . .'

'Lasers?' I said. 'How does that work?'

'They break up the cells that form the tattoo, so the ink disperses. Of course, the process leaves a scar – ' He broke off, shrugged.

'Could you do it today?'

He placed his cigarette on the groove in the ashtray. 'Show me the tattoo.'

I undid my trousers and pulled them down a little so he could see.

'You want to remove this?' he said.

I nodded.

'I'm not surprised.' He looked up at me. 'Did you do it?'

'No. Not me.'

Still looking at me, he eased back in his chair again.

'OK,' he said. 'I understand.' A distant smile appeared on his face, and I wondered what it was he thought he knew.

Later, while he was working on the tattoo, I felt the room shake slightly. Without looking up, he told me that the Metro passed beneath the building. He talked on, but I was no longer listening. I was thinking about the day when I had been allowed outside, to breathe fresh air, and how I had heard a train in the distance, the rhythm of its wheels laboured, tentative, as if it was slowing down, pulling into a station. Then I remembered church bells jangling . . .

A railway station, a church – these were co-ordinates, I realised. And if they were co-ordinates, then possibly, just possibly, I could use them to locate the house in which I had been imprisoned.

∼

For the next week or two I walked the streets, covering Amsterdam methodically, area by area. With each day that passed, I grew steadily more exhausted, more disillusioned. The co-ordinates weren't as useful as I'd imagined they might be. There were just too many places on the map where stations and churches coincided. The city began to irritate me.

The houses that lined the canals weren't houses at all, I felt, but façades built out of brightly coloured cardboard; the famous hump-backed bridges were equally two-dimensional. If I reached out with one hand, I could push the whole lot over. Only one area drew me back, exerting an uneasy magnetism I found it difficult to rationalise. It was in the east, near Muiderpoort. Immigrants lived there mostly – people from Morocco, Turkey, Surinam. Empty beer-bottles had been used to prop sash windows open, and wooden beads or strips of coloured plastic hung in place of the traditional Dutch net curtains. In the café where I stopped for something to drink, black women stood about in short leather skirts and sunglasses. Outside, I saw a tree with half a dozen children clustered in its branches, like birds or fruit. One road ran parallel to the train-tracks, which were raised high above it, on an embankment. The ponderous trundling of the wheels carried into the surrounding side-streets. There were three churches in the area, all within earshot of the railway, and I found two or three places where the sounds combined in a way that seemed familiar. But how to take it any further, how to narrow it down?

I was standing on the pavement, trying to think, when a hand wrapped itself around my forearm. I turned to see a man standing beside me, Turkish by the look of him, with a mournful droop to his jowls and a two-day growth of beard.

'*Zoeken?*' He paused, and then continued in English. 'What are you looking?'

It was hard to explain, of course. I hesitated.

'Here is Javaplein,' he said, and his free hand moved in a horizontal semicircle, the palm facing upwards, the fingers slightly curled.

'I know,' I said. 'Thank you.'

The man took a firmer grip on my forearm and peered at

me with a troubled expression on his face. He wanted to help me. I wasn't allowing him to.

'I'm looking for three women,' I said suddenly.

He wiped his mouth, an odd downwards motion of one hand, which, because of his stubble, made a soft scraping noise, like a match being struck on the side of a matchbox.

'Women?' he said.

'Yes.'

He looked at me for a moment longer, then he waved at me, a gesture that had a dismissive feel to it, and turned away.

But perhaps he had helped me after all, I thought – though not in the way he had intended. He had prompted me, given me something I could work with. I began to knock on people's doors.

My first encounter was with a black woman in her sixties. She opened her front door about a foot and peered through the gap. She had strange orange-gold hair which was probably a wig.

'I'm looking for three women,' I told her. 'Three women who live in the same house.'

The woman stared at me, her head wobbling a little.

'It's possible they don't live together,' I went on. 'It's possible they're just friends. Have you seen anyone like that?'

The woman was still staring, but the gap seemed to have narrowed.

'Three women,' I said. 'Dutch.'

The woman closed the door in my face, slowly though, as if she didn't want to be rude.

Further down the street I spoke to an old man in a cardigan. No, he didn't know anything. No, nothing at all. I had the feeling that he hadn't even listened to the question. In the next street a Moroccan answered the door. He didn't understand what I was talking about, even when I spoke to him in French.

143

Two houses further on I came across a young woman holding a baby. Before I could finish asking her about the women, she accused me of being a plain-clothes policeman. When I denied it, she called me a liar. The Turkish man's reaction turned out to be a sort of template for the various forms of suspicion I aroused in everyone I came across.

The encounter that put an end to my enquiries happened on a street that overlooked the railway line. When I rang the bell, a burly white man in a silk shirt and snow-washed jeans burst on to the pavement. He had opened the door as if the door was a steer that he was trying to wrestle to the ground. He was red in the face, and breathing hard. I could hear loud voices coming from inside the house.

'*Wat moet je?*' he said.

I asked if he had seen three Dutch women.

He looked down the street, first one way, then the other, then he put his red face close to mine. '*Rot op.*' When I hesitated, he leaned into me still further. '*Ben je doof? Rot op!*'

I had no choice but to turn round and walk away. On reaching the corner of the street, I looked back, over my shoulder.

He was still watching me.

~

It was that same week, curiously enough, that I met Mr Olsen. Bouhtala held a small cocktail party in his apartment to celebrate his birthday (no one seemed to know how old Bouhtala was, and he chose not to enlighten us), and Olsen was one of the fifteen or twenty people who had been invited. When I first saw him, he was standing by the window in a greenish-brown wool sweater, a glass of beer held in the air below his chin. He had an affable, slightly rumpled face, and

144

his wavy hair, once fair, was lightly dusted with grey. I suppose he was in his early fifties. Most of Bouhtala's guests had the look of dilettantes – one arrived in a maroon velvet jacket, with a yellow rose in his lapel; another leaned against the bookshelves in a tight black suit and a black shirt – and their jobs, if they had jobs, were as glamorous and mysterious as his. Olsen stood out because he looked so ordinary. Of course, at that point, I had no idea that he worked for the *Jeugdpolitie*, a branch of the Dutch police that deals with crimes such as child abuse and violence against women. If I had been asked to guess what his profession was I would probably have said schoolmaster.

I walked over and introduced myself. Olsen was Danish, from Arhus, but he had lived in Holland for the last ten years. Then we had something in common, I told him. His eyes wrinkled at the edges; he lifted his glass of beer and drank. We had Isabel in common too. He had met her several times, through Paul Bouhtala. She had impressed him greatly, he said, not only with her elegance, but with her discipline. Like most people, perhaps, he hadn't appreciated the amount of sheer hard work that went into the creation of a ballet. I asked him what he did for a living. The answer took me by surprise, and, wanting to hear more, I began to question him. At some point, he brought up the subject of unsolved crimes – and, more specifically, crimes that could not be solved because they had never even been reported. He called these crimes 'dark number cases', a phrase that has stayed with me ever since. Perhaps I drank too many cocktails that night – I have never been much good with alcohol – because I remember telling him that I knew of just such a crime. If he was curious he didn't show it. He didn't cock his head or raise his eyebrows, as some people might have done. No, that wasn't his way. He just watched me over the rim of his beer-glass, his grey eyes steady, intent. I told him that a friend of mine, a male friend, had been abducted by several women and held in a room for eighteen days. Olsen was silent for a moment, and then he laughed and said, 'That's terrible.'

I had never told a man the story before, but this was exactly the kind of reaction I would have predicted. Despite that, I found that I too was laughing. A few minutes later, though, I told Olsen that I needed another drink – he wanted one as well – and I left the room with both our glasses. In the hallway I hesitated for a moment, then I put the glasses down on the hall table, opened the front door and walked out of the apartment, closing the door behind me.

It was a misty night, more typical of October than July. I buttoned my jacket and, turning the collar up, set off through the orchard. For the past few years, it had been allowed to run wild: there was no footpath, and the grass had grown waist-high in many places. As I moved cautiously among the trees I trod on an apple; I felt it resist for a moment, then give beneath my weight, as if part of it, at least, had rotted.

When I reached the road I turned left, away from the house, and walked off down the hill. The fuzzy glow of a street-lamp, the tick of a bicycle freewheeling past . . . Why had I left the party so abruptly? Had I wanted Olsen to surprise me with his reaction, to confound my expectations? Or was it simply that I had said as much as I could say?

At the bottom of the hill I stopped beside a gate. Beyond it lay a narrow waterway. I gazed at the still flat surface, silence gathering around me. A rowing-boat glided towards me out of the fog. A man in a dark peaked cap, his shoulders hunched over the oars. The almost glassy trickle of water off the blades . . .

Perhaps it was the shock of mentioning it at all.

Later that night, lying in bed, I felt shaken to have come so close to a confession – and to a policeman, of all people! I heard his laughter, then my laughter. I heard him say, *That's terrible.* There had been a lightness about the exchange that I could never have anticipated.

The next day I apologised to Paul Bouhtala for leaving the party without so much as a goodbye. He smiled and said, 'Well, it's not as if we'll never see each other again,' a statement which, given what happened two weeks later, had a quality of tempting fate about it.

~

The summer was drawing to a close. One warm evening in August I sat in Bouhtala's apartment, listening to another of his stories. He was telling me how he came to own his cigarette lighter. This was no ordinary lighter. About four inches high, and made of steel, it was a black panther sitting on its haunches. Its eyes were real diamonds.

Bouhtala had just set the scene – a nightclub in Durban, 1962 – when I began to smile. He stopped in mid-sentence, one eyebrow lifting quizzically, and reached for his cocktail. In the gloomy half-light of the room his shirt-cuff was so white that it seemed an object in its own right, moving entirely independently of him.

'Why are you smiling?' he asked.

'I have decided to take a leaf out of your book.' I felt my smile widen. What was it about talking English to foreigners that made me use these old-fashioned idioms? I paused, and then I said, 'I have decided to travel.'

That morning something extraordinary had happened. By the time I got downstairs, the post had already been delivered. At first it looked as if there was just a postcard – the Munch painting on the front told me that it had come from Isabel –

147

but when I reached down I found a letter lying underneath. The handwriting was my mother's. That, in itself, was nothing unusual; she often wrote to me with news of home. I scanned Isabel's postcard quickly – *There's too much light in Norway*, she complained. *How on earth does anybody sleep?* – then I opened the letter. The first time I read it I wasn't certain that I had understood. I read it again, much more slowly. Afterwards, I walked out on to the terrace and sat there for a long time, staring into the pine forest. My great-uncle had died earlier that month, and he had left me approximately sixty thousand pounds in his will.

I told Bouhtala all this, and he listened intently, with his dark eyes fixed on me and his hands folded in his lap. Until he had started to describe Durban, I said, I hadn't been sure what I was going to do. Ever since the letter had arrived I had been wondering about it. But now, thanks to him, I knew.

Bouhtala did not appear particularly surprised, neither by the windfall, nor by my decision to travel, though something did seem to be weighing on him all of a sudden. His head had sunk into his shoulders, and he had settled a little deeper in his leather chair.

'You were close to your great-uncle?' he asked.

'No, we weren't close,' I said. 'In fact, I only met him once in my life. About five years ago. He came to see me at Sadler's Wells.' I paused. 'He lived in Canada.'

Bouhtala nodded, watching me. 'He must have approved of you.'

'It's strange,' I went on, 'but I was beginning to worry about money.' I paused again, and then added, 'Now that I'm not dancing any more – '

A silence followed. I could hear the house creaking, the hiss of drizzle on the trees outside the window. The room seemed to darken. It was the first time I had admitted it out loud, and the words sounded curiously awkward, even bogus, as if they had been spoken by a mediocre actor.

At last Bouhtala lifted his glass from the table at his elbow. Lips pursed, he watched the tiny strings of bubbles rise to the surface and then disappear. He asked me where I would go. Everywhere, I told him. I'd go everywhere.

Bouhtala smiled quickly, then drank. 'You will not regret it.'

He replaced his glass on the table beside him, and, sitting back, reached up with two fingers of his right hand and smoothed his moustache. It was a gesture I had become accustomed to, but one which, in the circumstances, seemed to take on special significance. In that moment I felt as though Bouhtala was bestowing his own personal seal of approval on me, a kind of unspoken blessing.

~

I knew I had to see my parents before I left. I didn't really feel ready, but I flew to England anyway, just for the weekend. Grey clouds flashed past the window as the plane shuddered and bumped through the air above London, and rain left slanting scratches on the glass. Though it was August, the lights had been switched on in all the airport buildings. The tarmac gleamed, slick and black, under a sullen sky.

On the train down to Hampshire I thought about my unlikely friendship with Bouhtala. I had seen him no more than once or twice a week, but I had seen almost nobody else; he had become the one solid point in my new fragile life, and I felt oddly indebted to him. I turned to the window. The rain was still coming down. A white horse stood under a tree in the corner of a field, its head lowered, its mane lank and matted. I smiled faintly as I remembered how Bouhtala had talked to me once about the beauty of English skin, and how one had to look upon it as some kind of compensation for the horrors of the climate.

There was no one on the platform to meet me when the train pulled in, but that wasn't such a great surprise. My father would still be at work, and my mother was never on time for anything. She drove into the station car-park twenty minutes later to find me sitting on a bench, reading a book. We embraced beside the car. Taking her in my arms, I kissed her on the cheek and breathed her in – the waxy, slightly theatrical scent of her lipstick, and the rain-soaked fragrance of her dark-brown hair, which she dyed to hide the strands of silver. She was so sorry she was late, she said. Had I been waiting long? I smiled down at her.

'I just got here,' I said.

'You've been here for ages.' Her grin was both knowing and guilty. 'I can tell.'

I put my bag in the boot and got into the car. Before she started the engine she turned in her seat so she was facing me.

'You look so well,' she said.

Her tone of voice gave something away, the feeling on her part that she had been expecting me to look otherwise, but I pretended not to notice, and, after a moment, she reached out, rubbed my shoulder affectionately, and told me how good it was to have me back.

∼

My parents had been married for thirty-five years, and they were easy in each other's company; they still made each other laugh, and still, or so I liked to think, made love. That weekend, though, I noticed a new restlessness in them. Like children at the end of a long day, they could not seem to settle. My father kept suggesting different outdoor activities – expeditions, picnics, walks – and this despite the fact that the rain was still falling, heavier than ever. *It's supposed to let up later on. Maybe then* . . . My mother rushed from room to room, as if she was permanently behind schedule – a schedule no one else could fathom. Once, just out of curiosity, I followed her. She hurried into the garage with a damp cloth and began to wipe dust off the bottles of fruit cordial she stored on the shelf above the freezer. Twenty-four hours into the visit, it occurred to me that my parents' behaviour might not be new at all. Maybe they had always been like this. Maybe I was the one who had changed. They seemed so bright-eyed, though, so tireless! They seemed constantly to be striving for an effect and falling short.

Only on Monday, after supper, did a kind of calmness finally descend. The rain had stopped, and the night was warm and humid. We took chairs out to the patio behind the house and sat there drinking tea, our faces starkly lit by the fluorescent glow that radiated from the kitchen window. I leaned back, my hands behind my head, and stared up into the sky. In nine days I'd be on a plane . . . I felt no excitement, only an awareness of what I was about to do, and how extreme it was.

'Your mother tells me that you're going travelling,' my father said after a while.

I nodded. 'That's right.'

'Is that a good move?'

I looked across at him uncertainly.

'At this point in your career,' he said.

I had prepared for this. The story I had invented had a convincing ring to it since it was just a slightly exaggerated version of the truth.

I was thirty years old, I told him, and had to face the fact that I was coming to the end of my career – my career as a dancer, anyway. For years now I had been working twelve-hour days, week in, week out, with almost no time off. Also, I had been having back problems. I leaned forwards, knowing how my father enjoyed anything technical. I had a stiff and immobile spine, I told him. Through repeated jumping, I had developed a condition known as spondylolisthesis. In layman's terms, this meant that one of the vertebrae in my lower back – L5, to be specific – had slipped out of position. The company physiotherapist had warned me that if I carried on dancing I would risk severe low back pain and even, possibly, disability. Thankfully, I had the choreography, though, and that would be waiting for me when I returned from my travels. It felt peculiar to say this because it was something which, until that moment, I hadn't even begun to think about.

My father ran one hand carefully over his thinning hair.

'And Brigitte?' he said. 'Is she going with you?'

Brigitte . . . I saw her as I had seen her last, sending one wild, despairing glance around the apartment. *I can't live here, not like this.*

'She's staying in Amsterdam,' I said. 'She has her dancing.'

I saw my father's chin lift a fraction, a kind of nod, but at the same time he drew his shoulders in towards his chest, almost as if he was cold. He had thoroughly approved of Brigitte. First of all, she was half French, and my father had always loved France (most summers, during my childhood, we would take the car over on the ferry, and then drive to Brittany, or the Dordogne, or Languedoc). She was pretty too, which counted in her favour, but there was more to it than that: she had what he called 'spirit', and that made her beautiful in his eyes. I watched him reach for his cup of tea and take a sip. He would miss her, I thought.

'And where will you go?' my mother asked.

'Mexico,' I said, 'to start with.'

'Mexico!' A short, delighted laugh came out of her, and she looked down into the lap of her dress and shook her head.

The people in the house next door had opened all their windows. Their TV was on, its volume turned up loud. I could hear the music that signalled the beginning of the nine o'clock news.

'You'll take good care of yourself, won't you,' my mother said.

'Of course.'

Staring into the darkness at the bottom of the garden, my father cleared his throat. 'You see, we worry about you . . .'

'I love you both very much,' I said.

～

Back in Holland everything speeded up. I had less than a week to prepare for my departure, and all of a sudden there were a hundred different things to do. Luckily, I had arranged my life in such a way that I didn't have to say too many goodbyes. On the Wednesday I spoke to Isabel in Oslo and told her of my plans. She wasn't due back until the second week in September, she said, which meant we would miss each other by a matter of days. The spare room would be there for me on my return, whenever that might be. I tried to thank her for her generosity, but, typically, she didn't want to hear it.

'Anyone would have done the same,' she said impatiently.

It was the first time she had referred, even indirectly, to the fact that I had been in trouble.

On one of my many trips into Amsterdam I met up with Stefan Elmers. He was excited that day because he was moving to a house on Prinsengracht which his father, a property speculator, had found for him. He would rent out half the house, he said, and live in the other half for nothing. This reminded me of the last conversation I'd had with Brigitte, and the question had left my mouth before I had time to think.

'Did Brigitte ever find someone to share with her?'

Stefan's eyes shifted sideways, and he plunged one hand into his curly dark-brown hair. 'Jean-Claude's moved in.'

Jean-Claude was a dancer at the company. And he was French too, of course, from Paris. Everything had worked out perfectly. I couldn't understand why Stefan was looking so uneasy.

Then I understood.

'Oh,' I said. 'I see.'

I stared through the café window at a woman who was chaining her bicycle to a lamp-post, but images of Jean-Claude rose up, blotting her out: the leather coat he always wore, the way his black hair seemed to accentuate the lean bones of his face, the time he did a *double tour en l'air* in dance class and loose change flew out of his pocket and rolled all over the studio . . .

'Maybe I shouldn't have told you,' Stefan said.

I turned back to him. 'What? No, it's all right.' I laughed, then swallowed suddenly and looked away.

That she should have a new man – Jean-Claude! – in her life. That I should be so easily replaced. I thought about the ballets I had made for her, and how I would have gone on making them for her, just to see her face glow when I first showed her the steps, just to see her body begin to inhabit what I had imagined . . . I ran my index finger along the edge of the table, backwards and forwards, backwards and forwards. Perhaps it was just that men took second place with her, I thought. She needed someone to be with her, someone she could rely on, but she wasn't too bothered about who it was. Her art took precedence. It was all that mattered. Her lover could have whatever was left over.

I looked across at Stefan, saw that he felt guilty.

'It's all right, Stefan.' I put a hand on his arm. 'It's not your fault.'

As we parted that afternoon, I promised to keep in touch with him, no matter where in the world I might be. I had just started to walk away when I heard him call my name. I stopped, turned round. He was standing on the pavement with both arms raised above his head, his jacket lifting into the air on either side of him. He looked as if he had acquired a pair of ill-fitting and ungainly wings. He was waving.

'Good luck,' he shouted. '*Bon voyage!*'

Then there was Paul Bouhtala. On my last night he invited me to his apartment for a farewell dinner. As he rose to serve coffee and liqueurs, I reached for the rectangular parcel I had secretly brought in with me.

'In return for all your kindness,' I said.

His eyes opened wide, and he stooped over the parcel and began to tear the wrapping off in a greedy, almost desperate way that I couldn't have anticipated. I sat back, smiling, as his hands unearthed the atlas I had bought while passing through London the week before, the largest atlas I had been able to find.

'This is marvellous,' he enthused, turning the pages. 'Such detail.'

'When I send you postcards from exotic places,' I said, 'you will be able to see exactly where I am.'

He looked up, his dark eyes glittering with mischief. 'And who knows,' he said, 'perhaps I will even join you . . .'

~

My flight to Mexico City left at ten-thirty on a Wednesday morning. I had set the alarm for dawn, but I was awake before it began to ring. I stood by the bedroom window, staring out over the garden. Each branch that I could see, each leaf, each blade of grass, seemed sharply drawn, almost enhanced. Somewhere deep in the forest a bird was making a sound which it repeated at regular intervals, a single note that was exactly like the first half of a wolf-whistle. There was a feeling in my stomach that I didn't recognise – a hollowness, a kind of grief – and I wondered if I would ever return to this house again, if I would spend another night in this room, with its powdery pale-blue walls and its monastic bed . . .

At that point I had no aims, no real purpose. All I had was a vague itinerary, though even that could change at any time. I wasn't looking for anything, least of all myself. I wasn't running either. I knew I couldn't leave my memories behind; they would come along with me, whether I liked it or not. Travel wasn't a solution. It was just a possibility – the only possibility I could think of. And that's what I would have said that Wednesday morning, if you had asked me. *It's possible, so I am doing it.*

I don't think I could have added much to that.

~

From Mexico I travelled overland to Guatemala. From Guatemala to Honduras. From Honduras, by steamer, to Costa Rica. Then eastwards, into Panama. While in Panama I worked as a guide, taking tourists on walks in the rain forest near Lake Alajuela. The American who had hired me called me Mark for some reason, and, finding the change of name oddly appropriate, I didn't bother to correct him . . . I lived in Panama City for about three months, then I moved on, into South America. I had money, after all; I just kept going.

In Venezuela I slept with a French girl called Monique. I say 'slept with'. We didn't actually make love, not even once. The first time she took off her clothes, in a hotel room in Caracas, I saw a white wall behind her, and, all of a sudden, my whole body was running with sweat, so much so that there were dark stains on the sheets. I bent over, retching.

'What's wrong?' Her eyes had widened. 'Is something wrong?'

Not wanting to offend her, I told her I'd had a sugar-cane drink with crushed ice in it that morning. The ice must have been dirty, I said. She believed me. The moment she went out to buy me some Coca-Cola, though, I packed my things and checked out of the hotel.

From then on, I avoided all such situations.

It was one of the ironies of my new existence that, despite my absolute and unprecedented freedom, I was more self-contained, more sealed off, than I had ever been before. I became a mystery to others. Where was I from? Why was I travelling alone? What did I do for money? I often had the feeling that people were making up stories about me, but I knew their stories wouldn't have been a patch on the real one, not even close. There was a part of my mind that I kept hidden, even from myself, and they wouldn't have been able to see into it.

They would never have guessed the truth.

Their imaginations would have failed them.

~

Three years passed. I went everywhere, as I had told Paul Bouhtala that I would. I ate fish jalfrezi in a rooftop restaurant in Zanzibar, fruit bats whirling through the darkness like dead leaves. I watched the sun setting from the deck of a cargo boat

157

as it sailed from Ujung Pandang to Surabaya. I drank *caipir-inhas* in a dirt-floor reggae bar in São Luís . . . Sometimes I found myself using the name that the American had given me. It was another way of securing privacy. Also, perhaps, I had grown into it. My hair had bleached in the sunlight and salt water, and, for the first time in my life, I had a tan. I was thinner too; after repeated bouts of diarrhoea, I had shed more than a stone in weight. Every now and then I remembered how I had stood outside that bar on the day of my release, and how I had failed to recognise myself. I now thought of that as a defining moment. During my time in the white room, I had started to undergo some sort of transformation. My blond hair, my brown skin – they were just superficial changes. More significant by far was the fact that my relationship with my body had altered, and altered radically. I was still fit – I walked and swam whenever I could – but it wasn't the exhaustive, unrelenting fitness I had been used to for so many years. My body was no longer the centre of my attention, no longer the instrument through which I expressed myself, and, as a result, my life had lost much of its focus. As I moved from place to place, I seemed to carry a peculiar, almost eerie sense of quiet about with me. I thought of ancient battlefields, and how their trenches are replaced by grass and wild flowers. I thought of abandoned factories occupied by rust and birds. You walk around, and there's just a wind blowing gently, and a piece of metal banging somewhere, and the wide blue sky above your head . . . There were times when I felt as if I was a stranger in my own body. As if I had been separated from myself. I would be crossing a street in broad daylight, and, although I knew I was walking, I would feel as though I was dropping through the air. The two sensations would happen simultaneously, and they would both be true. The people who passed me on the street at times like that would see a man talking to himself, making a desperate attempt to hold himself together.

~

So what do I remember of those years, the years I was away? The peaceful moments, mostly – the moments of contemplation.

The Mekong River, four-thirty in the morning . . .

I remember waking early, dressing in the dark. The guesthouse where I was staying stood on a red dirt track at the edge of a village. It was a two-storey structure made entirely of bamboo, and every time I shifted my weight from one foot to the other, the whole building seemed to shake. All around me I could hear the feathery sound of people sleeping. The darkness was soft with it. Once, the man in the next bunk took a deep breath, as if he was about to make an announcement, but then the air rushed out of him and he turned over, one arm flung out, the hand with its palm upturned, dramatic, reaching almost to the floor. I crept downstairs, each step silent, furtive, like someone leaving without paying.

Outside, light was already seeping into the sky. A pale light, milky, the colour of old-fashioned paper glue. Rolls of mist lay in the fields or hung in ghostly suspension over the river. Trees were just beginning to detach themselves from the dark mass of the jungle; I could see their trunks – the pattern of hoops, the alternating bands of black and grey. Somewhere a cock crowed, raucous and insistent. Though I must have heard the sound in England first, or on holiday in France, perhaps, when I was young, it always reminds me of South-East Asia now, that hoarse cry somehow at odds with the dreamy sluggishness of dawn . . . And then the smell, a kind of sweetness in the air, but thick too, cloying, like the scent of

159

certain lilies. There's nothing fresh, even at five in the morning, only the sense of something being brought back to life. It was always the same day, you felt – the same day endlessly reheated.

The strangest feeling. As if the place was trying to speak to me. *Look*, it was saying. *This is what you have become.* And the people riding along the dirt track on their bicycles, smiling and nodding at me . . .

I sat on the grass for at least an hour and watched the river slide from left to right. On the far bank I saw smoke rise from the jungle. That was Laos. The country was closed to foreigners that year, and it had the allure of the prohibited – that wall of undergrowth and foliage, that blue smoke rising, drifting . . .

This is what you are.

Below me, boats had been drawn up, propped against the wet black roots of trees. The boats were thin and curved, like ancient dried-up pods, like bits of rind. The beauty of those shapes as the sky brightened and the day began to impose itself . . .

Just then, I felt the edges of my flesh dissolving. I was the same as the wood the boats were made of, the same as the water of the river. One flowed straight into the other, with no frontiers, no distinctions. I was so wholly present that I was wholly absent. And yet, at the same time, curiously, I was able to register a feeling of relief. To be rid of myself, if only for a few moments . . .

The Mekong, at Chiang Saen.

That was one of the times when I understood the nature, the true weight, of what it was that I was carrying.

What else do I remember? Everything and nothing. So much happened to me that, in the end, I found that I could no longer take anything in (though, if you had read the postcards I sent, you could be forgiven for thinking otherwise because I filled them with the kind of jewelled details I knew my friends would appreciate). If a fellow traveller asked me what it was like in Sulawesi or Bhutan, I would use superlatives. *Incredible, fantastic. Great.* I became the type of person I had never understood – the person who has been everywhere, but cannot tell you anything. I had met people like that on holiday with Brigitte. We would have two weeks, at the most, and they would have been travelling for ever. And they would have nothing to say. What was the point of travelling, I used to think, if the experience could not be communicated? Ah. Well. Slowly, as my time away stretched into months, then into years, I began to understand. You take in so much. You're too full. Which is the same as being empty. That seemed to be the effect. As if the brain could only process so much information . . . That emptiness, though – that became the point. For me, at any rate.

At first I achieved the state unwittingly. Then I started to co-operate with it. I stopped keeping a diary; I gave my camera away. I travelled more and more lightly. I bought nothing, kept nothing. Because that was what I wanted. To journey beyond my skin. To forfeit all awareness of my blood, my bones – my soul. To disappear completely into what I was looking at.

Not destinations then. Not adventures.

Movement.

The feeling of a ship or a train or a bus beneath me, each with its different rituals, its different rhythms. A destination was useful because it was a substitute for purpose; it answered any question I was likely to be asked. Movement became my reason for being, my excuse. Movement for its own sake. I forget who it was who wrote about the importance of doing nothing, how the art of doing nothing is one that most people seem to have forgotten. Well, I decided to resurrect the art. In doing nothing, I would be reduced to what I was moving through. I would, quite literally, become part of the scenery. I would blend, immerse. Dissolve.

And wasn't this, also, in the end, a way of dealing with death? Death, which is the root of all anxiety. Death, which requires us to justify ourselves. Death, which makes us believe in God.

All that I could happily dispense with.

Do nothing. Whatever happens, happens. Let it come.

~

Perhaps it couldn't have gone on, though. I don't know. Perhaps I would have reached a point where I lost myself completely. Certainly I had no idea where the path I was following would lead me. At the same time, I couldn't imagine what it would take to make me think of going home – what conversation, what event, what set of circumstances . . .

After travelling for three years or so, I found myself in the village of Lovina on the north coast of Bali. I had rented the usual bamboo hut. It had a small terrace at the front, facing the sea, and a creaky double bed. The inside of the hut smelled of coconut milk and mosquito coils, and also of the coarse string they used instead of springs to support the mattress. At night the palm trees clattered in the breeze that blew in off the Sea of Java. I breakfasted on Nescafé and papaya, then spent the day walking on the beach, or swimming, or lying in a hammock, reading. In the evenings I would meet up with a German man, a taxi-driver from Munich, whose name I have now forgotten. We would drink beer together, and I would watch the whites of his eyes turn red as he smoked the local grass. It was a peaceful place, one of many peaceful places that I had seen, and I thought I would probably stay there for a week or two before moving on to Lombok, Flores, Ambon . . .

I never saw those islands. One evening, after swimming, I stopped at the bar for something to drink. Three white girls were sitting at a cane table, wearing sarongs. I said hello, and we started talking. They asked me where I was from, as people always do when you're travelling. I said that I was English, but that I'd spent almost ten years of my life in Holland. It turned out that they were Dutch. Two of them lived in Amsterdam, the other in The Hague. We knew the same café, in the Jordaan. We could have been there at the same time, all four of us, without knowing it.

'What a coincidence,' said the blondest of the girls, whose name was Saskia.

And suddenly it struck me.

Three Dutch girls.

For a moment the bar seemed to tilt away from me. My body became as weightless as the air itself. I couldn't feel my legs at all. I wonder if the girls noticed any alteration in my manner. Probably not. They were only three weeks into their travels, and still starry-eyed at being so far from home.

When the feeling had passed, I smiled faintly.

'Yes,' I said. 'A real coincidence.'

I slept with Saskia first, who was the most forward of the three. We stood in my hut one afternoon, facing each other, our hips almost touching. A breeze pushed through the window's tilted slats.

'Will you undress me?' she said. 'I like to be undressed.'

As I lifted her T-shirt over her head, revealing her breasts, I thought of the women in the white room. Parts of their bodies came tumbling into my mind, one after another, indiscriminately – the coin-shaped scar, the dark-red pubic hair, the mole . . . Without taking my eyes off Saskia, I dropped her T-shirt on the bed. No mole. I kneeled in front of her, unfastened her sarong. As the sarong came loose and slid to the floor, I ran my hands up the outside of her thighs until I reached her hips. No coin-shaped scar. I drew her closer and pressed my face into her pubic hair, which was dark-blonde . . .

After what had happened in Caracas, you might think there would have been some nervousness or apprehension on my part. But no. Not at all. In fact, much to my surprise, having sex with Saskia felt entirely natural and effortless. Almost preordained. What seemed to make it possible was the idea that it was connected in some way with the women who had abducted me. It was as if, in making that connection, I had managed to earth myself.

During the next ten days I slept with all three girls. I knew they weren't the women from the room, but I still had to see them naked. I had to examine each of them in detail. Just to be sure.

They all thought it was unusual, the way I made love to them. The shyest of them – Camiel – said she found it cold and unalluring; I made her feel self-conscious, as if she had been put under a microscope. The other two were strangely flattered, revelling in my eager exploration of their bodies, revelling in what they must inevitably have seen as adoration . . .

I left Lovina suddenly. The girls were out that day, visiting a village in the mountains. I slipped a note under the door of their hut, saying something like, *See you back in Holland, maybe* – I didn't leave an address, though; I didn't have an address – then I headed south to Denpasar, where I bought a one-way ticket to Amsterdam . . .

Oddly enough, about a year later, I did run into one of them again. I had just eaten lunch with Paul Bouhtala at the American Hotel and I was crossing Leidseplein when I heard somebody call my name. I turned round, and there she was, not brown any more, but still slim, still blonde.

'Saskia,' I said.

We kissed each other on the cheek. She seemed pleased that I had remembered her name, that I had not forgotten her.

'When did you get back?' she asked.

I smiled. 'I've been back for quite a while actually.'

'Really? I thought you were never coming back.'

She stood in front of me in her brown suede jacket and her jeans, with her blonde hair falling in a straight line to her shoulders. In that moment I thought she realised there was some kind of link between our meeting on the beach in Lovina and my decision to return to Amsterdam, and I saw a look rise on to her face, a frank, receptive look that seems to come naturally to the Dutch, a look that communicates both desire and availability. She seemed startled when I cut our conversation short without asking for her number. But I had already searched her body for evidence, and come away with nothing. There was no need to search again. She was innocent. How could I possibly have explained something like that to her? Instead, I told her that I was living with someone, which wasn't true, and that I was happy, which wasn't true either. Saskia became rueful, even a little misty-eyed, openly expressing the wish that she could find a man who wasn't immature, who didn't cheat on her – a man, she implied, who was more like me. If only you knew, I thought.

When I said goodbye to her a few moments later, she leaned towards me and kissed me slowly on the mouth, softening her lips so that they seemed to grow as they touched mine, then she drew back and, smiling, turned away, still unaware of the profound effect that she and her two friends had had on me. I watched her blonde hair swinging against her brown suede jacket as she walked towards Leidsestraat. All of a sudden I felt strangely burdened, old.

~

I had flown into Schiphol direct from Bali on a warm grey day in early August. The flight had taken thirteen hours, and I had hardly slept. I walked through the efficient, hygienic spaces of the airport, noticing brightness, order and purpose every-where I looked. This was something I hadn't come across for months, and a bleakness stole into my blood. I was glad Stefan had offered to meet me.

I had called him from Denpasar, asking if he knew of anywhere I could stay on my return. I was in luck, he told me. He was still living on the first two floors of the house on Prinsengracht, but the apartment in the attic was empty. His father wanted him to find a lodger, and this would save him the trouble. He had some other news. He was no longer working as a dance photographer, he said. He had started taking portraits for newspapers and magazines. He added that he had lost touch with Brigitte. I think he wanted to put my mind at rest, to reassure me that if I lived in the house on Prinsengracht I wouldn't have to see her, which was a relief, of course, but also, curiously, a kind of disappointment.

I saw him as soon as I emerged from Customs. Standing sideways-on to me, with his dark-brown hair as tangled as it had always been and his hooked nose aimed at the ceiling, he was studying the Arrivals on a TV monitor. I walked up to him and put a hand on his shoulder. He jumped. Then, laughing, we embraced.

166

'It was good of you to come,' I said.

He took a step backwards. 'You look wonderful.'

'Stefan, I've been away, that's all.'

'No, really,' he said. 'You look, I don't know, *famous*.'

Which was the one thing I no longer was, of course. His eyes slid sideways, as if he felt he might have said something tactless. He picked up my rucksack. 'Is this all you have?'

I nodded.

He shook his head, as if he despaired of me, then he took my arm and led me towards the short-term car-park. Though I didn't really know what to say to him I was still relieved that he was there.

Once we were on the motorway he said, 'This must feel very strange to you.' He glanced out of the window at the grey-green land and said, 'All this.'

'Stranger than you know,' I told him.

I slept for most of the next two days. On the third morning, after I had eaten breakfast, I sat down at the small table by the window. I felt artificial, as if I wasn't actually back in Amsterdam at all, but had been superimposed on it, somehow. The weather had improved while I was sleeping. Trees stirred lazily against a pale-blue sky, and a warm draught pushed into the room. If I leaned forwards, I could watch glass-topped tourist boats cruise past, opening a thick, creamy fold in the surface of the canal. Somewhere in the city there were three women who had held me in a room against my will for eighteen days . . .

At the time I had watched them closely, and I had been able to distinguish them, one from another, especially when they were naked. I had a good memory for people's bodies – after all, they were my raw material, my inspiration – but how much could I remember now, years later? I summoned the women, one by one. Gertrude came first, wearing her cloak and hood. That way of moving that she had – upright, measured, almost self-important. Like a judge. After the banquet, though, when she had showed herself to me for the first time, her body had not been heavy or fleshy at all, I remembered, but well made, solid, with skin that looked unnaturally white, almost translucent – and then that moment when a single hair of hers, a red hair, had come floating downwards through the air . . . Astrid appeared next, in boots with pointed toes and stiletto heels. She had had the kind of body most men fantasise about – her breasts, her thighs, her cunt like an exotic shell . . . I tried to recall a distinguishing mark, a defect, but there was only that scar on her hip, the size of a guilder, and, if I closed my eyes, it was her fingers that I saw, fingers that were strong but elegant, with nails filed square across the top . . . And what about Maude? Well, she was probably the easiest of the three. I could almost see her in her entirety. She had a lumbering, affectionate quality about her. Her shoulders sloped, and her feet turned inwards. She had a mole placed neatly just to the right of her navel. What else? She bit her fingernails. Her breasts were disproportionately small. And I could still hear her saying, in that halting, stubborn voice of hers, *My body is not exciting to you* –

Shivering suddenly, despite the heat, I got up from the table. I leaned against the windowsill and gazed down at the canal. Another tourist boat glided by, the sun glancing off its curved glass roof. In the end, I didn't have much to go on, and given the amount of time that had elapsed, even the little that I had could easily have changed. Moles could be removed, for instance. Scars could fade. Hair could be cut, or dyed. I remembered Isabel's story about the ballerina with the birthmark at the bottom of her spine, a pale-pink birthmark that was shaped exactly like a sea-horse. If only I had something as unique, as unmistakable, as that . . . I was beginning to realise the difficulty of the task that lay ahead of me.

~

Halfway through August I travelled down to Bloemendaal. Isabel had just returned from Budapest, where she had been teaching dance, and she had invited me to supper. It was another grey day, and, as the train slid through the dull wet countryside, I had an odd churning sensation in my stomach, as if it was trying to turn over or change shape. More than three years had passed since I had last seen Isabel, but it felt like nothing suddenly, and I wondered what I had done with all the time.

She had invited Paul Bouhtala to supper as well, she told me as I followed her into the living-room. It would just be the three of us. She hoped it wouldn't be too boring for me.

'Isabel,' I said, reproaching her.

She looked just the same, with her head set at that imperious angle and her hair coiled in a chignon, but she seemed different, less patient than I remembered, more demanding – almost querulous. She had altered in some small way that made her virtually unrecognisable, just as a mistake of a fraction of a degree when you are navigating can take you hundreds of miles off course.

It was an awkward evening altogether, and it ended with an argument. In Isabel's opinion, I ought to be dancing – or if I thought it was too late for that, then at least I should resume my career as a choreographer. I told her I didn't feel ready yet. She treated these words with something close to contempt. You're wasting your life, she said, your talent . . . She gave me a sideways look, the eyebrow nearest to me raised, then she turned away and lit one of her Egyptian cigarettes. We went

169

round and round in circles. We got nowhere. I felt sorry for Bouhtala, who had to listen to it all. I noticed that he watched the conversation closely, though, the way you might watch a precious object teeter on a high shelf, ready to reach out and catch it if it fell.

At last, at about eleven-thirty, Isabel threw her napkin on to the table and stood up. 'I'm feeling rather tired. I think I'll go to bed.'

Seeing that Bouhtala was about to rise out of his chair, she stopped him by placing a hand on his shoulder.

'Stay a little longer,' she said, 'and see if you can't talk some sense into him.'

I waited until I was alone with Bouhtala, then I looked at him. He gave me a rueful half-smile and reached for his drink.

'She thinks so highly of you,' he said. 'She has such hopes.'

'I know.' I sighed. 'But she doesn't seem to realise how far I've gone. From that whole world, I mean.' I looked past Bouhtala, into the dark corner of the room. 'I only danced once in all the time I was away.'

The diamond merchant waited, his sombre, heavy-lidded eyes seeming to draw words out of me.

'It was in northern Brazil,' I said. 'Belem. You know the place?'

'I was there once,' he said quietly.

And suddenly our roles of three years before were reversed, and I was telling Paul Bouhtala a story. One night, not long after arriving in the city, I went for a drink in the centre. It was an outdoor bar, next to a park, with old, bad-tempered waiters and wrought-iron tables that had been painted green. I was sitting by myself, drinking a beer, when a boy of about fifteen walked up to me. He stood there, right in front of me, just smiling. He had curly hair and sharp white teeth, and dark eyelashes that were so long, they almost touched his eyebrows. I remember thinking that it looked as if a devil's face had been laid over the face of a child. I smiled back, though. He sat down at my table and pointed at my beer. I nodded. He signalled to a waiter, asked for two more glasses. By the time the glasses arrived, a girl of about his age was sitting beside him. The boy poured the girl an inch of beer, poured himself an inch, then put the bottle back on the table. He began to talk to me in English. He was proud of his English. He had learned it in Fortaleza, which was further down the coast. Nice place, he said. Beaches. Many tourists. From time to time he leaned sideways and spoke to the girl in Portuguese. I watched her as she listened to the boy, her face angled away from him, his mouth close to her ear. Her skin had a glow to it, a fullness, and the whites of her eyes were as bright as her white T-shirt. She would look at me, then look away. Then she would look at me again. Her gaze had no amusement in it, no curiosity either, only a kind of steadiness. I had no idea what she was thinking.

'You are a dancer?' the boy said at one point.

I looked at him, surprised. 'I used to be.'

'I knew it.' He turned to the girl and translated for her. She listened carefully, with her head turned slightly to one side, then she looked at me again.

'How did you know?' I asked the boy.

'The way you sit.' He shrugged as if it was obvious. 'It is very – ' and he looked away into the dark trees of the park, trying to think of the right word. He didn't find it. Instead, he tilted his hand on one side and then moved it up and down in the air, a slow chopping motion. I understood that he was talking about my posture.

'Do you know any dancers?' I asked him.

'Yes, I know. In Fortaleza. His name was Peter.' The boy smiled at me furtively. 'But you stopped dancing? How can you stop? To be a dancer – ' and his arm lifted into the soft night air, and he looked at me again with that beguiling smile of his, which was too young for him, somehow, too innocent.

'It's a long story,' I said.

'You can tell.'

'No. It's too long.'

The boy spoke to the girl again, and she nodded, but this time she didn't look at me. Instead, she stared at her hands, which were resting in her lap. They looked very brown against the pale-blue of her jeans.

'We can buy cocaine,' the boy said.

I looked at him, but said nothing.

He shifted on his chair. 'But I have no money . . .'

I asked him how much money he would need. He shrugged and said thirty thousand. I told him I could give him twenty. I wasn't intending to do it myself – it was for him, for the girl too, perhaps – but when he came back ten minutes later he took my hand and led me off into the trees. The softness of the sky, the foliage so black above our heads, the girl's skin glowing . . .

When we were in the shadows, some distance from the bar, the boy opened a small envelope made out of a page torn from a comic book. He dipped the nail on his little finger into the powder and held it up to my nose. Then he looked me in the eyes and lifted his chin once, quickly.

Back at the table he grinned and said, 'It's good?'

'It's very good,' I said.

I called the waiter over and ordered another bottle of beer. The boy took the girl off into the trees. When they returned, I poured them both a drink. I had so many things to say, and yet I couldn't choose between them because they were all as interesting as each other.

'You will come with us tonight?' the boy asked after a while.

172

'Where are you going?'

'To the disco. You will come?'

'Yes, of course.'

It was an open-air club, not far from the river, with a concrete floor and a bar that was just a shed with a corrugated-iron roof. At midnight a live band played on a small stage under the mango trees. I remember seeing two girls in peach satin hot pants and stacked heels dancing with each other on the top of a wall, a lop-sided moon dropping in the sky behind them. Then everyone was dancing. The smell of hot skin, marijuana, rotting vegetation, and all the colours rich and bruised . . . The music was outside me and inside me, as much a part of me as blood or muscle. I couldn't resist it. I danced on my own, then I danced with a tall black girl in a yellow vest and a short skirt. Sometimes we were pressed together, our bodies touching. Other times we pulled apart, our arms out sideways, resting on the air. I didn't feel that I had bones or joints or anything like that. I had no sense of being made of more than one pure thing. All the movement from the waist down, hips like water. Everything flowing and swirling and only held together by the music . . . I wiped my forehead on my wrist, then on my forearm, but they were both already wet. I bought a beer, drank half of it straight down. I danced until my shirt stuck to my chest, and my hair hung dripping in my eyes. The tall girl was gone, and I was by myself again, deep inside the crowd. Once, I looked for the girl in the white T-shirt and the boy, but they were nowhere to be seen. Probably it was enough that I had paid for them to get in. Two days later I left the city on a boat bound for Manaus . . .

My story told, I looked across at Paul Bouhtala. He was staring at me.

'It's not like one of your stories,' I said. 'It doesn't really have an end.'

Bouhtala took a cigarillo out of the flat pale-yellow tin that lay on the table beside him. 'The boy. He sounds fascinating.'

'Yes.' I smiled gently, without innuendo. 'You would have liked him.'

'And the dancing,' Bouhtala said, 'you enjoyed it?'

'Yes. God, yes.'

Bouhtala smiled and nodded. 'The cocaine.' He leaned back, lit his cigarillo and smoked for a while. 'Interesting,' he said eventually, 'the way you buried one story inside the other. The story you tell, and the story you don't tell . . .'

~

One evening in late August I was sitting in Stefan's kitchen when he asked me if I would like to go to a party that his girlfriend Madeleine was giving in her apartment just behind the Concertgebouw. She had a roof terrace and a barbecue, he said. She shared the apartment with another girl, some kind of nurse. This last and seemingly innocuous detail had a dramatic effect on me. I suddenly remembered the argument that had taken place in the white room not long after Maude had given me that primitive tattoo. I remembered particularly something that Maude had said when she lost her temper. She had used the word *ziekenhuis*, which was the Dutch for *hospital*, then she had stopped in mid-sentence and hung her head. The other women swung round and looked at me, a reaction I could make no sense of at the time. What if Maude had accidentally let slip a vital piece of information? What if the hospital she had referred to was their place of work? *What if the women were nurses?*

All this occurred to me in the space of a few seconds, but it was enough to lift me from my chair and send me to the window where I stood looking out into the dark. It might still be true that the three women were bound together by damage that had been done to them. They had something else in common, though, something so obvious that I hadn't thought of it before: a job. If my new hypothesis was correct, it would explain why they had stared at me like that. They were hoping I hadn't understood what Maude had said. It would also explain why they had let me go so unexpectedly. They thought Maude could no longer be trusted. Suddenly I had the answer to questions I had never even asked. How had they got hold of the anaesthetic in the first place? How had they known what dosage to use? And how had they administered the anaesthetic without me noticing? No ordinary member of the public could have been so deft with a syringe. And what about the atmosphere in the room, that almost surreal climate of care . . . ? There was also the time when Astrid dressed up in a nurse's uniform in an attempt to arouse me . . . As a double-bluff, this was so bold that it took my breath away.

I turned round to see Stefan staring at me.

'So would you like to come?' he said.

'I'd love to.' I smiled at him. 'When did you say it was?'

The idea that the women were all nurses opened up a whole new angle of approach for me. The next morning I bought a Falkplan of Amsterdam. I turned to the page that listed the city's hospitals. There were nineteen of them – nineteen! – though, on closer inspection, I was able to reduce the figure to eleven, since differently named institutions were sometimes located at the same address. Imagine my excitement when I noticed that there was a large general hospital near Muiderpoort station, the area I had searched so fruit-lessly three years before! The fact that nurses usually lived close to their place of work on account of their long hours seemed to lend credence to my initial gut feeling – namely, that they lived somewhere in the Muiderpoort area. After all, the hospital, the station and several churches all lay within the same two-inch radius on the map. Though I was acting on nothing more solid than intuition and coincidence, it seemed a promising framework for my first tentative investigations.

~

The following night I showered, then I put on the simple white cotton shirt and trousers I had bought in India. My tan hadn't faded yet, and my hair was still bleached from the sun. Though I would never again reach the peak of fitness I had achieved while I was dancing, my body was still in shape from all the exercise I had taken during my years away. Studying myself in the mirror as I dressed, I thought I looked good – which was just as well, given what I had in mind.

Stefan had gone over to Madeleine's apartment in the afternoon to help with the preparations, so I was alone as I set out for the party. I cycled up Spiegelgracht, then through the Rijksmuseum, that stretch of chilly, dimly lit road that runs under the building. A man in a fedora stood in the shadow of the arches playing a tenor saxophone. I rode past him and out into the night, leaving the music floating eerily in the cavernous gloom behind me. The moon was rising in the sky to the south-west. Only a few days short of being full, it had a rich, buttery tint to it, not unlike the saxophone I had seen just moments earlier.

I arrived outside the house as ten o'clock was striking. After chaining my bicycle to the high black railings, I pressed the top bell. Someone buzzed me in. It was an old building, with a tall, cool hallway, reminding me of an embassy or a museum. A flutter went through me, as if some winged creature had stirred beneath my ribs and taken flight, and I realised that I was trying not to think about the nurse. It was a party, I told myself. It was only a party.

I climbed the marble staircase slowly, noting the name-plates of other residents – Korzelius, Camacho, D'Amore . . . The door to Madeleine's apartment had been left open. I walked inside. There was an immediate and unexpected sense of space. The main room stretched into the distance, its walls looking as though they had recently been white-washed, its stained wood floor the colour of caramel. Forty or fifty people stood about, talking and drinking. Nobody I knew.

I found Stefan by the french windows that led to the roof terrace. His eyes were slightly glazed, and his mouth was set in a mischievous half-smile. His nostrils, which had always been curved, now had the elaborate, almost ridiculous complexity of the toes on a pair of Turkish slippers. He had already drunk three or four cocktails, he told me, and he had smoked some pot as well. At that moment a girl with short black hair and a red mouth seemed to float out of the darkness behind him. Resting one forearm on Stefan's shoulder, she gazed at me steadily with dark-brown eyes.

'You must be Madeleine,' I said.

She smiled. 'I've heard all about you. You're a dancer.'

'I used to be.'

'What happened?'

'It's no good asking,' Stefan said. 'He won't tell you.'

Madeleine lit a cigarette and blew the smoke out in a slow, thin stream.

'This apartment's beautiful,' I said. 'You share it, don't you?'

'Yes, I share it with Jeannine.' Madeleine looked past me, into the room. 'I'm not sure where she is . . .'

So that was her name. Jeannine.

After a while I slipped away, saying I should get myself a

177

drink. I walked through the room, wondering which one she was, wondering if I had already set eyes on her without knowing it. I drank a fruit punch and talked to several people, but I didn't come across anyone called Jeannine.

Two hours passed. At midnight I ran into Stefan again. This time he was outside, on the terrace. As I moved towards him, he tipped his head back and stared up into the sky. 'What a night.' He dipped his mouth into his glass and drank. 'You're lucky, you know.'

'Lucky?' I said.

'To have been away. To have seen the world ...' He gestured with one hand – a sloppy semicircle. The world.

This was a conversation I had already had at least once that evening, and I didn't want to have it again. Since Stefan was so obviously drunk and stoned, I thought I could risk being blunt.

'Have you seen Jeannine?' I said.

'Jeannine? She's over there.' He stood up straighter, swayed a little, then pointed across the terrace at a group of people talking.

'Which one?'

'Red hair.'

The dark air seemed to shudder suddenly. I turned away. The city stretched out below me. I stared down into a space where there were hardly any lights. The Vondelpark. Named after a seventeenth-century dramatist whose play *Lucifer* had been banned because he had dared to portray heaven and the angels on a stage. Beyond the park, a bright strip of motorway – a ring-road which, if you followed it, would lead eventually to Rotterdam, The Hague –

A nurse, red hair ...

I took a deep breath, faced back into the terrace. Stefan was going on about my luck again. Only half listening, I leaned against the railing and watched Jeannine. Her hair was long and fine, and it flowed over her head, showing the shape of it, as water might. She had white skin, as red-haired people often do. Could she really be the leader of the women? Could she be Gertrude? I moved closer, watched her lift a cigarette towards her mouth. I saw the tip of her cigarette glow like a cinder as she inhaled. She wasn't wearing any nail-varnish. Well, these things change.

For the next half-hour I followed her as she moved through the party. She drank and smoked. She laughed. She was confident. I didn't think she had noticed me yet, but then it occurred to me that if, by some bizarre coincidence, she actually was Gertrude, then she must be *pretending* not to have noticed me, she must be *pretending* that she didn't know who I was. In that case, we would both have been watching each other, but without appearing to . . . What would she do when I approached her? Presumably she would behave like somebody who had never met me before. The women were gamblers, after all. They knew how to take risks. They had nerve. Still, I couldn't imagine what would happen after the first few moments . . .

I had been wondering what to say to her, how to effect a meeting, but in the end she did it for me. At about one in the morning I was following her downstairs for the second time when she suddenly stopped, turned round. She must have forgotten something, or remembered something. At any rate, it all happened so abruptly that we collided. She apologised in Dutch.

'That's all right,' I said. 'You're Jeannine, aren't you?'

She registered surprise with a slight backward movement of her upper body and a twist of her head, her cigarette held out sideways, at shoulder-height.

'You're a nurse,' I said.

179

'You seem to know all about me.' There was a wariness in her voice, as if she hadn't yet decided whether my knowledge was a good or a bad thing.

I introduced myself. 'I'm living with Stefan.'

'Oh yes,' she said. 'Haven't you just been away?'

'That's me.'

To give myself some time, I asked her where she worked. She wasn't really a nurse, she said – at least, not any more. She was attached to a psychiatric clinic, doing research into the treatment of depression. While she talked about her job, which she did quite naturally, I tried to form a picture of her body. She was dressed in a see-through turquoise shirt with a black bra underneath, and a pair of black hipsters that flared slightly towards the ankles. Though her clothes could be said to be revealing, it was surprising, in the end, how little they actually revealed. I could see her collar-bone, and the beginning of a cleavage, both of which seemed unfamiliar – as did her wrists, her hands, her fingers . . . But if she took off everything she was wearing, then I would know for sure. Something primitive would flash through me. My body would remember. If I saw her naked I would know.

'You're not listening,' she said.

'I'm sorry,' I said. 'I was looking at you.'

An odd expression rose on to her face, a mixture of amusement and confusion. She didn't know what to make of me. She dropped her cigarette into the empty glass she was holding. A quick hiss as the cigarette went out. Downstairs they were playing the club re-mix of a song that had been famous that summer.

'Would you like to dance?' she said.

I shook my head. 'No, not really.' Then, almost without thinking, I leaned down and kissed her. Though I had surprised her, she had let it happen.

'Is there somewhere we could go?' I asked.

'You don't waste much time, do you.' Once again, she seemed more amused than anything, as if she had never come across someone like me before.

Taking my hand, she led me down to the next floor. During our conversation on the stairs I must have changed my mind at least a dozen times. One moment I was disappointed because she obviously wasn't one of the women I was looking for; the way she was behaving, wary and yet provocative, was entirely natural, I felt. The next moment, imagining that she was Gertrude, I silently applauded her extraordinary skill in dissembling. She should have been an actress, not a nurse . . .

I followed her along a corridor lined with books, through an unlit hallway, then down another, smaller corridor and into an oblong room with a high ceiling. She stood aside to let me go in first, then locked the door behind us. There was a washbasin against one wall and a toilet in the corner. Was this a reference on her part, a sign of guilt? I turned round. In the darkness I could hardly see her – just the outline of her head and shoulders, and the almost metallic gleam of her teeth when she spoke.

'The light doesn't work,' she said. 'Do you mind?'

I said I didn't.

She moved towards me until she was only inches away from me. Each time my heart beat, the air behind her appeared to contract. I put my hands on her hips. We kissed two or three times, quickly, as if touching something that we feared might be hot, then we kissed more slowly, and for longer. Her mouth was sweet from the alcohol, though I could also taste the charred flavour of cigarette smoke. I guided her towards the window, which was tall and set deep in the wall. Lights from outside showed through the old-fashioned frosted-glass like fireworks frozen in mid-explosion. She seemed to know what I wanted her to do. When she felt the gap behind her, where the window was, she hoisted herself up on to the sill. She was even harder to see now that she had her back to the light. I knew her face was plain – not ugly, but not memorable either – and I found, strangely, that that excited me. I unfastened the buttons on her turquoise blouse and watched it float away from her shoulders, then I undid her bra. Her breasts were round and resilient, with tiny nipples. I kissed them gently. Her head snapped back, banged softly against the glass. From somewhere inside her came a murmur, almost as if she was humming to herself.

I pulled her trousers and pants down to her knees, then I eased her forwards until the tops of her thighs were level with the thick lip of the windowsill. Again she seemed to anticipate me, reaching upwards and backwards, and gripping the sash of the window with both hands. She was looking down at me, her hair falling across her face. Her breasts shone where I had touched them with my tongue.

Her pants and trousers had gathered around her ankles in an untidy heap. I could see her pubic hair now, darker than the darkness. I couldn't tell what colour it was, though. Thinking I would have to be with her at least once more, I put my tongue in her belly button, then ran it slowly down into the first tight coils of hair. Then further down, to where the flesh parted, opened, turned to liquid . . .

Later, as she closed the bathroom door, she said, 'I hope you don't – ' Then she stopped herself.

'Don't what?' I asked.

She shook her head. 'Nothing.'

I told her that I ought to be leaving. Walking out of the apartment, I heard myself apologise, make an excuse – I had to be up early, I said, which was a lie, of course – but I promised I would call her in the week. Stefan would give me the number. As I rode off on my bicycle I glanced over my shoulder. She was standing on the top step, waving.

~

During the five days that elapsed between Madeleine's party and the next time I saw Jeannine I slept with three other nurses. In a bar on Sunday night I talked to a girl whose sloping shoulders reminded me of Maude. In bed she turned away from me, as if from a bright light. Very faintly, in the distance, I thought I heard a voice murmuring. *Don't worry. It's only a dream* . . . I leaned up on my elbows, looking down at her. I could see the curve of her left buttock, a handful of coarse brown hair. The skin at the base of her neck was milky, almost greenish in colour, like mould. Her body shook, as if she was crying. I tried to comfort her, but it was no use.

'Do you want to go?' I asked.

She didn't answer. She just lay on the bed, with her back to me, naked and trembling.

'Perhaps you should sleep,' I said.

I drew the covers over her and turned out the light.

In the morning we passed Stefan, who was outside the house, unlocking his bicycle. He peered at us through the light rain, raising his eyebrows slightly, in surprise. Probably Madeleine had told him that I was seeing Jeannine. Or perhaps it was simply that we looked like such an unusual couple.

On Tuesday I slept with two nurses who worked at the hospital near Muiderpoort station. I met them in the Oosterpark, which was just across the road from the hospital. They often went for walks during their breaks, they told me, or, if the weather was warm, they lay on the grass and sunbathed. When the three of us were naked in their two-

183

room apartment in De Pijp, they mixed French martinis, then turned on MTV and rolled a joint. They seemed just as interested in each other as they were in me, which suited me perfectly: it meant I could examine them both in detail. There was nothing remotely familiar about their bodies, nothing at all, and, as I lay beside them, noticing the differences between them – differences in build, differences in colouring and texture – I thought of Julia who used to work for the company, in the costume department. Once, when I was up there for a fitting, she had showed me her notebook. It was a record of the skin-tones of every dancer in the company. Sometimes the difference was dramatic – the difference between Tyrone, a black American, for example, and Suitsugu, who was from Japan – but what interested me most was the difference between people I had always thought of as more or less identical. Julia found the swatch that represented my skin, then she turned to Marcel, a French dancer, who was on the next page. *You're both white*, she said, *but you're so unalike. Marcel has more pink pigment in his colouration, you see? And here*, turning another page, *is Jorg. Something almost yellow* ... At the time I had seen the notebook in almost metaphorical terms, as a testament to individuality, as proof of everyone's uniqueness – and so concise, so precise, in the way that it distinguished one person from another. Lying in bed with the two nurses, though, I came at it from a new angle. A notebook like that could be practical, I thought. It could help you find somebody. It was a means of identification.

By the time I met Jeannine on Thursday I was feeling awkward. Despite having sex, I had to avoid all personal involvement, and, unlike most men I have talked to, this did not come naturally to me. Ironically, it was those men I was now beginning to resemble. On one occasion that week I was sitting in a café watching students walk in and out of the medical faculty across the road when I happened to notice two builders at the next table. They were doing exactly what I was doing. I suddenly realised that, to an impartial observer, to somebody who had no inside knowledge, I was no different to the men with the dirty low-slung jeans and the cement dust in their hair. I was just a man watching women. And, like the builders, I wanted to go further, of course. In the case of Jeannine, though, I had the feeling that I had been clumsy. Our encounter at the party had had the excitement of the illicit. It had been too charged. Perhaps, also, I had allowed her to think that I felt something for her. But I couldn't afford to have a relationship with her. I couldn't afford to have a relationship with anyone. There was no room for it, no time for it. I walked towards the restaurant, knowing it would not be an easy night.

I saw her before she saw me. She was sitting at right-angles to me, against a dark-yellow wall. She was wearing a brown, long-sleeved T-shirt and a pair of jeans. Her face was pale, clean and plain, and she had put her hair up in a bun. I felt she was someone I had never met. I had nothing in common with her. My presence in the restaurant seemed unlikely, inexplicable.

I sat down. She gave me a watery smile. We didn't kiss. I ordered a carafe of red wine and some olives. It was loud in the restaurant, the waiters shouting and gesturing and elbowing their way through the smoky, ochre-coloured air. Sitting at the table next to us was a Spanish couple, the woman middle-aged, black-haired, grand, the man in a tight-fitting pale-grey suit. The man leaned towards her, as if what he was talking about was either private or of huge importance, and, every now and then, he fell silent suddenly, looked down and, with raised eyebrows, twisted the signet ring on his little finger. I drank a mouthful of wine, which tasted sour, and

185

glanced at Jeannine. She was smoking. I had no idea what to say to her.

Then, as she reached out to extinguish her cigarette, she asked me what South America was like.

'What?' I said. 'All of it?'

And suddenly we were both laughing.

It wasn't too bad after that. She had a dry, self-deprecating sense of humour that I had seldom come across in Amsterdam. She told stories against herself, and yet she didn't come across as pitiful or unlucky. Instead, you thought she was probably a survivor. Perhaps it was the wine, but, as the evening wore on, she grew in confidence, so much so that when we stood outside the restaurant, unlocking our bicycles, she was able to say, half jokingly, 'My place or yours?'

We cycled to Prinsengracht, which was closer. The night was cool, and a mist had risen off the canals, turning the trees into grey blurred shapes. It was after one o'clock by the time we walked into the house, and though a thin strip of light showed under Stefan's bedroom door we decided not to disturb him. We climbed to my attic apartment in silence. While Jeannine was in the bathroom, I undressed and slipped under the covers. A few minutes later she appeared, wearing a white vest and a pair of knickers. She asked me if I wanted her to turn the light off. I shook my head.

'I want to see you,' I said.

She climbed into bed beside me. Her skin was cold to the touch. She kissed me on the mouth, then leaned on one elbow, with her head propped on her hand, and looked down at me.

'Your body,' she said. 'It's like the body of a samurai.'

I laughed quickly. 'Is it?'

Her face had a kind of stubbornness about it, a complacency, and I knew then that I should never have allowed things to go so far.

'Wide shoulders,' she went on, 'a narrow waist . . . long thighs – you're very beautiful . . .'

A man coughed in the street below. I felt awkward, almost embarrassed, as though the man was in the room with us. Jeannine kissed my shoulder, then my neck. Her hair, loose now, brushed against my chest.

I ran one hand into the hollow of her waist, then over her left hip, taking her knickers halfway down her thighs. I noticed at a glance that she had no scars of any kind, and that her pubic hair was brown. Well, I suppose I had known it all along, really. She could join the list of women whose innocence had been established. It was still a short list, I realised, and the thought tired me suddenly.

'What is it?' she said.

'Nothing.' I lay back. 'Did you ever dye your pubic hair?'

She laughed. 'What a strange question.' Then she saw that I was serious. 'No,' she said, 'I've never done that.' She paused. 'Would you like me to?'

I shook my head. I wasn't even sure why I had bothered asking. Perhaps it had just been something to say.

She reached out and touched my penis. It didn't respond. She started to pull at it, which only made it worse. I took hold of her hand, moved it away.

'Don't you want to?' she said.

I sighed. 'I don't know.'

'You don't know?' She laughed quietly, and then she lay back, staring at the ceiling. 'I think I'll go to sleep now, if you don't mind.'

In the early morning I felt her wake and ease out of the bed. Through half-closed eyes I watched her dressing by the window – the pale curve of her spine, her hair black in the dim light and hanging perpendicular to the floor as she bent down to pull on her tights.

187

Before she left the room she leaned over me and kissed me. I opened my eyes.

'You going?' I said.

She smiled faintly, sadly, as if she knew I had been deceiving her.

'I'm working today,' she said, 'and I have to go home first.'

I nodded.

'Goodbye,' she said.

~

If Stefan knew anything about what had happened between myself and Jeannine he did not refer to it. Though we often talked about the party afterwards, what a success it had been, Jeannine was never mentioned. Perhaps she never spoke about it to anyone. Or perhaps he simply hadn't noticed. In the meantime, while walking in the Vondelpark one afternoon, I had met a tall, dark-haired girl who worked at the Alexander van der Leeuwkliniek on Overtoom . . .

I was beginning to spend a lot of time in hospitals, or in the neighbourhood of hospitals. At first I would pretend to be visiting a sick relation, which allowed me to loiter in different wards and then fall into conversation with the nurses working there, but I realised that, before too long, I would be found out. I needed a legitimate excuse. It was then that I had a stroke of luck. One morning I saw a flyer on a notice-board, advertising a Hospital Visitors programme. Why hadn't I thought of that before? During the next few weeks I signed up with programmes all over Amsterdam, and, from that point on, my presence in hospitals was justified. No, more than justified. It was actively encouraged. After all, I was contributing something to the community. I was doing good. When Stefan asked me what I did all day, I told him that I had become involved in charity work. And it was true! I would spend hours with old people, or people who had no families, and I would listen to their complaints, their dreams, their reminiscences – sometimes it reminded me a little of sitting on the brown velvet sofa in Paul Bouhtala's apartment – but all the time I would keep a close watch on the nursing staff, scanning them for attributes or qualities that seemed familiar.

That winter I often found myself in awkward situations. I remember one nurse in particular. I had noticed her in a hospital ward, wheeling a silver meal trolley, and I had stopped to talk to her. She had agreed to meet me in a bar after work. When she walked in through the door, she was wearing a black plastic raincoat belted tightly at the waist, and she had painted her fingernails cobalt-blue. Though her face was delicate, her eyes had a jaded look, as if she had seen everything there was to see. It was her eyes that had brought her to my attention. We drank shots of neat vodka, then she took me back to where she lived, a squat on the top floor of a derelict container terminal in East Amsterdam. I followed her through dripping corridors to a room that overlooked an industrial canal. I remember the water, how thick it looked, and how it smelled of rust and oil, and I remember the yellow weeds that nodded in her window. She offered me some pills, which she had stolen from the hospital pharmacy. I refused, but she took three, knocking them to the back of her throat with the flat of her hand, then washing them down with the dregs from a can of Coca-Cola. When we were lying together on her mattress, she crouched beneath me, tearing at my body with her tiny blue nails, as if she wanted to open me up and look inside. Later, in a slurred, sardonic voice, she told me she had been abused by her father, but no one had ever believed her because he was such a friendly man, so popular, he worked for the fire department, she said, and it

189

suddenly occurred to me that I was not alone: there were others like me, people who were operating in the fourth dimension, a world that was parallel to this one, a kind of purgatory. Oddly enough, she had a little round scar too. It was on her arm, though, halfway between her elbow and her shoulder. Still, I let out a gasp when I saw it. She asked me what was wrong, but I just shook my head and told her it was nothing.

~

Towards Christmas I came home one evening to find Stefan sitting at the kitchen table, working out his accounts. Standing in the doorway, looking at the piles of invoices and receipts, I realised that I would have to find a job before too long. My uncle's money had not run out yet, but it wouldn't last for ever.

Stefan leaned back in his chair, his hands behind his head, and studied me for a few moments, then he smiled and slowly shook his head. 'You know, you really are something.'

I didn't follow. 'What do you mean?'

'You're so successful with women,' he said. 'Every time I see you, you're with somebody different.'

I frowned. It was true that I had slept with a lot of women since returning to Amsterdam, but I didn't think of myself as successful, not at all. In fact, that was the last word I would have used. As far as I was concerned I had failed miserably.

'You're like some kind of playboy,' Stefan said.

'Stefan,' I said.

'I'm serious,' he said. 'It's extraordinary.'

His face showed elements of both admiration and disbelief, but, underneath, I saw a kind of bewilderment, as if something was dawning on him, and I thought I knew what it was. It had just occurred to him that Brigitte might have been right to suspect me. It had just occurred to him that I could have been unfaithful to her after all. Well, there wasn't much I could say about that. I turned to the window and watched the rain running down the glass.

'The thing is,' I said quietly, 'I'm looking for someone.'

Stefan chuckled. 'Aren't we all?'

'Stefan,' I said.

Still amused, he looked up at me. 'What?'

'It's not what you think.'

~

I lived in the house on Prinsengracht for fourteen months, and during that time I slept with one hundred and sixty-two women. Most of them worked in hospitals or clinics, but there were some who had nothing to do with the medical profession at all. Perhaps I saw them from a certain angle, or in a certain light, or perhaps it was the mood I happened to be in, but in each case they appeared to be in possession of a secret, or harbouring some kind of guilt. It was a quality they all had, of seeming to conceal something from me, of being impenetrable, unknowable.

I had developed a new approach to the task I had set myself: I began to see it as a process of elimination. The more women I slept with, the more likely I was to find the women I was looking for. The longer I went on, in other words, the shorter the odds became. It wasn't so much a quest as a dismantling. The three women were like soldiers whose cover was being gradually but systematically eroded. In time they would become visible to me. That's what I kept telling myself. It was just a matter of time.

One hundred and sixty-two women in fourteen months . . .

I don't remember any of them now. No, wait. That's not quite true. There is one I remember.

Daphne.

Because she peered at my scarred penis in the half-dark-ness of her bedroom, and then turned to me and said, *You haven't got syphilis, have you?*

~

On a bright, cold October afternoon I moved into an apartment in the Kinkerbuurt, not far from where I had lived before I met Brigitte. Though small, it was three floors up on the corner of a street, which meant I had plenty of light, and the rent was reasonable, less than eight hundred guilders a month. From one of my living-room windows I could see a segment of the Jacob van Lenneykade; I could watch the heavy, sluggish barges pushing past, their loads covered with tarpaulins and lashed down with ropes, their hulls low in the water . . . On my first morning, as I was looking for a place to buy fresh bread, I saw a notice in the window of a local bar. They were advertising for staff. While living in Stefan's house, my Dutch had improved, and I now felt confident enough to apply for a job. The bar had a row of tables on the pavement, facing a quiet stretch of water, and a beer-garden at the rear, with wooden benches and an ancient lime tree. It was so close to my apartment that I could walk to work and back. That night I had an interview with the owner, a blonde woman in her mid-fifties. Her name was Gusta. She wore mauve eye-shadow, and her wrists were as plump as a baby's. In the sixties and seventies she had been a jazz singer. She had known Chet Baker. She had smoked a joint with him just hours before he fell from the window of that hotel – the Prins Hendrik, wasn't it? –

and died. I let her talk about the old days and by closing time the job was mine.

A week later, when I had settled in, I called Isabel. I wanted to give her my new address and number. To my surprise, Paul Bouhtala answered the phone.

'You were lucky to catch me,' he said. 'I just dropped in to collect a few of Isabel's things.'

'Why?' I said. 'Where is she?'

'She's in hospital in Haarlem. She has cancer.' He was silent for a moment. 'Didn't you know?'

After speaking to Bouhtala, I put the phone down and stared out of my living-room window. The sun was shining. White clouds hung in a blue sky, motionless and two-dimensional. They looked like targets in a fairground rifle-range. Below the clouds, there was a row of houses. A bathroom-fittings shop. A tree.

Nothing seemed to be moving. Nothing seemed real.

It was only when I arrived at the hospital in Haarlem the following afternoon that I realised what a vicious echo of my life this was, a parody of that period when all I wanted was an excuse to spend time in medical institutions.

Well, now I had it.

I came to a standstill in reception. Looking at the floor, I felt a sense of shame sweep over me.

~

When I walked into Isabel's private room that day I was shocked by the change in her appearance. Her face had tightened, withered, aged. I could see right through the skin to the structure that lay beneath: I could see the joins in her skull. I laid my flowers at the foot of her bed and sat down beside her. I had a feeling in my throat, as if I couldn't swallow.

'Beautiful flowers,' she whispered. 'Thank you.'

She used her eyes to smile with. It seemed there was something painful about the inside of her mouth.

I could think of nothing to say.

I noticed her arms, which were resting on the outside of the blanket. Her left arm was almost impossibly thin, just skin and bone. All the muscle tone, all the sinew she used to have, had been wasted by chemotherapy. Her right arm was in plaster to the elbow.

'What happened?' I said.

Isabel looked where I was looking. 'I leaned against the wall to steady myself,' she said, 'and it just broke.' She paused for breath. 'Isn't that ridiculous?'

'Oh, Isabel.'

'I must look dreadful. Like one of those shrunken heads you saw in South-East Asia.' She tried to laugh, but no sound came. 'You sent me a postcard, remember?'

Her hand moved fractionally across the blanket towards me. I took it in both of mine. I looked down at her skin, which was as fragile as wafer. I looked down at her veins. Wiry. Almost black.

'I can feel the strength in you,' she whispered. 'Strange how strong people feel . . .' Her eyes closed for a moment, then they opened wide, and she looked around, as if uncertain of her whereabouts.

'It's all right, Isabel,' I said. 'It's all right.'

She smiled up at me. I sensed that she was trying to tighten her grip on my hand, but the difference was barely discernible.

'Paul says you've moved . . .'

I described my new apartment to her, in detail. I told her that, although the living-room was small, it had windows that faced both south and west, which meant it would be flooded with sunlight in the summer. From the west-facing window I could see a bathroom-fittings shop, which never seemed to open. From the south-facing window I could see a small section of canal. I told her that my kitchen had green walls and a green ceiling; it was a shade of green I had never seen before, somewhere between lettuce and eau-de-Nil. It looked perfect at two in the morning, though, which was when I sat at my simple wooden table, drinking herb tea and reading the newspaper. I told her about the plumbing, and how the water crackled and crunched when it ran down the pipes, as if there was a dog gnawing on a bone inside the wall. I told her about the person who played the piano at the same time every evening. There was something poignant about it, I said, because, although the playing was technically proficient, there was no emotion in it whatsoever. I told her about the bar round the corner, and how the owner had wrists like a baby's and a nest of brassy hair, and how she drank crème de menthe at ten o'clock in the morning.

I didn't tell her I was working there.

After a while she closed her eyes again, and this time they did not open. I thought she must have fallen asleep, though it's difficult to tell with people who are very ill: the gap between the two states narrows, and they can slip from one to the other and then back again without you noticing.

Outside, the light had faded, though it wasn't even four o'clock. From my chair beside the bed I could look out of the window, look down on a main road that was filled with rush-hour traffic. The road ran past the hospital, then curved slowly away into the distance, the unknown. Most cars had their headlights on, as if they had come from a place where it was raining heavily, or already dark.

~

Standing outside the hospital, I couldn't feel the world at all. The cold wind, the car-park. The buildings. They were just the same, and yet I was receiving them in a new way. They seemed at one remove from me, and utterly without significance. I noticed something similar in the taxi that took me to the station. The driver talked to me the whole time, his eyes shifting between the rear-view mirror and the road, one hand lifting off the steering-wheel to emphasise a point. I had the distinct impression that he was reciting lines, and if he seemed pleased with himself, even a little smug, it was only because he had learned them perfectly.

On the train to Amsterdam this sense of dissociation stayed with me, so much so that when the black girl sitting on the other side of the carriage spoke to me I didn't notice, not until she reached across and touched my shoulder.

'Are you all right?' she said.

I looked at her blankly. 'Yes, I'm fine. Why?'

'You were talking to yourself.'

'Was I?' I stared straight ahead. I had no memory of talking to myself. 'What was I saying?'

'I don't know. Just words. Like people talking in their sleep.'

I looked at the girl again and saw that she was beautiful. Her eyebrows arched disdainfully above her oval dark-brown eyes. Her lips were soft and full. She had straight hair, which was exactly the same colour as liquorice. She had drawn it back in a short ponytail, the end of which stopped in the air an inch or two above her collar. Something about this beauty of hers released the truth in me.

'A friend of mine is dying. I've just been to see her.'

'I'm so sorry.' The girl looked down at the book she was holding in her lap. Her fingers were long and slender, with dark-pink nails. 'Is she a close friend?'

'In some ways, she's the closest.'

I turned to the window. It was dark now, but I could just see the land stretching away – land that should have been invisible, under water. Somehow, this angered me, though the anger quickly passed.

'She looked after me a few years ago,' I said. 'When I was going through a bad time.'

'There aren't many friends like that,' the girl said.

'No.'

'What's wrong with her?'

'Cancer.'

'Oh. I'm sorry.'

The train's announcement system crackled, and then we heard the conductor's voice, a lifeless monotone: 'Amsterdam Central Station. . . This is Amsterdam Central Station. . .' The girl gave me a resigned expression, then she closed her book.

'What's your name?' I asked her.

'Juliette,' she said. 'Juliette Voerman.'

I told her my name, and, reaching across the aisle, we shook hands. 'Would it be strange if I asked you for your number?' I said.

She smiled faintly. 'No, not strange.'

She wrote her name and number on a piece of paper and handed it to me. I looked at it, to make sure I could read it, then I pushed it deep into my trouser pocket.

'We could have a drink sometime,' I said.

She nodded.

The train drew into the station, slowed, then stopped. We both stood up.

'Thank you for talking to me,' I said. 'It made things better.'

She smiled again, but said nothing.

I saw her once, inside the station. I caught a glimpse of her short, dark ponytail about twenty yards ahead of me. Then I lost her in the crowd.

Later, in my apartment, I stood by the window and studied the piece of note-paper again. I was struck by the neatness and elegance of her handwriting. A phone number. Like dozens of other phone numbers I had asked for during the past eighteen months. And yet, this one seemed different . . .

I stared down into the empty street – the street-lamps, so evenly spaced, and where they ended, a section of canal. A cold night. Motionless. As if the city lay beneath a crystal dome.

In the winter months in Amsterdam there were nights of such perfect stillness that, if you were out walking, you could hear the ticking of bicycle wheels in the next street, or a couple talking in their bedroom three floors up. This stillness had always reminded me of the fairy-tales I had read when I was young.

Juliette.

Of course, I knew what was different about her. I suppose I must have known it as soon as I looked at her. She could never have been one of the women in the room. She was innocent, in other words. And there was no doubt about that, not even a shadow of a doubt.

It was the colour of her skin that proclaimed her innocence.

It was the colour of her skin.

~

In the middle of November I came home from the bar at one-thirty in the morning to find a message on my machine from a woman who said her name was Else. She was calling to tell me that Isabel was in remission. Isabel had returned home, to the apartment in Bloemendaal, and would like me to visit her. When I knocked on the door two days later, in the middle of the afternoon, it was Else who let me in.

'You'll find Isabel in the living-room,' she told me.

Isabel was lying on the divan, propped up on half a dozen pillows, with a Guatemalan quilt thrown over her. She wore a turban of amber silk, and her fingers glittered with valuable rings (*the only glamour that old women have left*, she had said to me once – and, naturally, I had disagreed with her).

'Isabel,' I said.

I walked up to her and kissed her on the cheek, then I sat down in the chair that had been placed close to the divan. The last of the day's sunlight slanted across the wall of books behind her.

'You look so much better,' I said.

Isabel made a face, drawing down the corners of her mouth in a haughty, disbelieving mask.

'Really,' I said, 'you do.'

'I'm a corpse,' she said. 'But what about you?'

I told her how my apartment was coming on, and then I told her I was working in a bar, just to make some money, then, all of a sudden, I found that I had run out of things to say. Embarrassed, I looked down. Isabel put a hand on my wrist. Her hand felt so insubstantial, almost weightless. I looked up at her.

'What are you doing to yourself?' she said.

I laughed nervously. 'What do you mean?'

She repeated the question. 'What are you doing to yourself?'

'I'm not doing anything,' I said in a low voice.

Isabel considered me for a moment, then she reached sideways for her glass of water. She swallowed a tablet and leaned back against her pillows.

'I know something bad happened to you,' she said.

I could not speak. All I could do was stare at her.

'I know something about it,' she said, 'because that policeman mentioned it. What's his name? Olsen.'

'But I didn't tell him anything – not really . . .' I thought back to the conversation I had had at Paul Bouhtala's birthday party. I could still see Olsen's sympathetic face, the glass of beer held just below his chin . . .

Isabel gave a little shrug. 'Well, you must have said something.'

The bookcase behind her head was plunged in shadow now. Outside, beyond the terrace, the sun had dropped so low in the sky that it lit only the tops of the pine trees, staining the foliage a bright burnt orange, almost exactly the same colour as the turban Isabel was wearing. Turning back into the room, I saw her reach up with one thin arm and pull the string of metal beads that switched on the lamp.

'I have said this before,' she said slowly, 'but I'm going to say it again, and if it sounds harsh, forgive me. I don't have the time or energy for subtlety. Whatever happened, it's behind you now. You have to move on. I can understand if you feel you can no longer dance, but what about your choreography? You were such a talented choreographer. Young, of course, but very talented.' Her smile was sly, half held inside her mouth. Even in her weakness, she could tease me. 'Everybody in the world is looking for someone who can – ' She broke off for a moment, to think. Then she said, 'Someone who *has* something. Don't you see that?'

I nodded, then I was quiet for a while.

'I don't know whether it's behind me,' I said at last. 'Sometimes it doesn't feel as if it is.'

We sat in silence, each caught up in our own thoughts. My mind drifted. I pictured Paul Bouhtala sitting in his study, the diamond eyes of his cigarette lighter glittering on the table beside him . . .

The door opened, and Else's pale face appeared in the darkness at the edge of the room. It was time for Isabel to rest, she said. I rose to my feet, preparing to leave, but Isabel held on to my wrist.

'Stay the night,' she said, 'in your old room. Then we can talk again tomorrow.'

~

There are days when the landscape of Holland suits your mood. On the train back to Amsterdam the following afternoon, I sat by the window and watched the neat, flat countryside fly past, and I was soothed by it. There was nothing miraculous about its appearance. What was miraculous was that it was there at all. Once, in the distance, I saw a copse that looked wild and natural, as if it had sprung up haphazardly, but by the time the train drew level with it, the trees had resolved themselves into straight lines, into a grid, in fact. Order had been there all along. It was like a Dutch joke, and I found that I was smiling.

That morning Isabel had talked about my ballets, praising my imagination, my exuberance, my wit. This was untypical of her, and I realised that, in reminding me of my past, she was trying to return me to myself. It didn't have the effect that she intended. As I listened to her, I saw how much had been taken from me: I bore no more than a passing resemblance to the person she was describing. She insisted that I could use dance to exorcise the things that were troubling me. I responded by saying that the things that were troubling me made the thought of dance impossible. You have to work with it, she said. You have to move forwards. What I didn't tell her was that I *was* working with it, I *was* moving forwards. Each woman I slept with was a step closer to the truth. Or so I believed. I still felt compelled to close that gap between myself and what I had experienced. What would I do if I was actually confronted by one of the women who had been in the room with me? I had no idea. Perhaps nothing. It wasn't a matter of wanting answers. It wasn't even a matter of asking questions. It was a matter of regaining proximity.

During the last few months I had widened the net. I was no longer looking specifically for nurses. I was just looking. After all, given the amount of time that had elapsed, it was conceivable that the women no longer worked as nurses – if indeed they ever had. My interpretation of the scene that had taken place in the room was only one of many possible interpretations. What if the women had broken into a hospital and stolen the anaesthetic? What if they were not nurses at all, but thieves? So, yes, the net had widened, and my methods had become entirely instinctive. If I had a gut feeling about someone I acted on it. I had gone to bed with all kinds of women – fat and thin, old and young. They assumed I wanted to have sex with them. They were wrong. In fact, once they had taken their clothes off and I realised they weren't who I had thought they were, I often lost all interest in them. There they would be, on a sofa or a bed, in a cheap hotel in the dead hours of the afternoon or an apartment late at night – moonlight on the floor, the radiators cold – or in the back of a car parked in an alley, on a blanket under a tree or among the sand dunes or beside water – a canal, an inland sea – there they would be, naked, unfamiliar and, above all, innocent. A complicated moment, this. Mostly, they would turn on me. They would accuse me of attempting to humiliate them. They would tell me I was only interested in power. They would ask me what I was trying to prove (now there was a pertinent question). They would say I was impotent, pathetic, cowardly – and they would also, as you might well imagine, call me a misogynist. They could become violent too. One woman had pulled a knife on me. I can still see her standing in her bedroom with nothing on, her face twisted, unsteady with rage. I can see the curtains behind her, drawn against the daylight, a burnt look to their brown and orange flowers. I can see the six-inch blade protruding from her fist. It took me an hour to calm her down. But sometimes – and this was worse, far worse – a terrible sadness would come over them, as if being rejected by me, which was how they always saw it, fitted some idea they already had about themselves. I felt so cruel as I watched them gather up their clothes, their bodies meagre suddenly, poignant – almost meaningless, somehow. What could I do, though? Say I was sorry? Say it was all my fault? I doubt that would have changed anything.

The train slowed as it pulled into one of Amsterdam's suburban stations. There were times when I had almost given up, when I felt I could no longer face the anger, the tears, the silent resignation . . . But then, I didn't appear to have a choice. I knew no other way to live. Some kind of transmutation had taken place. I had become as monstrous as the women I was looking for. That was their effect, their legacy. Like vampires, they had turned me into another version of themselves.

~

As I climbed down on to the platform at Central Station, something else occurred to me, and I was surprised I had not thought of it before. I stood on the platform, under the high curved roof, with people streaming past me. How accurately could I remember the bodies of the women in the room, I asked myself, now that almost five years had passed? I had been clinging to a few details, the way a shipwrecked man clings to pieces of wreckage, but what else, if anything, did I actually remember? There is something that I believe to be

203

true, and it is this: it's just about impossible to remember the bodies of people you have slept with in the past, no matter how long you were together. As soon as you are separated from each other, their bodies start to shed detail. They become incomplete. They assume an abstract, almost ghostly look. Yes, you still retain a generalised idea of how that person looked, but can you picture them in their entirety? I don't think so. So there's one form of decay, which takes place in the memory. And then there's another, more obvious form of decay, of course, which is physical, and which takes place in real life, real time. In five years the body alters. Maude might have put on weight, for instance. Astrid's skin might have lost some of its resilience, its gloss. The question was, in the face of all this change, could I be confident that I would be able to identify the women if I saw them? If they were standing in a police line-up, with hoods over their heads and no clothes on, would I be able to pick them out? Or would I hesitate in that tense darkness behind the two-way mirror?

I began to walk along the platform, which was now deserted, pigeons squabbling in the iron rafters overhead. A sudden bitter smell of urine burned the lining of my nostrils. There was a third form of decay, now I thought about it. The bodies of the women I had seen in the white room five years ago were beginning to merge with the bodies of women I had been with since. They were being super-imposed, one on top of the other. Their outlines were becoming blurred. It was as if I had taken a slide of each woman I had been with, put them in a pile, in chronological order, and then, by shining a light down through the pile, tried to see the three women who were lying at the bottom.

Impossible.

Halfway along the murky tiled tunnel that leads to the

station concourse, I came to another standstill. I realised I was involved in a process that was completely self-defeating. Every time I saw a woman's body naked, it acted as a kind of acid, corroding the bodies of the women I was looking for. Far from exposing them, as I had thought it might, the process was actually protecting them from exposure. To put it more bluntly, my initiative had the seeds of its own certain failure implanted within it. I thought once again of what Isabel had said. She knew nothing of my true situation, and yet, in telling me to move on, she had given me advice that now seemed peculiarly relevant. I was about to reach a saturation point, a point beyond which it was useless, absurd, perhaps even hazardous, to go.

∼

I use the word 'hazardous' advisedly. That winter I had contracted NSU. I had never had a sexually transmitted disease before, and my reaction was probably a typical one: I felt dirty, ashamed.

I was treated at a clinic in the city centre, not far from the Muziektheater. The doctor who saw me was a woman in her late forties. She wore a white coat, which she left unbuttoned, and a pair of glasses with narrow, oblong lenses. She asked me a series of personal questions, one of the last of which concerned the number of sexual partners that I had had during the past six months. I hesitated for a moment, not knowing what to say, then I told her that I wasn't sure.

'You're not sure?' She peered at me over her glasses, the expression in her eyes opaque, unreadable.

'A lot,' I said.

'More than ten?'

I nodded. 'Yes. More than that.'

'Do you use protection?'

I looked at her, but didn't answer.

'In that case, you're very lucky,' she said. 'If that's all you've got, I mean.'

Though it might seem hard to believe, the possibility of serious infection had never occurred to me, not until that moment. I could only assume it was because I had been so single-minded, so blinkered, as I went about my task of trying to uncover the three women.

'You know,' the doctor said quietly, 'you really ought to take more care.'

To be told to take care of myself, after all I had been through – well, it amused me, and I suppose I must have smiled.

The doctor leaned forwards. 'It's not you I'm thinking of,' she went on in the same quiet voice. 'It's the people who might come into contact with you . . .'

I swallowed quickly, then looked away.

She wrote me a prescription for some antibiotics. In less than two weeks all evidence of the disease had gone. It did not recur. Her words stayed with me, though, and from that point on I acted in a more responsible manner.

~

Apart from anything else, there was Juliette to think about. I had come to believe that Juliette – or rather, the idea of Juliette – had a direct bearing on my predicament, on my whole frame of mind, in fact. Three days after we met on the train, I called her at home. She told me it was good that I had got in touch with her. She was a drama student, she said, and she was about to go away on a course. She hadn't wanted me to think that she had given me her number and then just disappeared. She laughed quickly into the phone. We arranged to meet the following day, in the Café Luxembourg. We had both remembered that it was often fairly empty in the middle of the afternoon.

She was already there when I arrived, sitting at a table towards the rear of the café. She was leaning back in her chair, reading a book, her legs stretched out in front of her, and crossed at the ankles. She smiled up at me as I walked over. 'So,' she said lightly, 'are you still talking to yourself?'

'I wouldn't know, would I? Not unless you were there to tell me.'

'Me,' she said, 'or someone else.'

I smiled. 'There isn't anyone else.'

I don't remember much of what we said that afternoon. I just know that, for the first time in what seemed like years, I felt entirely relaxed. Here I was, out with a girl, and there was no agenda. I didn't need to see her naked body; the colour of her face was enough. The one moment that stood out – and I found it touching, confirming, as it did, an innocence that had already been established – was when I noticed the scar on her left hand, a burn, presumably, because the skin looked as if it had melted and then set. I chose not to ask her about it. I didn't want to disrupt the atmosphere, which was so easy, so calm, so utterly new to me.

One month later, when she returned from the Côte d'Azur, I took her out to dinner in a small Italian restaurant I knew in the Jordaan. It was a cold night, and she was wearing a black ribbed sweater, which, together with her short ponytail, gave her an appropriately French look. Her lipstick was a lush bruised purple. On the third finger of her scarred hand she wore six thin silver rings. She looked even more beautiful than I remembered, and yet she did not appear to be aware of her beauty – or, if she was, then she treated it with a tolerant amusement, the way you treat children when they ask too many questions. This seemed unusual to me, given how young she was. I didn't think she could be more than twenty-five; in fact, she was probably nearer twenty.

She told me that her course had taken place in a converted farmhouse in the hills above Nice. Some evenings they drove into the town in an old American station wagon that belonged to one of the drama teachers. They had cocktails at the Negresco. They danced at a club in Cap d'Antibes. On her last night a man asked her to sail to the Greek islands with him in his yacht. She turned him down. He was too pretty, she said. He had no character. He was like a dummy in a shop window.

'A rich dummy, though,' I said.

She shrugged, but said nothing, and, once again, I was struck by her air of self-possession. She seemed to stand on her own, without illusions or dependencies. She saw everything with such clarity.

We talked about the South of France, which I also knew, of course, from the years I had spent with Brigitte. Once, while she was filling our wine-glasses, she noticed I was looking at her hand.

'Do you find it ugly?' she said.

'No, not at all. I was just curious.'

'People always want to know about it, but they almost never ask.'

She studied it dispassionately, tilting it one way, then the other, as if it was not her hand she was looking at, but the rings on her fingers.

'How did it happen?' I asked.

'My older sister did it.'

'It was an accident, I suppose – '

'No. She did it on purpose. She was jealous.' Juliette lifted

208

her eyes to mine. 'My father was a Dutch businessman and my mother was from Surinam. I don't think I was,' and she paused, 'intended.' She gave me a wry smile. 'In any case, I was given up for adoption when I was still a baby. The people who adopted me already had one child, a girl called Taiana. I think she became jealous of the attention I was getting. One day, when I was five or six, she put my hand in a pot of boiling water and held it there – '

'She held it there?'

'Well, only for a second or two. I screamed so loud that she got frightened.' Juliette smiled again and drank from her glass of sparkling water. 'We get on quite well now. She has no memory of doing anything to my hand. Sometimes I see her looking at it in a puzzled way, as if she's wondering what happened . . .'

Though Juliette was no longer upset by the incident, she still carried a trace element of sadness in her, and, in telling the story, her voice had buckled slightly, despite itself. I put my hand over hers. I could feel the smooth, shiny skin against the inside of my fingers.

'You see photos of me as a little girl,' she said, looking out into the restaurant, 'and I'm always standing there with one hand in my pocket. Or else it's summer and I'm wearing gloves.' She laughed quietly and shook her head.

After dinner I took her to a bar where she ordered an Amaretto. We sat by the window and stared out into the streets, which were cold and colourless, the cracks between the paving-stones inlaid with frost. Sometime during the last few days the temperature had dropped below zero, and all the canals in Amsterdam had frozen over. Later, as I walked her to her tram-stop, we passed a flight of steps that would normally be used by people who owned small boats. We climbed down to where the dark bricks disappeared into the ice. I reached into my pocket and took out a coin.

'Listen to this,' I said.

I sent the coin skimming across the frozen surface of the canal. I had always loved the chattering sound it made, half musical, half metallic, a little like the electric whiplash of tram-rods sliding along their power-lines.

'Did you hear it?' I said.

Juliette smiled. Then she stepped past me, on to the ice.

'Careful,' I said. 'It may be thin in some places.'

'I had an idea,' she said.

I watched her as she stood there in her long black coat.

'I thought we could go and find your money,' she said. 'I saw where it went.'

'You're crazy,' I told her. 'What if it breaks?'

'We'll get cold and wet,' she said, with a kind of restrained delight, 'and then we'll have to go to a bar and have another drink to warm us up.'

'You're crazy,' I said.

But I was already stepping out on to the ice.

Juliette took my hand. 'It's this way. Come on.'

We began to walk, following the diagonal path that the coin had taken when it flew out of my hand. People had thrown all kinds of objects on to the newly frozen canal. We passed a milk crate and a metal dustbin lid. We passed a bicycle with no front wheel. The ice winced and creaked, but it held. Usually I wasn't superstitious, but a thought kept repeating in my head. If we find the coin, I thought, then something will have been decided. If we find the coin . . .

'Are you sure you saw where it went?' I didn't really want to know. I just needed to be saying something, to be talking. It was nerves, I suppose.

Juliette seemed to understand because she just smiled at me and didn't bother to reply.

And then, about two-thirds of the way across, she took two or three steps to her left and bent down quickly. She turned to face me, holding up one gloved hand. Something silver glittered between her finger and thumb. I took the coin from her and stared down at it.

'It's the same one,' I said.

'Of course,' she said. And then she said, 'You mustn't spend it.'

'No, I'll keep it. As proof.'

'Of what?'

'I don't know. Of something.'

There was an eerie brightness out there in the middle of the canal. The lights of the city rebounded between the low cloud cover and the ice that was all around us, achieving a kind of concentration, an intensity of effect. As I brought my eyes back down, I saw that Juliette was looking at me.

'Do you think I'm attractive?' she said.

I laughed. 'Yes, of course.'

She remained serious. 'As a woman?'

'As a woman,' I said.

'Would you like to kiss me?'

She watched me lean towards her, tilting her face upwards to meet mine. As I kissed her I could feel the ice through the soles of my shoes, which contrasted oddly with the heat of her mouth. I stepped back and looked at her.

'How was it?' she said. 'Was it nice?'

I smiled, but did not answer. My heart was beating loudly. Almost loudly enough, I felt, to crack the ice beneath us. To be dangerous.

I saw a man cross the hump-backed bridge behind her on a bicycle. He was singing to himself, his voice a fine, deep baritone. Somehow, it made me realise how late it was. I took Juliette by the hand and turned towards the steps.

'We should go,' I said, 'otherwise you'll miss your tram.'

~

It was a time in my life when I seemed to be holding my breath. I was living within myself, waiting for the future to be revealed. Most days I talked to either Isabel or Juliette. I thought they were both, in their different ways, trying to show me the paths that were open to me, and, though I listened to them both, I still held back. The memory of the walk across the ice had stayed with me. I had to move carefully because there was always the possibility that something might give way, but, equally, I felt that confidence would be rewarded.

One night, after the bar closed, I had a beer with Gusta and a friend of hers called Renate who had just returned from India.

'You've travelled, haven't you.' Renate turned to me greedily, wanting to establish common ground.

The three of us walked to Renate's houseboat, which was filled with incense candles, gold Buddhas, and cushions that had miniature mirrors sewn on to their covers. We drank more beer. I asked what the strange smell was. Renate explained that it was perfume she had bought in Varanasi. She showed me several small glass phials, each one containing a different brightly coloured liquid. We smoked grass through Renate's home-made bong, and all of a sudden I was alone with her. Apparently Gusta had left. I hadn't noticed.

'Yeah,' and Renate chuckled huskily, 'this is good pot.'

She was sprawling on a couch, watching me through half-closed eyes.

'You can fuck me if you like,' she said.

'I don't know . . .'

'You fuck everybody else,' she said. 'What's wrong with me?'

I shook my head. 'I'm too stoned . . .'

'Oh well. Just thought I'd ask.'

And there was a time when it would probably have happened. Because, now I thought about it, she did remind me a little of Maude. She had the same sturdy ankles, the same coarse hair . . . But I had reached the end of something. I was exhausted. As soon as it was possible to imagine walking home – a distance of no more than a few hundred yards – I rose to my feet and said good-night. Still lying on the cushions, Renate gave me a mocking, dismissive smile.

About three days later I met Juliette for lunch. This was unusual because Juliette's acting classes lasted all day, while I worked in the bar most nights and then slept until one or two in the afternoon. Also, since that kiss on the ice, I had been trying to discourage her – or if not discourage her, then at least move slowly, give myself more time to think. It might have been the weight of everything I was carrying, the thought of having to explain it all to her (she knew almost nothing about me; she didn't even know I used to be a dancer). Or perhaps sex had been a means to an end for so many years that I could no longer equate it with closeness or with love. I don't know. In any case, though it was only a twenty-five-minute tram-ride from my house to hers, I behaved as if she lived in a different country. We talked on the phone, for hours. We had the heightened intimacy of people living thousands of miles apart. The distance I put between us intrigued her, though. She thought I was mysterious. Once, she even told me I was cruel. She didn't have to explain that. I understood. I realised that my strategy, if you could call it that, was only binding her more tightly to me. By resisting her, I was making myself irresistible. There was a sense in which I was only delaying something that was bound to happen.

That lunchtime I was in the middle of telling Juliette about Isabel's recovery when I sensed somebody standing to one side of me. I glanced round. It was a girl of about twenty-five, with short blonde hair. I knew from the look of contempt on her face that she must be someone I had slept with, though I had no memory of her.

'So this is what you've been doing,' the girl said. 'So it's black girls you go for now.'

'This is Juliette,' I said. 'We're just friends.'

'*Juliette.*' The girl spat the word out as if it was something rotten she had eaten by mistake. 'No wonder you haven't called me for so long. No wonder you just dropped me like a stone . . .' She brought one hand up to her face. Suddenly she looked as if she might be about to cry. 'Don't you have any feelings?'

'It wasn't like that – '

'I bet you don't even remember my name. What's my name?'

She was right, of course. And she saw that she was right.

'Fuck you,' she said, and walked out of the café, slamming the door behind her.

I looked down at the table. When I lifted my eyes again, Juliette was staring at me in bewilderment.

'I'm sorry about that,' I said.

She tried to laugh the whole thing off, but the laughter caught on something in her. With a kind of shocked wonder in her voice, she said, 'What did you do to her?'

'I can't explain it.'

'You went out with her, though?'

'No. Not exactly.'

Juliette looked at me, then slowly shook her head.

'Juliette,' and I took her hand, 'you have to believe me. There was nothing between us. Nothing at all.'

I suppose I could have used the sudden intrusion of the blonde girl to discourage Juliette for good, but what I learned from the episode, even while it was happening, was that I didn't want to discourage her. I now felt that Juliette was closer to me than anybody else I knew, and I could not afford to lose her.

By the time we left the café, I had succeeded in persuading her that I was innocent of any wrongdoing, though I could tell by the look she gave me as she walked away, just one look, over her shoulder, that I was more of a mystery to her than ever.

~

Later that week, on my day off, I travelled down to Bloemendaal to visit Isabel. Else let me in, as usual. Isabel was still in remission, she told me, and growing stronger every day. The doctors were cautiously optimistic.

For the first half-hour, though, Isabel just complained. She thought chemotherapy was barbaric. With all the recent advances in medicine, she found it hard to believe that treatment was still so primitive. She wished Else didn't fuss so much. Else was always fussing. And as for her doctors, they were tyrants because they had forbidden her to smoke. Then, as the light outside began to fade, she asked if I had ever heard of Nova Zembla. I shook my head.

In the Middle Ages, she said, if you wanted to travel to China, you had to sail south, past the Cape of Good Hope. It was a long and dangerous voyage. Towards the end of the sixteenth century, however, a Dutch explorer tried to change all that. He sailed north instead, hoping to establish a shorter, safer route. The explorer's name was Willem Barentsz, and there was a street in Amsterdam named in his honour. There were also streets named after his captain, Van Heemskerck, and Nova Zembla, the island which played such a big part in their story.

Barentsz's last expedition had left Amsterdam on 18 May 1596. Some weeks later, his ship became trapped in ice off the north coast of Russia, and Barentsz and his crew found themselves marooned on Nova Zembla. In pictures, the island appeared to have a certain stark beauty. The ice that surrounded it for most of the year was pale-blue, almost turquoise, and sculpted into strange shapes by the elements. The sunsets could be breathtaking – bands of crimson folding into deepest black. To Barentsz, though, it must have seemed like the end of the world. There were no trees, only stones, and, from August onwards, it was dark almost all the time. Using materials commandeered from the ship, the men built a makeshift camp. They called it 'Het Behouden Huys', which meant 'The Sheltered House' or 'The House That Remains'. They spent the entire winter there, living on a diet of Arctic foxes and polar bears, which they shot with the muskets they had brought with them. Finally, in June of the following year, they managed to row to the mainland. They did not reach Amsterdam until 1 November 1597. Only twelve of the crew survived.

In 1871 a Norwegian expedition discovered the remnants of the camp where Barentsz and his men had lived for so many months. On the ground were books, tools, clothes, ammunition, cutlery and navigation equipment, all of which had been lying undisturbed on Nova Zembla for almost three centuries. But, to this day, the ship that had been captained by Van Heemskerck, and the grave of Willem Barentsz, who had died on the homeward journey, had never been found.

When Isabel had finished talking, I sat quite still and stared into the fire. While I was being held in the white room I used to think there was a place inside my body that the women could not touch. I used to see this place as a house. A house inside my body where I lived. Where I was safe. From its windows I could look out over land that was flat and featureless. I could see the women, but they were tiny figures, far away. They were always there, but they were always in the distance, and they never came any closer. Even if they had come closer they couldn't have entered. I don't know how I knew that, but I did. And now, after hearing what had happened to the Dutch explorer and his crew, I realised that that was how I had survived . . .

At last I looked away from the fire, and I felt as if my eyes were glowing, as if they were sending beams of bright, pale light into the room.

'What do you think of the story?' Isabel asked.

'It would make a great ballet,' I said, surprising myself. The thought and the words seemed to have arrived simultaneously.

But Isabel was smiling, as if I had given her the answer she was looking for.

'I think so too,' she said.

When Else walked in a few moments later, to persuade Isabel that she should rest, we were both still smiling at each other.

'You should see yourselves,' she said. 'You're like a couple of conspirators.'

That was exactly what we were. As a result of our various misfortunes, Isabel and I had become inextricably linked, and during the next few weeks, the weeks that led up to Christmas, we began to discuss a project that would bring us still closer together. The ballet would be based on the story of Barentsz, but only in the loosest sense; it would also draw heavily on my own experience. I wanted to use just four dancers – one male, to represent the explorer and his crew, and three female, to represent the various forms of hardship they endured – and Isabel agreed. I had even thought of music: at home, in my apartment, I had been listening to Jean Barraqué's Piano Sonata, which was like a landscape in itself, with its dramatic storms of sound and its desolate silences. Though we had neither commission nor deadline, though the world knew nothing of our collaboration, we worked eagerly. Isabel took notes, using Labanotation, an old-fashioned method of transcribing movement that she had taught me several years before. I cleared a space around the divan so I could develop my ideas in front of her. I wanted to invent steps that captured the shock of being plunged into the unknown. They would be steps taken in the dark, in other words, steps that sought enlightenment. They would reveal how foreign we are to one another. They would illustrate the paradox that when we are naked we become less knowable, and that our skin is the greatest mystery of all.

It felt strange, after so long, to be producing choreography again, and I sometimes caught Isabel giving me an oddly satisfied and yet shrewd look, which it took me a while to dissect. I thought she was probably congratulating herself on having lured me back to work. That was part of it. But she might also have been wondering whether she would live to see the ballet finished. Or perhaps that did not matter to her. She had been the impulse behind it, the catalyst, and that was enough; she expected me to see it through on her behalf – or, even, in her honour. For, although she was stronger than she had been in November, she still tired easily. When she needed rest, I would put on my coat and walk out into the landscape I had grown to love, the pine forest that stretched behind the house, or the sand dunes, and I would return an hour later with my ears ringing from the wind, and nothing in my mind, nothing except the bleakness of the place and the purity of light – the peace.

～

That Christmas I flew home to see my parents. We had a relaxing, enjoyable few days together. I was able to talk about my collaboration with Isabel, who was, after all, one of the most famous choreographers in Europe. I told them about Barentsz and Nova Zembla, realising, as I did so, that I was giving them a coded version of my own story. I saw once again how much I owed to Isabel. In telling the story of Barentsz, I could give him emotions I had experienced myself – shock, bewilderment, fear, hope, shame. This was as close as I would ever come to telling my family what had happened to me, and perhaps, in the end, it was close enough.

On Boxing Day I met up with Philip, a cousin of mine who I hadn't seen for years. Philip was already drunk when he arrived at the pub. As soon as he sat down he started telling me about how he was having trouble finding a girlfriend. It was all he wanted, he said, to be married, to have children, but no one was interested in him. He swallowed a third of his pint, sighed deeply, and then said, 'What about you?' Suddenly I found myself talking about Juliette. I talked about how we had met, on the train to Amsterdam, and how sympathetic and intuitive she had been. I talked about the quality she had, of seeming to stand all alone in the world, and how I thought it might be to do with her having been adopted. I talked about her beauty, and how lightly she carried it, as if it was a joke someone had played on her. I had never talked about her before, and though it seemed tactless, in the circumstances, I went on talking about her because I felt I was making discoveries. When I stopped, Philip looked at me, his face quite still for a moment, and then he said, 'Well, it's all right for some,' and plunged forlornly back into his beer. Later that night, as I prepared for bed, I leaned on the sink and looked deep into the mirror. Beyond my face. Into the space behind it. The space where we keep secrets, even from ourselves. It's all right for some, I thought. And then I said the words out loud: 'It's all right for some.' In that moment something was decided – in a way I felt it had been decided for me – and, two days later, on the flight back to Amsterdam, I could scarcely contain my impatience. At last the plane begin its descent, and the clouds parted, and I caught a glimpse of the North Sea, cold and sluggish, and the strip of palest yellow that was the coast of Holland. Then the runway was flashing by, beneath the wing . . .

As soon as I was inside the airport I went to a pay-phone and rang Juliette. She wasn't there, so I left a message. *I'm back. I need to see you. Call me.* I rang her again when I reached my apartment, and this time she answered. She asked me what Christmas had been like. I told her that my parents had given me a towel, a tie and three pairs of socks. They had always been hopeless at presents. She laughed.

'Perhaps you're a mystery to them as well,' she said.

'Perhaps.' I swallowed quickly. 'That's why I'm calling, actually. I wanted to tell you. All that's over.'

Juliette was silent, and I could see her face, eyes lowered, as she weighed up what I had just said.

I asked her what she was doing for New Year.

'Oh, you know,' she said, 'there are some parties –'

'I had an idea,' I said. 'I thought we could walk down to the

Nieuw Markt, just the two of us. They have fireworks down there, don't they?'

'You know, I've never done that,' she said, 'not in all the years I've lived here. Not even when I was a child.'

'So would you like to?'

'Yes, I would.'

'What about the parties?'

'What parties?' she said, and laughed.

~

I left my apartment at just after half-past eight on New Year's Eve. The canals had thawed a few days before, and everything that had been thrown on to the ice had sunk swiftly to the bottom, never to be seen again. This seemed to augur well. It was strange. I had become superstitious for the first time in my life. I was seeing omens everywhere.

I had arranged to meet Juliette in a bar not far from the red-light district, and I walked quickly, wanting to get there first. As I crossed Marnixstraat I saw somebody aim a rocket out of the window of a passing car and light the touch-paper. For one extraordinary moment the car seemed to be attached to a nearby tree by a frayed bright-orange rope, then the car raced on, making for Leidseplein, and I stood and watched as the tree showered sparks in all directions, like a dog shaking water off its coat.

When I arrived, Juliette was already there, sitting on a tall stool at the bar. She was wearing a new black leather jacket and a short red mini-skirt with black wool tights. She sat very upright, which gave her a haughty, almost majestic air.

'I thought I was early,' I said as I walked up to her.

She looked at her watch, then smiled. 'You are early,' she said, 'but I was even earlier.'

Instead of the usual three kisses on alternate cheeks, I

221

leaned forwards and kissed her lips. They were softer than I remembered, and sweet from the hot chocolate that she was drinking. I stood back. She looked both surprised and curious, and yet there was still the ghost of a smile on her face.

'I've missed you,' I said. 'I really have. It's been so long.'

'Do I look the same?'

'More beautiful, if anything.'

I ordered a whisky and stood beside her, aware that my leg was touching hers. All around me people's faces glowed, as if lit from inside. The last night of the year.

'What's in the bag?' Juliette asked, touching the small backpack I was carrying.

I handed it to her. 'Have a look.'

She undid the drawstring, reached inside and took out a bottle of champagne. 'For us?'

I nodded. 'For later. Midnight.'

She reached inside again. This time she found a small white packet tied up with silver ribbon.

'That's for you,' I said. 'A present.'

This was not something she had been expecting. I watched her untie the ribbon, then undo the wrapping-paper. Inside was a small square box. She lifted the lid off the box and there, lying in a bed of cotton-wool, was a silver chain with a 2½-guilder coin attached to it. It was the coin I had skimmed across the canal, the coin she had led me out across the ice to find. I wondered if she would understand what I meant by it. I hoped she would. I watched her as she looked down at the present, which was now coiled, glinting, in the palm of her hand.

'You trust me,' she said.

~

Though it was only a short distance to the Nieuw Markt, it took us twenty minutes, the crowd thickening as we drew closer. Once, somebody lit a firecracker that must have been at least fifteen feet long, and people scattered in all directions. I felt Juliette tighten her grip on my hand as we backed against a wall. We watched from a distance as the firecracker writhed and twisted and flung itself about, loud as a machine-gun in the narrow street, then the crowd flowed on, laughing, drinking, making jokes, and, all of a sudden, we were in the square . . .

The atmosphere was jubilant, chaotic. Bonfires had been built on the cobblestones, using whatever came to hand: cardboard boxes, broken chairs, fruit crates – even a row-ing-boat. We passed two men who were wearing giant, painted papier-mâché heads. We saw a girl on stilts stalking through pale, drifting clouds of smoke. Fireworks fizzed horizontally through the darkness, missing people by inches, and the air shook with constant explosions.

We sat down by the fountain and opened the champagne.

'I've got some pot,' Juliette said.

She took a joint out of her pocket, lit it and passed it to me. I drew the smoke into my lungs and held it there.

'Look,' I said.

From where we were sitting, at the base of the fountain, we could see two transvestites, one dressed in a full-length black ball-gown, the other one in white. They wore extravagant, eighteenth-century wigs, with heavy rolls of hair that tumbled halfway down their backs, and, judging by the way they lurched and tottered across the cobbles, their heels were six inches high. They called out to each other in raucous voices, trading obscene remarks and grimacing theatrically through layers of foundation. Small kerosene lamps arranged in a wide circle marked their territory.

Juliette was smiling. 'They're wonderful.'

We stood up and walked over. The transvestite in the black dress was drinking from a champagne bottle. The one in white blew smoke rings and winked at men whenever he caught them watching. They took turns lighting the fireworks that were placed haphazardly on the ground all round them.

As I passed the champagne to Juliette, the transvestite who was wearing black swayed over to her. Up close his dress looked exactly like charred newspaper. I had the feeling that if I touched the fabric it would crumble into dust.

He raised his bottle and touched it against hers. The weighty clink of thick green glass.

'So who are you with tonight?' he said.

Juliette grinned, but didn't answer.

The transvestite turned to me. His teeth were gappy and rotten, and his hollow eyes glittered with an almost sub-terranean light. He spoke to me in Dutch, putting his mouth close to my ear, so close that I could smell the alcohol and tobacco on his breath, and the sickly, sodden perfume of his skin.

'She's beautiful,' he said. 'Look after her.'

Then he staggered away across the cobblestones, stooping once to light another firework with the tip of his cigarette.

'What did he say?' Juliette asked.

I smiled. 'I can't tell you.'

'It was about me?'

I nodded.

'Was it nice?'

I looked at the transvestite. He was twenty yards away, flirting with a group of boys who were drinking beer out of cans. His champagne bottle was empty now, and he held it by the neck like a juggler's club. I let my eyes drift beyond him. The sky flashed mauve and white and crimson above the rooftops as fireworks exploded in the side-streets behind the square.

'It was perfect,' I said.

Just then all the clocks began to strike. It was midnight, and we hadn't even realised. I laughed and took Juliette in my arms and when the last note sounded, a roar filled the square, as if a furnace door had been opened, or a great wind had descended, and we clung to each other, and we kissed for so long, my tongue touching hers, that when I opened my eyes I was dazzled by the eerie silver light that seemed to surround us. I stood back and looked at her and even though I was stoned by now, drunk too, I still had the same feeling of absolute certainty that I had had while I was looking into the mirror at my parents' house five days before.

At half-past twelve we left the square and walked back to my apartment in the Kinkerbuurt. The streets were covered with the remnants of firecrackers, scraps of dull-red paper that lay in heaps, like autumn leaves. We passed a young couple dancing slowly on a bridge. The girl was humming a tune I didn't recognise, her eyes closed. The boy's leather coat had the gleam of chrome.

'I used to be a dancer,' I said suddenly.

Juliette turned and stared at me.

'I was a choreographer as well. I used to be quite famous.' I smiled at the thought of that.

She asked me what I had done, and I mentioned the titles of my ballets.

'You know, I think I saw one of them.' She was standing in the middle of the street, between the tramlines, nodding to herself. 'My father took me. I must have been about fifteen.'

She began to describe a ballet, which I scarcely recognised.

'It's funny,' she said, 'but when I first saw you, on the train, I thought there was something familiar about you. It made it easier to talk to you, somehow.'

I had to smile at that. It was her very unfamiliarity that had attracted me to her. It was the fact that I knew for certain that I had never seen her before.

'But you work in a bar now . . .' She left the sentence hanging in a such a way that it became a question.

'It's temporary,' I said.

'Will you go back to dancing?'

'Not dancing. Choreography maybe. In the last few weeks, it's surfaced again, the urge to do something . . .'

On Jacob van Lennepkade there were lights burning in most of the apartment windows, though the canal was quiet and still. We turned into the street where I lived. As I took out my keys, Juliette put a hand on my arm.

'Let me,' she said.

She took the keys from me and opened the door. Inside, she found the light-switch. There was a dark-green door to the left and, beyond it, a narrow flight of stairs leading steeply upwards.

'Which floor?' she said.

'Third.'

We climbed the stairs in silence. On the third floor she hesitated, studying each of the doors in turn.

'It's on your right,' I said.

The light on the stairs clicked off as she turned the key in the lock. She pushed the door open cautiously and stepped inside. A ghostly rectangle rose out of the darkness beyond her like a photograph developing. The living-room window. Outside, on the street, there was a plane tree, and the intricate shadow of its bare branches covered one entire wall and all the furniture in that half of the room.

I followed Juliette into the apartment, closing the door

behind her. The air smelled of the jute matting I had put down and also, faintly, of dried flowers. In the middle of the living-room she turned to me, her face serious, intent, but apprehensive, as if she was about to attempt something dangerous.

'I'm in love with you,' she said.

Putting one hand on my chest, she reached up and kissed me. Her mouth was relaxed, cool. She kissed me again, slipping her leather jacket off her shoulders, allowing it to fall on the floor behind her. We were still in darkness. On the wall the mirror glinted, alive and silvery, a magnet for what little light there was.

I drew her close to me. She pressed her body into mine, as though she wanted to leave an imprint of herself on me. There was an urgency about her, an insistence, which made me feel that I was less experienced than she was. Faintly, in the distance, I heard the whistle of a rocket.

In the bedroom we undressed each other, taking the same care that she had taken with her present earlier that evening. It was the only thing she was wearing that she would not part with. As she lay down, I watched the coin slide between her breasts and settle in the hollow of her collarbone. In the darkness, naked, she looked so black. Like something I could disappear into.

'Kiss me,' she whispered. 'Kiss me all over.'

I started with her feet, moved slowly upwards.

I had seen so many women's bodies, even in that room, that bed, but always in a highly twisted state of anticipation. I was always looking for marks, for signs – for evidence. I had been a detective, eliminating suspects. Now, though, with Juliette, I knew there would be nothing I had ever seen before. Everything was strange. Everything was new.

'Your hair smells of fireworks,' she murmured.

227

I wanted to delay the moment that I entered her. I wanted to please her endlessly before that happened. Because, for once, there was no reason not to. Because, at last, I could.

I remember that she reached out and touched my wrist and that the clock on the bedside table said twenty-five-past four. She held her face quite still below me, as if it was full to the brim, as if it might spill.

'Put it in me now,' she whispered.

~

At the beginning of January in Amsterdam there are images of abandonment and desolation almost everywhere you look. After the New Year people put their Christmas trees out on the street. The trees lie on their sides, shedding scores of brittle, bright-orange needles. They quickly become skeletal. Clogging the gutters are the remains of all the Chinese firecrackers, another kind of foliage, faded and soggy, but still red. Dead trees, dead leaves . . . It's a dead time, perhaps, in any city. The holiday is over, and most people go back to work, with nothing to look forward to for months. It's a strange time to be in love. You feel as if you're going against the grain. You feel chosen. Lucky.

That year the weather was cold and grey. When the bar closed, I would walk home to find Juliette asleep in my bed. Sometimes she woke when she heard the door, and she would rise up out of the bedclothes, eyes wide open, and say my name. She wasn't awake, though, not really. I would stroke her hair, and kiss her, and she would soon sink back among the pillows. When her breathing had deepened, I would go into the kitchen, with its green walls, and make myself a cup of herb tea. I would sit there quietly, reading English newspapers. Outside, it would be silent except for the late-night traffic two or three streets away, a soft rushing sound that reminded me of air-conditioning, and, every now and then, there would be a rustle of sheets as Juliette turned in the bed. After an hour, when I had left work far behind, I would slide into bed beside her, fitting my body against hers, one hand resting on her upturned hip. There were nights when I lay there in the darkness, in the silence, and my thoughts slipped their moorings. Time slowed down. Opened out. I felt myself float free. I was happier than I had ever expected to be, given the circumstances. But also, curiously, I felt as if my happiness was earned. I had waited so long for it. I deserved it. Which gave it a different quality, a different value, to any happiness I had known before.

In the mornings, if I woke first, which was unusual, I would watch Juliette sleeping. Her face had a dull gleam to it, as if, deep down, it contained a seam of gold. I loved the dark lines on the palms of her hands, and I loved the sweet smell of her, a mixture of parsnip and oat biscuits. If it was a weekend, we would stay in bed until eleven or twelve, sometimes just holding each other, or talking. Outside, it would be so gloomy that the bathroom-fittings shop would have its lights on . . . Later, wearing a kimono I had bought in Osaka years before, Juliette would walk into the kitchen and put on the coffee. While she was waiting for the milk to heat in the saucepan, she moved idly through the apartment, looking at things. I would see her pass the bedroom doorway, the kimono much too big for her, trailing along the floor behind her like a bridal train. Sometimes she lost herself in a book, or in the view from a window, and there would be a sudden cry, and I would hear her run back into the kitchen to find that the milk had boiled over. She never bothered to tie the kimono at the waist, so when, eventually, she came towards me with the coffee, an upright section of her, the middle part, would be exposed – the smooth space between her breasts, her stomach with its slightly protruding belly-button, her pubic hair, which was as straight and black and shiny as the hair on her head, the insides of her thighs, her narrow knees, her feet . . . If it was a weekday, and Juliette had drama classes, I would often drift off to sleep again. Later, we would meet in a café, or see a film. Afterwards I would cook an early supper, then I would leave the house and walk to work. Though she didn't care for Gusta, Juliette sometimes came to the bar at midnight. She would sit at a round table in the corner with a *witbier*, reading a play or a script. Every now and then I walked round, collecting glasses or emptying ashtrays, and she would look up with a smile that seemed to say, *Isn't it strange, that I should be here? Isn't this unlike me?* She always seemed to have that view of herself, that she was unexpected, out of place – a surprise both to herself and others.

Of course, we were not dissimilar in that respect.

~

One Saturday in the middle of January, I took Juliette to Bloemendaal with me. I had to smile when I saw Isabel that afternoon. Though she was lying on her divan, as usual, she had put on an elegant white dress and a headscarf of mauve silk, and her wrists and fingers glittered with an array of jewellery, including the bracelet Balanchine had given her as a token of his admiration. She had known I was bringing Juliette, and it was for Juliette that she had dressed. She looked so striking, in fact, that it was a while before I noticed Paul Bouhtala sitting in the shadows on the far side of the fireplace. After the introductions, I left the two women together and sat down next to Bouhtala. He seemed more than usually subdued, his eyes shifting from myself to Juliette and back again without so much as a flicker of curiosity or feeling. I asked him if he knew Paris. I wanted to take Juliette there for the weekend. He muttered something about a cemetery called Père Lachaise, and then he shrugged and, glancing downwards, removed a speck of dust from his lapel.

'It was you who brought us together,' I heard Juliette tell Isabel in the silence that followed. 'We have you to thank.'

'I think you're probably exaggerating my part in it,' Isabel replied, though I could see the idea appealed to her. Her life had been so restricted by her illness, so pared down. To have some influence – any influence – on events that happened beyond her living-room . . .

But she was tired that afternoon, and we stayed for less than an hour. As I bent down to kiss her goodbye, she held on to my wrist, making me promise to visit her again before too long. Even if it was only for a morning, or part of a morning. It was all she was good for, anyway. We had to continue with our ballet, she said. I told her I'd come down as soon as I returned from Paris. I had a new beginning, which I wanted to try out on her.

On the train home I asked Juliette what she thought of Isabel. Juliette was leaning against the window, watching the darkness rush by.

'She's very grand, isn't she,' Juliette said. 'I always thought that people who were grand were only interested in themselves. She wasn't like that, though.'

I smiled. 'She can be.'

But Juliette didn't seem to hear me. 'Now I know why you were talking to yourself that night,' she said. 'To lose someone like her . . .' She stared out of the window for a moment longer, and then turned towards me, her eyes lit with sudden wonder. 'Did you see that bracelet?'

∼

We arrived in Paris on a Friday, checking into a small hotel not far from the Gare de l'Est. Our room was on the top floor, with big red roses on the wallpaper – like explosions, Juliette said – and a bed that creaked and twanged whenever we made love, or even moved. That night we ate in a brasserie just off the Rue du Faubourg St Martin, and then, at eleven-thirty, we took a taxi to a club Juliette had heard about. The entrance had been roped off, and a crowd of people waited on the pavement, their eyes fixed on the swaggering, tuxedoed doorman, but when he saw us climb out of our taxi he signalled to us, and the crowd parted obediently, and we walked right in. It became a joke between us, how fashionable we were. We returned to the hotel at three in the morning and sprawled on the bed, a little drunk. Juliette peeled off my shirt, which was still damp from the dancing, her hand pausing as it passed over the oblong, shiny patch of skin where my tattoo used to be. 'Funny, isn't it,' she murmured, 'how we both have scars . . .' But that was all she said, which came as a relief to me. Many of the women I had slept with had asked about the scar, and I had invented all kinds of stories – a car-crash, a sporting injury, a bungled appendix operation; I had never told anyone the truth, and I didn't want to tell it now. At some level I suppose I must have realised that the love I felt for Juliette was rooted in ideas of escape and safety. While I was with Juliette I felt protected from the past, and I had no desire to jeopardise that feeling; I was happy where I was, sealed in a present that was continuous, unending . . .

They were simple, memorable days. We walked through the cold, sunlit streets until our feet hurt, we asked a Japanese woman to take our photograph beneath the Eiffel Tower, we drank *pastis* at zinc-topped bars. We even visited Père Lachaise, the cemetery that Paul Bouhtala had mentioned, and were astonished by the size and grandeur of the place, which looked more like a city than a cemetery, its cobbled pathways lined with graves built in the style of mansions or temples, and, every now and then, an obelisk, or a pyramid, or some other exotic, unexpected monument. Slowly, I was learning to know Juliette better. Though she could be strangely methodical, almost, at times, pedantic – she stood in front of Edith Piaf's memorial with her head lowered for exactly a minute – she could also have moments of pure spontaneity. She had revealed that side of her once already, when she led me out across the ice. On Sunday night, which was our last night in Paris, she revealed it again. We had been invited to dinner by Madame Soffner, who was an old friend of her father's, and thinking we should not arrive empty-handed, we had bought a bunch of crimson roses that reminded us of the wallpaper in our hotel room. In the 7th arrondissement, not far from where Madame Soffner lived, we saw a black limousine pull up outside an apartment building. The car door opened, and Catherine Deneuve stepped out. I thought it had to be her because of her hair, which was moonlight-blonde, and because of the clarity of her skin. Before I could say anything, though, Juliette was crossing the street. I watched her hand Deneuve the bouquet that we had bought for Madame Soffner. Deneuve looked down at the flowers, then she looked at Juliette and smiled. As Juliette walked back towards me, Deneuve vanished into the apartment building, followed by two men in dark suits.

I turned to Juliette. 'What did you say to her?'

'I told her she was a great actress. *Magnifique*, I said. I told her I wanted to become an actress too.' Juliette frowned suddenly. 'Is it all right to say "*magnifique*"?'

'It's fine. What did she say?'

'She said the roses were very beautiful. She wished me luck with my career.'

'So it really was her?'

'Yes.'

Juliette glanced at the entrance to the apartment building, which was now deserted, the lobby filled with an expensive, pale-gold light.

'We haven't got anything for your father's friend,' I said.

'Yes. That's a problem.' Juliette spoke so earnestly, and with such a look of concern on her face, that I had to laugh.

In the end, though, it wasn't a problem. We bought Madame Soffner a bottle of champagne from a shop that just happened to be open, and the brand we chose turned out to be her favourite.

There are times when the world is kind to you, when you cannot wrongfoot your good fortune, no matter what you do, but it was so long since I had lived that way that I felt as if my life had been dipped in syrup, as if it was deliciously, almost unbearably, sweet.

∼

One Tuesday towards the end of that month Juliette decided to spend the night in her apartment. She had an audition early the next morning, and the theatre was close to where she lived. At six o'clock that evening we said goodbye outside my house. It was only our second night apart since New Year's Eve, and I remember holding her so tightly that she murmured something about me crushing her. I wished her luck, kissed her one last time, then watched her as she walked away, a slender, upright figure in a long dark coat, her black hair shining as she passed beneath a street-light.

A young Scottish couple came into the bar that night. They

had flown to Amsterdam for a week's holiday. He worked for an oil company, as a geologist, and she was a make-up artist. Their names were Bill and Emma. At closing-time they told me they were going to a club, and asked if I wanted to come along. Usually, I made a point of never going out with people from the bar. Also, by one-thirty in the morning, I would be looking forward to the peace and quiet of my apartment – and since the beginning of January, of course, there had been the added incentive of seeing Juliette, even if she was asleep. That night, though, with Juliette not there, I thought, Why not?

The weather had turned colder, and we walked fast, our breath clouding the air. Emma was wearing heels, and she kept stumbling on the cobbles or the tram-tracks and saying *Shit*, or *Fucking hell*, or *Wait for me*. She didn't lose her temper, though. In fact, she was always grinning when she caught up with us.

We went to a club on Singel first, then to another club on Reguliersdwarsstraat. Bill and Emma danced. I drank a beer and watched. It was hot in the club, but I was enjoying myself. I did not regret my decision to come out.

By three-fifteen we were sitting in an upstairs lounge. It had dark-red walls and muted lighting, and there were blue velvet sofas that looked like scallop shells. Emma was talking about the time she worked with Liza Minnelli, and I was just thinking I could tell the story about Juliette and Catherine Deneuve when I noticed that Bill's glass was empty.

'Same again, Bill?' I said.

Bill nodded. 'Cheers.'

'Emma?'

She shook her head. 'I'm fine.'

I walked over to the bar, which was curved, fitting snugly into the corner of the room. The barman wore a black waistcoat and a spangled royal-blue bow-tie. Behind him were rows of bottles on glass shelves, all illuminated from beneath. I edged between a man and a girl, and ordered two more beers.

I was staring down at my hands, I remember, when something moved at the edge of my field of vision. It was almost as if the air had warped for a moment, as if it had shuddered in slow motion. Then I saw a hair land on the bar, about six inches to the right of my right hand. The bar had a black, lacquered surface so the hair showed up clearly. It was about the length of a finger, with a slight curve to it. It was red.

I was standing so still now that I felt that the air around me was solid, enclosing me. Inside the stillness, my heart was beating loudly, and I saw the sound as a soft black circle appearing and disappearing before my eyes . . .

As I turned to face the girl who was standing beside me, she stepped back from the bar and walked away. I watched her cross the room and sit down on a sofa, then I looked at the hair that had just fallen from her head. I touched it cautiously with my forefinger. A thrill of recognition darted through me.

'Two beers.'

I looked up. The barman had placed the drinks in front of me, and he was waiting for me to pay.

Back at the table, I sat down. The girl was behind me now, under the window.

Slowly I leaned back, looked round. She was sitting on a sofa with two other people, her face angled away from me. Not that her face mattered. She had Astrid's body, and this confused me for a moment. I had always thought that it was Gertrude who had red hair. But then, given the state I was in when they held me in that room, was it any wonder if I had got things wrong?

'Are you all right?' Bill said.

236

I heard the words I had heard in the room, just after I had watched that red hair drift slowly downwards through the air. *Tell me what you'd like for your reward.*

I stood up. 'Excuse me a moment.'

I walked over to the girl and stood in front of her. Her blouse was black, with long, see-through sleeves. Her skirt was also black. On her left thumb she wore a wide silver ring. She could have been in her early thirties, but, equally, she could have been twenty-five. She looked good. She had always looked good. Perhaps she always would.

'Don't I know you?' I said.

Her eyes lifted to mine. They were shiny and utterly incurious. They didn't waver. I watched her light a cigarette. The people she was with, a man and a woman, turned to each other and started talking. The man sounded American.

'We know each other,' I said, 'don't we.'

This time I wasn't asking a question, but if she was surprised or disconcerted she didn't show it.

'I don't know what you're talking about,' she said, inhaling. She let the smoke drift out of her nostrils, then, turning sideways, she tapped her cigarette against the edge of the ashtray.

I watched her slim forearm move beneath the gauzy fabric of her blouse. I watched her fingers, elegant but strong. I watched the ash fall from her cigarette and shatter into fragments. I was watching her closely, and nothing that she did seemed unfamiliar.

Then her face tilted upwards suddenly and seemed to open, revealing a much harder surface.

'Get lost,' she said.

Her two friends looked round sharply.

That flashed anger, the same as in the room. I smiled at her. Her eyes were a muddy green colour, the colour of

237

camouflage. It seemed strange I hadn't noticed this at the time. It was perfect, though. I smiled down at her and shook my head.

'I'll call security,' she said.

Still smiling, I turned away. I sat down next to Bill, with my back to the girl, as before. Bill broke off in the middle of a sentence.

'What was all that about?' he said.

Emma was looking at me curiously.

'Do you know her?' Bill said.

I picked up my drink. My heart was beating again, but at least I could no longer see that soft black ball in front of me. I was thinking of all the women I had been with – and here she was, almost five years later, one of the women I had been looking for, one of the three. Now what? I was thinking. *Now what?*

I looked at Bill.

'I know who she is,' I said.

'Sounds mysterious,' Emma said.

'Yes.' I laughed. 'Yes, it is.'

I drank some beer. It tasted warm and frothy, like saliva.

I left Bill and Emma talking on the sofa and walked out into the main part of the club. I had told them I was going to the toilet, but really I just wanted to be on my own, with no one watching me. I leaned on the matt silver railings that formed a gallery above the dance-floor and looked down at the people dancing below. The music was loud – funk and disco from the seventies. I wanted to be thinking clearly, but my mind felt tangled, slow. I couldn't have been drunk, though. I had only had three beers.

Then, looking up, I saw the girl from the lounge. She walked out on to the gallery and then turned right, moving in the direction of the toilets. She hadn't noticed me. She was alone.

I put my drink down and followed her along the gallery. I passed through a pair of black swing-doors. I found myself standing in a short corridor lit by infra-red. A thin man in a vest loped past me, scarlet cheeks and forehead, black hollows instead of eyes. The gust of air that hit me smelled of hash and bitter sweat and after-shave. Should I follow the girl into the toilets, or should I wait where I was?

I walked up to the door that said *Women* and pushed it open. It was a big square room with strips of ultra-violet in wire cages on the walls. The girl stood to my right, fifteen feet away. Otherwise the room was empty. I could hear the water spilling through her hands and down into the basin. More distantly, through the floor, I could hear the dull, muffled thud of music coming from downstairs . . .

The girl had her hands over her face as I crossed the room towards her, as if she was playing a game, as if she was going to count to one hundred, then come and find me. She saw me in the mirror as I walked up behind her. I didn't speak to her this time. I didn't think there was anything to say. Instead, I put a hand over her mouth and pulled her backwards, into one of the empty stalls. Once the door was half closed, I grabbed at her blouse. It was a flimsy thing; it came away like paper. I could see her breasts. They looked familiar, but that wasn't enough. I had to prove it to myself beyond all doubt. I needed solid evidence.

I reached for her skirt. The girl's mouth was open, and I thought she must be screaming; somehow, I couldn't hear it, though. And anyway I needed both my hands. I tugged hard on the skirt and something ripped. She was trying to fight her way past me, hands flailing at my face, sharp fingernails, but I forced her back against the cistern. She was straddling the toilet seat, off balance. Her pubic hair was abundant, almost black. I didn't remember it. What about the coin-shaped scar?

It had to be there – surely. Which leg, though? I pushed one hand against her throat as I bent down. There was no scar. Perhaps I had got it all mixed up. Perhaps it was one of the others who had had the scar. I heard water trickling out of a pipe, and I seemed to see the flow of it close up, twisting down into the cistern, swirling as it hit the surface. It had the beauty, the complexity, of blown glass.

My hand lifted away from the girl's neck, and I stared down at her body, naked except for her skirt and tights, which clung to her knees, and the remains of her blouse, which hung in tatters from one shoulder, one cuff still buttoned, neatly enclosing her left wrist. The shape of her breasts, her hips, her thighs . . . I stood in front of her, trying to remember. But there had been too many bodies. I was looking at this girl through the bodies of a hundred other girls. They were all still with me, inside my head, like interference. There was no clarity of signal, no clarity at all.

I heard voices in the room behind me, and somebody shoved hard against the door. I half fell against the girl, who was slumped on the toilet seat with one hand clasping her throat, a pose that struck me as incongruously refined, almost aristocratic. I stepped back, turned, opened the stall door. A man stood there, his face stupid with surprise. He wore a blue tartan shirt with the sleeves cut off. I thought I recognised him from the lounge.

'Hey!'

I pushed past him. Somebody shouted the Dutch word for police, and I began to run. Out into the infra-red, black holes instead of eyes. Through the swing-doors and along the gallery, one hand skimming the silver rail. Then down the stairs, too many people suddenly, too many faces, one drink spilled and then another, almost tripping, falling, but out on to the street at last, a shock as the cold air closed over me, it was January, after all, and I had forgotten to collect my coat.

I walked towards the lights of Rembrandtplein. I was shivering. My coat was in the club, on a blue velvet sofa, but I could hardly go back for it, not now. Perhaps it was that sense of loss, trivial though it was, that feeling of being separated from something that was mine, but I felt as if I didn't know myself. I felt like somebody who had no name, no home. It wasn't that I was outside myself and looking down, as people sometimes are when they're close to death. I wasn't outside, and I wasn't inside either. I wasn't anywhere.

I stopped walking and stood quite still, outside a sports shop. There were golf clubs and hockey sticks and skis. Tennis rackets fanned out like a peacock's tail. I heard the trundle of a tram behind me, the clang of its bell. I instinctively stepped closer to the window of the shop. In that same moment I was struck between the shoulder-blades. Time blackened. I thought the tram must have hit me after all. But then I heard somebody swearing at me. The voice was behind me, above me. I recognised the accent. American.

I lay face-down on the ground, not feeling any pain, just cold. The street smelled of chewing-gum and metal. I could still see Rembrandtplein, though it was tilted on its side. Green neon, yellow neon. One sign had a cowboy on it. The cowboy drew his gun, and then leaned forwards. Then he was standing upright, with his gun back in its holster. Then he drew the gun again, leaned forwards. This would go on for ever, I thought, and there was nothing the cowboy could do about it. He would never actually fire the gun, for instance. He would never ride a horse. He would never stretch out on his bed-roll and tip his Stetson over his eyes and go to sleep. There were so many normal, ordinary things that he would never do.

I was lifted to my feet by two policemen. Their white car stood nearby, its blue light spinning in the street. They took told of me, one arm each, and led me back towards the club. The American walked slightly ahead of us and slightly to one side. Every now and then he turned and looked at me, and his face was bleached out, blank with anger. In a way, he was just like the neon cowboy.

A small crowd had gathered outside the entrance to the club. I wondered where Bill and Emma were. The policemen led me up the steep flight of stairs, past the ticket booth, then through a door into an office. Dark-red walls, grey blinds. Two yucca plants in tubs. The girl was sitting next to a water dispenser with a blanket wrapped around her. The policemen stood me in front of her, but she would not look up. She was twisting the ring on her thumb, twisting it and twisting it as if it had the power to change things, to transport her to another place, a different life.

'Is this him?' one of the policemen said.

I stared at the girl's ring turning on her thumb. Round and round it went. I thought I could hear the sound of metal on skin – a faint chafing, like a fly rubbing its legs together.

The policemen repeated the question in the same quiet voice, and this time she looked at me quickly, for no more than a second.

'Yes,' she said.

FOUR

L ook at a map of Amsterdam and you see it right away: the city is a fingerprint. The four principal canals form a series of concentric semicircles that are echoed further in by streets like Damrak and Nieuwezijds Voorburgwal. Right in the middle, the area the red-light district occupies, is a slightly more compacted section, the whorled heart of the print, where the lines are no longer curved, but tightly packed together, almost parallel, as if they have been subjected to some kind of pressure: Warmoesstraat, Oudezijds Voorburgwal, Oudezijds Achterburgwal, Kloveniersburgwal.

The fingerprint is not complete, though. It is partial, smudged, the kind of print found on a window-frame or a door-knob or the edge of a desk drawer. Would it be enough to allow the police to make a positive identification? Probably not. Would it lead to a conviction? Unlikely. Whoever left that fingerprint behind, whoever committed the crime, would almost certainly go free.

There was a sense in which the city had been trying to tell me something all along. *You'll never solve this case. You might as well forget it.* But I had not been listening, of course.

Look at the map. It's all there, in a way.

The whole story.

~

I sat on a hard chair under bright fluorescent lights and waited. On the wall directly opposite me was a white electric clock. I watched the second hand sweep past the numbers, smooth as a knife spreading butter. Quarter to five.

They had taken me to a police station just behind Leidse-plein. As I sipped the coffee they had given me, which was weak, black and scalding hot, I thought of my kitchen and how I should be sitting at the table, a pool of lamplight on the plain wood surface, the green walls shading into darkness near the ceiling. I could hear the gentle crash and rustle as I turned the pages of my newspaper. I could hear the chuckling of the water-pipes inside the wall and the creak of the window as cold night air leaned against the glass. I could see the dark bulk of the house across the street and, to the left of it, in the distance, I could see the blushing of car brake-lights on the main road. And if I leaned back in my chair and looked over my shoulder I could just make out the shape of Juliette sleeping in my bed – though not tonight, of course . . .

I sipped the coffee. Five to five.

At last a police officer came over and told me I could not be registered until nine o'clock. He seemed almost to be apol-ogising for the delay. He had bloodshot eyes and a face that was smooth and slightly shiny, as if he had just shaved. It would be best if I slept now, he said. Taking hold of my arm just above the elbow, he led me through a series of doors and into a cell that had one narrow bed in it and a metal toilet with no seat. He took my shoes, my watch and my belt, and dropped them into a transparent plastic bag, which he then sealed.

'What's going to happen?' I asked him, fearful all of a sudden.

He misunderstood my question. 'Nothing will happen,' he said, 'until the morning.'

I suppose I must have slept because I remember that I jumped when they opened the door. When I realised where I was, a flash of heat passed over me. If only I could have dreamed the girl on the blue velvet sofa, the girl in the toilet stall, the girl wrapped in the blanket. And her smudged eyes lifting. *Yes. That's him.* Surely it should have been the other way round. Me wrapped in a blanket, me accusing her . . .

I couldn't understand how things had gone so badly wrong.

I was shown into a large grey room that had no windows. I sat down and waited. My eyes felt more watery than usual, which was probably tiredness, and my knees and elbows were bruised from when I had been knocked to the ground outside the club. After a few minutes the smooth-faced policeman appeared. I was glad to see him. Somehow, I felt as if we had a bond. I watched him walk round the table. In his hand was a sheaf of forms and documents, which he arranged in front of him.

'A long shift,' I said.

He looked up. 'Excuse me?'

'You work long hours.'

'Ah. Yes.' He studied me for a moment and smiled faintly, then he glanced down at his papers.

The door opened again, and another policeman walked in with a tray of Danish pastries and coffee, which he placed carefully on the table between us. The smooth-faced policeman extended one hand, palm upwards, to indicate that I was free to help myself. I poured some coffee, added milk, then took a pastry. It tasted delicious, and, oddly enough, I was reminded of the beer I had drunk on the day of my release from the white room five years before.

While I was eating, the policeman informed me that, under Dutch law, I could be held in custody for one period of six hours, followed by two periods of twenty-four hours, starting

247

from the time of registration. After that, I would either be released or charged. This was standard procedure. If I was charged, he said, I would be entitled to a lawyer. What he was saying sounded so reasonable that I just nodded, unable to think of any questions.

For the next half-hour he took down my details, filling endless boxes with neat, clear handwriting that had a slight forward slant to it. After the registration, I was fingerprinted and photographed, then I was escorted back to my cell. The policeman told me that I would be interviewed later that morning, and that I would be required to make a statement. It would be advisable, he said, if I prepared for this.

When I left my cell again, towards lunchtime, the mood in the police station appeared to have altered. One or two of the officers gave me thinly veiled looks of disapproval as they passed me in the corridor. Others studied me with a curiosity that seemed cold, aloof, as if I were a specimen in a laboratory. There was no sign of the smooth-faced policeman who had treated me with such consideration.

This time there were two policemen sitting at the table when I was shown into the grey room. One had a long face and narrow shoulders. His name was Snel. He was smoking a cigarette, exhaling through his nostrils in two disdainful streams. The other one, Pieters, was balding, with a square head. They both seemed exhausted, bored. They would rather have been anywhere but in this room, and their presence there was something for which they were holding me personally responsible. As I took a seat in front of them I felt guilty and on edge.

They wanted to hear my version of what had happened the night before. I gave them the bare facts, in so far as I could remember them. When I had finished, Pieters began to tap his biro on the notepad that lay in front of him. The top page was still unmarked, quite blank. I found it slightly insulting that he hadn't bothered to make a single note. Snel rose to his feet and began to pace back and forwards with both hands thrust deep into his pockets. He was unusually tall, I noticed, and his body tilted forwards from the waist. Sideways-on, he looked like a ski-jumper in mid-flight.

'You have told us what you did,' Snel said in a nasal voice, 'but you have not told us why you did it.'

'That's not something I can explain,' I said.

Snel looked at me askance, his chin aligned with his shoulder. 'You can't explain why you did it?'

'No.'

'According to information we received this morning,' Pieters said, 'you assaulted the girl and attempted to rape her.'

I shook my head. 'I had no intention of raping her. It wasn't rape.'

'But you tore off all her clothes,' Pieters said.

'Yes.'

'If that isn't rape,' Snel said, 'what is it?'

I stared at him as he leaned against the wall, both hands in his pockets. I couldn't think of an answer to that question. Though my hands and feet were cold, I felt sweat collecting on the back of my neck and on my chest.

'Why did you assault the girl?' Pieters said.

'I told you,' I said. 'I can't explain.'

Back in my cell I fell into a deep sleep. I dreamed that Stefan Elmers was married to a big buxom woman in a tight-fitting pale-pink dress and high-heeled silver sandals. To watch her walk across the room was to witness the most astounding feat of balance. Smiling fatalistically, he told me that he already had five children, and that his wife was now pregnant with the sixth. Then I dreamed that a man was cutting my hair. He botched the job completely, shaving my head in some places, but leaving clownish clumps of hair in others. *Usually, I work in the zoo*, he said. I woke to the sound of my cell door banging open. It was a policeman I had never seen before, bringing me some lunch.

That evening Pieters and Snel interviewed me again. They wanted me to make a statement before I left the room. While the facts seemed beyond dispute, they were still puzzled by the motivation. If only I could give them a clearer picture of what had been going through my mind at the time . . .

'It might make your statement easier to write,' Snel said.

He sat on the corner of the table, one leg dangling, one foot on the floor. He offered me a cigarette.

I shook my head. 'Thank you, but I don't smoke.'

'Did the girl make any advances?' he said. 'Did she encourage you in some way? After all, you're a good-looking man . . .'

He lit a cigarette with a crisp snap of his gold lighter, exhaling through his nostrils as usual, then stood up and walked to the far side of the room.

'No,' I said. 'She didn't encourage me.'

Pieters seemed surprised by my answer. His big square forehead creased as he leaned over his pad of paper and jotted something down.

'What about this?' Snel said. 'You saw her in the club and you liked the look of her immediately. You don't know what came over you. You couldn't help yourself.' He brought his cigarette up to the corner of his mouth and inhaled deeply. 'You wanted her.'

This was such an obvious and yet, to me, unlikely version of events that I must have smiled.

'Did I say something amusing?' Snel was leaning against the wall now, with one hand in his pocket.

'In a way,' I said.

'But you can't explain it?'

'No.'

'So you didn't find her attractive?' Snel said. 'You didn't find her,' and he paused, 'irresistible?'

'No.'

Snel walked back to the table, crushed his cigarette out in the ashtray and then sat down. 'How do you feel about women?'

'I'm sorry,' I said. 'You'll have to be more specific.'

Snel leaned forwards. His hands lay folded, one on top of the other, limp as gloves. 'Do you have a grudge against women?' He paused, and then distilled the thought. 'Did you have a grudge against this woman?'

'I wouldn't call it a grudge exactly,' I said, 'but it's an interesting question.'

'What would you call it?'

I stared down at the table, its grey metal surface freshly painted, free of blemishes. I didn't see how I could be of any further use to the policemen. I had gone as far as I could go. Why were they so obsessed with motivation? Were they trying to do me a favour by finding me an escape-route? Or were they intent on trapping me?

'Well?' Snel lit another cigarette.

'I'm sorry,' I said. 'I can't go into that.'

Some air rushed out of Pieters' mouth, almost as if he had just been punched in the stomach. It was involuntary – part sardonic laughter, part disgust.

'One final question,' Snel said. 'Do you have a girlfriend?'

I nodded. 'Yes, I do.'

'What will she think about all this?'

My voice rose suddenly. 'She's got nothing to do with this.'

'No?'

'No. They're two completely different things.'

251

Pieters turned sideways and muttered something rapid that I didn't quite catch. Then he selected a form from the pile in front of him and slid it contemptuously across the table.

'Here,' he said. 'Write your statement.'

~

I must have woken up a dozen times that night. My right elbow had stiffened, and it was hard to find a comfortable position on the bed. Also, I was aware of doors slamming in the distance, and the constant murmur of voices. A police station is never quiet. I lay there under the fluorescent light and went back over my statement. I had been unable to avoid using words like 'tore' and 'ripped'. The word 'dragged' had appeared too. The whole thing looked so much worse when you wrote it down. What's more, I had been unable to give any reasons for my behaviour, although, at the end of the statement, I did say that I realised I'd done wrong, and that I deeply regretted any injury or offence that I had caused.

After reading the statement, Snel looked up sharply. *Is there anything you want to add?* The way he asked the question made me think that I must have left out something important. But I couldn't for the life of me think what that might be. Perhaps there was something about my expression of remorse that seemed inadequate, that didn't quite feel genuine, but I couldn't improve on it, so I just shook my head.

I lay on my narrow bed and stared at the ceiling, feeling as if I had sleep-walked through the day. I had concerned myself only with my most immediate reality – the look of the police officers, the taste of a Danish pastry. Perhaps there was a kind of comfort or distraction in these details, but they were minor, inconsequential, and had no relevance. Now, though – finally, you might say – the gravity and hopelessness of my situation

252

were beginning to filter through to me, and what happened in the middle of the following day stripped away any last remaining layers of delusion I might have had.

I had just woken from a light sleep when a policeman unlocked the door of my cell and told me that I had a visitor. I would be allowed ten minutes with her, he said.

Her.

I swallowed nervously. My face flushed and, for a few moments, the floor seemed to tilt, as if I was falling forwards.

Juliette was already sitting at the table when I walked into the interrogation room. I hesitated behind her, taking in the healthy shine on her black hair and the shape of her shoulders under her black ribbed sweater. Though I had known it would be her, her appearance was so unlikely, so incongruous, somehow, that it had the quality of a hallucination.

I walked round the table and sat down opposite her. The policeman who had escorted me into the room stood by the door, his eyes unblinking, his mouth pressed shut, like a child pretending to be invisible.

'Juliette?' I said.

She had been staring at her hands. Now she looked up. She seemed tired, dark smears reaching from the corners of her eyes. A greyness lay beneath the surface of her skin instead of the gold that I remembered. I tried to smile.

'Did you get the part?'

She looked puzzled.

'That audition,' I said. 'Did you get the part?'

'Oh, that. Yes.' She nodded. 'Yes, I did.'

'That's wonderful.'

I watched her as she slowly pulled off her gloves. When she looked up at me again, her eyes had filled with tears.

'What did you do?' she asked in a small, strained voice.

It wasn't a question. It was just the closest she could get to an expression of her bewilderment. I wondered how much she'd been told.

'Juliette?'

She shook her head and, glancing downwards, touched one of her eyes with the back of her wrist.

'Juliette, listen. It's not what it sounds like.'

'Isn't it?'

'No.'

I stared down at the table. Juliette sniffed twice, then blew her nose. It struck me that this was the first time I had ever seen her cry.

'It's not what you think,' I said.

I had used the same words before, and though they were as true then as they were now, I remembered how unconvincing they had sounded, how inauthentic. How guilty. I also remembered that they hadn't worked. It was as if my life consisted of a series of desperate and ineffectual repetitions.

No, it was worse than that. I was like someone with a market stall who brings out the same fruit day after day until, eventually, what he's selling is rotten to the core, nothing more than putrefaction.

I looked up at Juliette.

'Nothing's changed,' I murmured.

But I knew I was wrong. The ice had cracked and we had fallen through. There was a distance that could be measured by such things, a distance that could not easily be closed.

Of course, I could have told her the whole story. It wasn't as if I hadn't had the opportunity. In our hotel in Paris, at three in the morning, red roses exploding silently behind her – her fingers hesitating on the scar . . . But she hadn't asked, and I hadn't answered, and we had made love with the unspoken hovering between us . . .

Juliette was saying that she had brought some letters from

my apartment. They had been confiscated at the front desk, but they would be given to me later. As she was talking, the police officer who was standing by the door stepped forwards and informed us that our time was up. I did not ask Juliette to come again. I simply repeated what I had said earlier, that none of this was what it sounded like, and when she looked at me, her eyes reluctant, forlorn, I told her that I loved her, and I saw her nod gravely before she turned away.

It was only later that I wondered whether the police had asked her to visit me, thinking it might throw some fresh light on my character.

~

On Thursday evening, some thirty-eight hours after my arrest, I was summoned to the interrogation room by Snel and Pieters. Snel was smoking, as usual. In a voice that was both soft and urgent, he told me that I was being charged with aggravated assault and attempted rape. They had received a statement from the girl in question. Though still shaken by the experience, she seemed determined to press charges, and there was nothing in my statement to suggest that she might not be fully justified in doing so. In fact, Snel said, inhaling, our statements were remarkably consistent with one another, almost as if we were in collaboration. He looked up at the ceiling, expelled smoke from his nostrils in two flamboyant streams, and then repeated the words 'remarkably consistent'. It was clear that my behaviour intrigued him.

An hour later I received a visit from the lawyer who had been appointed by the state to represent me. He was a short man with a ruddy, good-humoured face, and from the first moment I saw him, I knew I had virtually no chance of winning the case. Alone in my cell with him, I told him I would plead guilty to the assault charge, but not guilty to the charge of attempted rape. I told him there was no evidence to suggest that I had tried to rape the girl. He disagreed.

'You followed her to the toilets,' he said. 'You forced her into an empty cubicle. You tore off all her clothes. The circumstantial evidence is overwhelming.' He smiled, which, in the circumstances, seemed both inappropriate and condescending.

'I didn't touch her,' I said.

'You were interrupted,' the lawyer said.

I stared at him. 'Whose side are you on?'

'I am only saying what the prosecution will say.' The lawyer clasped his hands on the table in front of him, as if he was about to say grace. 'I am on your side, of course I am, but you must give me some assistance.'

I could not satisfy him, though, and he left shortly afterwards, looking at the floor and shaking his head. At that point I was tempted to contact Isabel or Paul Bouhtala and ask for their advice, but, in the end, I just didn't feel as if I could bother either of them. They had done too much for me already.

Early the next morning, after a surprisingly deep sleep, I was informed that, as a result of a consultation with the Public Prosecutor, I was to be interviewed by an investigating judge. Once again, I was taken to the interrogation room; I knew the route so well by now that I could have walked it with my eyes shut. The judge was a well-built man with a head of creamy white hair, and he swept into the room with the sudden energy of a wave breaking over rocks. He asked me the same questions that Snel and Pieters had asked me, only his manner was both more formal and more distracted, and as I was led back to my cell fifteen minutes later I couldn't help but feel that the interview had gone badly. Even so, I had no way of predicting what the eventual outcome might be. Events were speeding up in a way that seemed both orchestrated and vertiginous. People appeared and disappeared in front of me with dizzying rapidity, and I was supposed to impress each one of them. I found that I could hardly catch my breath – and this, oddly, despite long periods in my cell, alone. I was being asked to assume full responsibility for my past actions, and yet, at the same time, I seemed to have forfeited all control over the present.

~

The post that Juliette had brought from my apartment was delivered to me in the evening. The envelopes had been torn open, as I had expected, but, so far as I could tell, the contents had not been tampered with. Most of the letters were routine, mundane, fit only for the waste-paper basket – a statement from my credit-card company, an offer of a bank loan – but, among them, there was a postcard from Stefan. He had written to me from New York, where he was working on a photographic assignment. His assumption that my life was going on as always – *How's the bar? Hope you haven't slept with Gusta yet!* – made me realise how drastically everything had altered, and it was several minutes before I was able to turn to the last of the envelopes, which was rectangular and white, and which had the address of a firm of lawyers printed in the top left-hand corner. The letter was from a Mr Werkhoven. He wrote that, as executor of Isabel van Zaanen's will, it was his responsibility to inform me of her wish that I should inherit her apartment in Bloemendaal. For a moment I could make no sense of this. I had to read the sentence again. Even then, its meaning seemed partial, incomplete; it left a smudge in my brain, like a poor-quality Xerox or a piece of rain-blurred ink. I put the letter down and lay back on my bed, and my mind seemed to empty all of a sudden, the space that thoughts usually inhabit taken up by just two words: *Isabel's dead.* Just those words repeating silently, endlessly, until they lost their meaning altogether . . .

I had last seen Isabel halfway through January. Juliette and I had taken the train to Bloemendaal, and we had spent an hour with her – though I had hardly talked to her at all. There had been a certain tension in the air that afternoon, I remembered, which I had put down to the fact that two women who were both close to me were meeting for the first time. I also remembered that, on our way back to Amsterdam, Juliette had turned to me and said, 'Isabel must have been beautiful when she was young,' a remark which made me smile. I told Juliette about the photograph Isabel had showed me once when, uncharacteristically, she had drunk two brandies after dinner. In the photograph – taken at the Waldorf Astoria, in 1953 – Isabel was wearing a white evening gown, with diamond earrings and a diamond choker. Her skin was flawless, and her black hair slanted, gleaming, across her forehead, covering her right eyebrow . . . 'She's still beautiful, of course,' Juliette added quickly, sensing she might have sounded tactless. 'I only meant it's a pity when you meet someone and they're already old. You realise you've missed something, and that can sadden you.'

I thought back to my own first meeting with Isabel. She was in her late fifties then, and at the height of her fame. I had walked up to her backstage at Sadler's Wells and told her how much I admired her work. I was studying at the Royal Ballet, I said, but there was a dance company in Amsterdam that I hoped to join. We spoke for less than five minutes, and I remembered nothing about her afterwards except for her perfect English and the seemingly disparaging way in which she had looked me up and down. Towards the end of that year, a scout from the Dutch company visited the Royal Ballet, and I was one of the dancers he chose to audition. You cannot imagine my excitement when he took me to one side afterwards and asked if I would be interested in becoming a member of the company . . . One afternoon the following autumn, when I had been in Amsterdam for about six months, a message came over the studio PA, saying there was somebody to see me in reception. It was Isabel. I was sweaty and dishevelled, in a ripped T-shirt and Lycra cycling shorts, and she was wearing a Chanel suit and sunglasses. She kissed me three times, and then stood back and looked at me. 'So,' she said with just the faintest trace of a smile, 'you're dancing in the Netherlands, just as you planned.' At the time, of course, I had no idea how she had found me, and it had seemed like the most extraordinary coincidence. It was only years later that I discovered that it was Isabel who had sent the scout to audition me, Isabel who had stage-managed the whole thing . . .

I picked up the lawyer's letter again. In writing to me, Mr Werkhoven had assumed that, as one of Isabel's close friends, I would already have heard about her death, and this gave his letter a matter-of-factness, an abruptness, that had only added to my shock, my confusion. After all, it was little more than two weeks since I had seen her last. Her decline must have been sudden, rapid – almost brutal.

I turned on to my side and stared at the wall, which was disfigured by obscene messages, drawings of male genitalia, cigarette-burns. My vision blurred. I felt that I was sinking, sinking into dark, dank sediment . . . There was only one consolation in all this: at least she had been spared the news of my latest humiliation.

~

That night, half awake, half dreaming, I opened the door to Isabel's apartment. I moved slowly across the entrance hall, dimly aware of the paintings on the wall, and the crisp, fragrant heads of dried roses in the silver bowl under the mirror. I felt my way down the passage that led to the living-room. All the rooms lay in darkness, their furniture invested with the mystery and ambivalence of neglect. Outside, there was no moon, but a kind of dusty greyness spilled through the french windows, allowing me to see the swept fireplace and the cushions stacked neatly on the divan. I sat in the chair Isabel had always sat in when she was well, a chair with a high back, upholstered in fabric that was subtle, lavish – a blend of yellow, green and gold. On the table beside the chair lay a pile of loose pages, her record of the ballet we had been developing together. Though I was familiar with the type of notation she had used, it always looked intriguing to me, even a little sinister, like inscriptions found on rune-stones or plans for an experimental prison. We had made progress, I realised, but there was still work to be done and only I could do it. As I was reading what she had written, a faint aura of Egyptian cigarettes encircled me. It must be left over from the early autumn, I thought, before the cancer surfaced. A few sheets of paper crowded with pencil marks, a trace of cigarette smoke in the air – and that was all that remained of her. How quickly, how utterly, we are gone . . . Sitting in her chair, I began to speak to her. I was saying things I had never had the chance to say when she was alive. I was also saying things she would never have allowed me to say if she had been in the room with me. But that's the whole point of a vigil, perhaps. It's a monologue, not a conversation. The person I was talking to no longer existed. She could not interrupt or disagree; she could not even answer me. The solitary nature of the act, the fact that it is so one-sided, makes you realise exactly what it is that you have lost.

The floorboards stretched away, black in the half-light, and, through the windows, I could just make out the dim shape of the forest, one shade darker than the sky. There was a wind blowing out of the north-east, but no other sound from anywhere. Though it was the middle of the night, I thought Bouhtala would be awake upstairs, in his leather armchair, with a glass of cognac at his elbow. He would be studying the atlas I had given him, or leafing through his photographs of tattooed men, and the only movement in the room would be the smoke from his cigarillo spiralling upwards through a pyramid of lamplight, or his white shirt-cuff lifting as he reached out to turn a page, or smooth down his moustache . . .

The next time I looked up, it was morning. I yawned, then stretched. Opening the french windows, I stepped on to the terrace. I leaned on the wooden rail, looking out across the garden, into the trees, and let the cool, damp air pass over me.

Later, after breakfast, I went for a walk along the beach, my hands in my coat pockets, my collar turned up. The wind pushed against my back, pushed so hard at times that, despite myself, I broke into a run. Loose sand whipped past my feet in lines that were long and sinuous, like snakes. There was no one else about. It was winter, after all. To my right, the sea unrolled against the shore. The low thunder of waves ex-ploding, grey smashed into creamy white –

The scratch of a key in a lock, the creak of my cell door opening . . .

I slowly swung my legs on to the floor. I sat on the edge of the narrow bed, quite still, so as not to dislodge the memory of inhabiting the rooms where Isabel had lived; if I moved too much, it would all disintegrate, like a piece of five thousand-year-old wood that is suddenly exposed to light and air. I felt a calmness flow into every part of me, as if my body had been plunged in cool water. Perhaps it was simply the knowledge that I could sink no further, that I had reached a place, at last, some kind of solid ground or bedrock, on which it might be possible to build.

~

That morning I was summoned to the interrogation room where the two policemen, Snel and Pieters, and my lawyer were waiting for me. Snel selected a cigarette from the packet lying in front of him and tapped it thoughtfully on his gold lighter. My lawyer watched Snel with an eager, patient expression which only confirmed my lack of faith in him.

'You look pale,' Snel said.

'I'm all right,' I said. 'It's nothing.'

I sat down at the table.

Snel lit his cigarette and inhaled with relish. 'Bad news, I'm afraid.'

I felt a bitter smile surface. 'It never rains but it pours.'

'I'm sorry?' Snel said.

'Nothing,' I said. 'Please go on.'

Snel said that the judge who had interviewed me the day before had found me uncooperative. Subsequent to the interview, he had recommended that I should be remanded in custody until my court appearance, which would take place in about two months' time. In his report he claimed that I represented a danger to the community. It was possible, he said, that I would commit the same offence again.

I began to laugh. And once I started laughing I couldn't stop, even though I saw that it shocked the three men who were sitting at the table. It must have been at least a minute before I brought myself under control. Still gasping, I apologised. Snel passed me a tissue. I thanked him.

When I had fully recovered I sat back in my chair and turned to Snel again.

'Do you think I could make a phone-call?'

The policeman considered my request for a moment, then he signalled to Pieters, who hauled himself noisily to his feet. While Pieters was out of the room, my lawyer leaned forwards, his ruddy face exuding its usual incongruous good-humour.

'I should remind you,' he said, 'that you have the right to remain silent.'

Of course, he couldn't have known what was in my head, but, all the same, the announcement seemed so ill-timed, so utterly inappropriate, that I began to laugh again. I couldn't help it. My lawyer sat back in his chair, bemused.

The door opened. It was Pieters, returning with a phone. He plugged the jack into a socket low down in the wall and placed the phone in front of me.

'I need a number,' I said.

Pieters frowned. 'What number?'

'I need the number of Police Headquarters,' I said, 'in Marnixstraat.'

Pieters turned to Snel, who slid a hand into his inside jacket pocket and took out a small black notebook. He turned a few pages, then looked up and, studying me across two streams of exhaled smoke, read the seven-digit number out loud.

The three men watched me carefully as I dialled. I listened to the ringing tone. At last a woman answered. I took a deep breath, composed myself.

'Good morning,' I said. 'Could I speak to Mr Olsen, please?'

There was a brief rustling sound, not unlike paper being crushed, then the line cleared and I heard him, very close, almost as if he had been there the whole time.

'Olsen here.'

'Mr Olsen. Hello.' I gave him my name. 'We met at Paul Bouhtala's birthday party. It was quite a while ago – nearly five years . . .'

'Ah yes,' he said. 'The dancer.' A few seconds passed. 'You never brought me that drink.'

The sharpness of his memory unsettled me. At the same time, though, I felt it might work in my favour.

'That was rude of me. I'm sorry.' I paused, and then I said, 'I owe you one.'

Olsen laughed. 'So,' he said, 'what can I do for you?'

'It's a long story, I'm afraid . . .'

'That's all right. I'm not in a hurry.'

I began to describe the events of Monday night, the events leading up to my arrest, but I had been talking for less than thirty seconds, I had just reached the point where the girl's red hair landed on the bar, when Olsen interrupted me.

'You've started in the middle,' he said gently. 'Go back to the beginning.'

A NOTE ON THE AUTHOR

Rupert Thomson is the author of five previous
novels, *Dreams of Leaving, The Five Gates of Hell, Air
and Fire, The Insult* and *Soft.* He lives in London.

A NOTE ON THE TYPE

The text of this book is set in Linotype Janson. The original types were cut in about 1690 by Nicholas Kis, a Hungarian working in Amsterdam. The face was misnamed after Anton Janson, a Dutchman who worked at the Ehrhardt Foundry in Leipzig, where the original Kis types were kept in the early eighteenth century. Monotype Ehrhardt is based on Janson. The original matrices survived in Germany and were acquired in 1919 by the Stempel Foundry. Herman Zapf used these originals to redesign some of the weights and sizes for Stempel. This Linotype version was designed to follow the original types under the direction of C. H. Griffith.